Praise for Sami Lee's
Erica's Choice

"This book, featuring a fascinating look into a polyamorous relationship, is hot! The characters are distinct and interesting... With a lot of heart and heat, this book will have you on the edge of your emotional seat."

~ *RT Book Reviews*

"*Erica's Choice* is a sexy, heart wrenching story about love, self acceptance and honesty that will have you falling in love with each turn of the page... With raw emotion, hardcore sexual tension and a three way relationship that will make you melt, this story is a must read!"

~ *Guilty Pleasures Book Reviews*

Look for these titles by
Sami Lee

Now Available:

Born Again Virgin
Fijian Fling
Chasing Sunset
Sunset Knight
Moonlight Mirage

Print Anthologies
Sand, Sun and Sex
Bandicoot Cove: The Wedding

Erica's Choice

Sami Lee

SAMHAIN
PUBLISHING

Samhain Publishing, Ltd.
11821 Mason Montgomery Road, 4B
Cincinnati, OH 45249
www.samhainpublishing.com

Erica's Choice
Copyright © 2013 by Sami Lee
Print ISBN: 978-1-61921-271-8
Digital ISBN: 978-1-60928-964-5

Editing by Anne Scott
Cover by Angela Waters

First Samhain Publishing, Ltd. electronic publication: August 2012
First Samhain Publishing, Ltd. print publication: July 2013

Dedication

First of all this book is for my editor Anne Scott. Without her insightful suggestions, it may well have languished on my hard drive unpublished, unread and unloved. Thanks for being the left brain to my right.

To my family, who allow me the space to write and love me despite my frequent bouts of distraction.

To the girls in my local writing group, the Romantix, who commiserated with me through two years of writer's block and reminded me that I am never alone in the struggle.

And finally to the Divas, who commiserated with me through two years of writer's block...then told me to suck it up and write a book already. Here are your bloody firemen.

Chapter One

The beveled glass doors of the Sovereign Hotel swung back with a *whoosh* as Erica Shannon shoved them open. Stalking through the breach, she was assailed by noise and light, the typically boisterous ambiance of Friday night revelry at an inner-city Brisbane pub.

She halted in the foyer, taking a moment to catch her breath. Glancing around, she realized no one had noticed her theatrical entrance. The crowd of mostly men stood in groups talking and laughing, drinking beer from brown-tinted bottles and arguing jovially over a game of rugby being played out on a massive plasma screen in the corner. Nobody turned to look at her.

Perhaps her arrival hadn't been dramatic at all. It simply felt that way because she'd never come to a pub by herself, and her agenda was pounding in her ears like the rush from some illicit drug, amplifying every sound, every smell and every sight.

Or at least that was how Erica imagined the rush from an illegal substance would affect her. She—sensible English teacher, loyal niece, staunch obeyer of road rules—had never done anything taboo in her life, chemical or otherwise.

That was about to change. Tonight.

Heart pounding impetuously in her chest, she weaved her way through the crowd, heading for the area at the back of the establishment that housed the pool tables, dart boards and jukebox. This was the section of the Sovereign where her quarry tended to hang out, as though the tables were permanently reserved for the firefighters of Ashton Heights.

Through the throng, Erica easily spotted the familiar outline of Corey Wachawski's wide shoulders and the dark swatch of hair on his head. His back was to her, but she knew his eyes were as warm and blue as the summer sky. She'd snagged his gaze once or twice in the past few months—or rather, Corey had caught her staring. If he'd detected the longing in her scrutiny, it had never prompted him to approach her.

Tonight, Erica was not in the mood to be dismissed. She would make a move on him, no matter the potential for embarrassment.

The very thought made her heart rate triple. Her palms grew slippery against the tweed fabric of her skirt. *Tweed.* Erica would have laughed if her lungs were capable of expelling air. She was the kind of woman who wore tweed and modest button-up blouses, who stayed home most nights rereading her favorite Jane Austen novels instead of venturing out to experience life. Was she out of her mind even to daydream a man like Corey Wachawski—local hero, calendar model, Adonis—would want to take her up on a sexual proposition?

Steeling her resolve, Erica relentlessly pushed forward. After all, she had little left to lose now.

A large hand clapped Corey's back. The sound of the other man's laughter moved through Erica like a fast-flowing tide, the sight of his lean, muscle-packed body in a navy-blue T-shirt and faded jeans made something wicked and needy pass through her erogenous zones.

Dale Griffin.

There were photos of him all over the pub walls. Some in which he wore his firefighter's uniform, in others he was listed as a member of a local football team. One was a framed clipping from the newspaper which detailed his heroics in saving a local man from a fire. And on the ladies' room wall, his picture from an old Queensland Firefighters Charity Calendar was pinned, right beside Corey's more recent one.

Erica was both exhilarated and terrified to see Griff—whenever she'd heard one of his colleagues call out to him above the usual cacophony of pub noises, they always called him Griff—here as well.

There was nothing to stop her living out her ultimate fantasy.

Nothing except it required her to sexually proposition not just one man, but two. Twenty-eight years old and she'd never so much as initiated a coffee date with a member of the opposite sex.

That's right, Erica. You haven't been living at all, and now it could be too late.

The reminder refueled the anger and frustration that had brought her here. She could do this. There were worse things than being embarrassed.

Much worse things.

She wet parched lips with the tip of her tongue as she drew nearer to the back corner. She kept her gaze fixed on Corey Wachawski's massive shoulders, focusing on them as she drew closer and closer...

Suddenly, her view was obstructed by one of the sharks.

Oh darn.

How had she not factored in the sharks? That was how her female colleagues, who often stopped in at the Sovereign on their way home from a hard day at school and who'd recently begun dragging Erica with them, referred to the beautiful, sexily clad women who routinely circled the group of handsome firemen. Hunting them like sharks on the lookout for their next meal.

Not that Griff, for one, seemed to mind being fish food. He'd left the pub with two of those women only a few weeks ago.

Two.

It was the event that had made Erica start thinking about threesomes. What was good for the gander had to be allowed for the goose, too. It was only feminist, and her Aunt Claire had raised her to be an independent woman, aware of her rights and willing to fight for them.

That was all well and good, until you had to battle a woman who looked like Miranda Kerr on a good hair day.

Erica's steps faltered. The very blood seemed to drain out of her as she watched the tall, willowy brunette slide her arms around Corey from behind and whisper something in his ear. Whatever she said made Corey blush. The shark was stunning, flawless in looks and manner. And Erica stood there gasping, as graceful as a flounder that had been washed up on shore.

From the corner of her eye, Erica saw a couple work their way out of a booth in the corner. She made a dash for it, sliding into one of the olive-green vinyl bench seats before anyone else could claim the table. She hoped it looked natural, more natural than turning around and walking straight back out. Like her intent all along had been to find a table to herself and sit quietly.

Without a drink.

Dear Lord, she must look like an idiot.

Perhaps there *was* something worse than facing your most frightening demons. Being completely and utterly humiliated first.

Corey Wachawski watched as the woman of his dreams took a book out of her large black shoulder bag, opened it to a dog-eared page and began to read. It was a big book, the kind he'd never get through if he had a year to kill, which only reminded Corey how out of his league the pretty redhead with the big brown eyes truly was.

"Are you sure you don't want to come out with us, Corey?" Madison purred the invitation into his ear while she stroked a fingernail up and down his forearm. "Vibe is the hottest club in the Valley right now. We're going to have the best time."

It was clear from her tone that the club wasn't the only thing offering a good time. It would be easy enough to take Madison up on it, but Corey found girls like her a little intimidating—and a lot scary. He got the feeling if he went home with her he'd wake up naked, tied to a bed and minus the one credit card he owned. "No thanks. I'm going to have an early one tonight."

Madison stuck out her bottom lip in an exaggerated pout. "They work you boys way too hard."

Corey wasn't about to tell her work had nothing to do with his refusal. He simply didn't want to spend the night with Madison.

The woman he did want to spend some quality time with was sitting across the pub right now with her nose in a book, her sleek red hair sweeping down to conceal her face, as out of reach as the moon. She probably thought he was some kind of man-slut because every time she came in here some random woman slipped him her phone number, or even her panties. Jeez. What did girls think he was going to do with a pink satin G-string?

Madison finally gave up and left. Corey's sigh of relief was audible and beside him Griff laughed. "That was piss weak."

"She isn't my type."

Griff remarked with a lopsided smile, "With an ass like that she doesn't need to be. Besides, you might as well dip your wick somewhere. You won't do anything about the girls who are your type, either."

Corey didn't pretend ignorance. His gaze once again strayed to the corner booth and the woman sitting there. She wore an ordinary grey skirt, black heels and a plain white blouse, the collar trimmed in lace. Her haircut was of the sensible, I'm-not-the-type-to-primp variety, a chin-length bob that framed her high cheekbones and wide brown eyes. She exuded none of the glamour of a woman like Madison yet she fascinated Corey on a level that went beyond appearances. He wanted to get to know her better, had since the first time she'd come in a few months ago.

But the idea of approaching her made his palms sweat, so he'd settled for watching her from across the room, waiting for...*something*. A sign maybe. Some kind of magic that would make everything click into place.

He offered Griff his excuse. "She's really into that book."

"She's *alone*. Nobody comes to a noisy pub to read. She's probably dying for you to go over and talk to her, dickhead." At Corey's skeptical look, Griff insisted, "Look, she doesn't even have a drink. Go buy her one before somebody else does."

Corey scowled. "Who's going to buy her a drink?"

"Maybe I will."

Corey wouldn't have been more surprised if Griff had punched him in the gut. "You wouldn't."

"Why not?"

"She's not *your* type."

Griff laughed. "And that means?"

Corey didn't know how to express what he meant without dissing his friend's usual taste in women. Eventually he settled for, "She's delicate."

Griff raised a brow. "I like delicate. I like soft women. Hell, I just like women. Matter of fact, I'm talking myself into it. I'm going over there."

"No." Corey stood at the same time Griff did. They met eye to eye, Griff's hazel irises twinkling with amusement. Corey figured his own expression was less jovial. His voice came out sounding threatening, which surprised him more than it seemed to surprise Griff. "I mean it, Griff. Don't you hit on her."

"What's to stop me?"

"The guy code," Corey said. "I saw her first."

Griff chuckled. "You've gotta actually do something about it in order to activate the guy code. Sitting here with your thumb up your ass does not constitute staking a claim, so stand back and start taking notes. I'm about to show you what a move is."

Griff strode past him with ease. Corey was bigger physically but Griff was more brazen. Corey knew the second Griff introduced himself to the mystery woman his own chances would be all shot to hell. Females usually proved susceptible to Griff's particular type of brash charm. And if Griff found out her name first, he'd probably insist the guy-code privileges reverted to him or something like that. Griff would find a way to get what he wanted. He always did.

Damn it. It was do-or-die time. Corey had to get over to that booth before Griff or he was going to lose his fantasy woman before he ever caught her.

"White wine and two beers—one light." Griff flashed the blonde bartender the grin that usually procured good service. "Take your time."

The woman returned his smile and gave him a quick once-over before moving off to fill his order. Griff returned the compliment, admiring the way the mounds of her ass were accentuated by the tight black pants she wore. Nice, but for some reason she didn't stir his blood.

What did, however, was something, someone—okay, *two* someones—he was going to have to stay away from.

Griff slid a glance over to the corner booth. Corey stood beside the table offering his hand to introduce himself. He had finally gotten up the balls to approach Red, and all he'd needed was a mighty shove in that direction. Griff had never intended to make a serious play for his friend's fantasy woman, but *something* had to be done. Griff couldn't go through another night watching those two making hopeless goo-goo eyes at each other.

"There you go." Griff turned back and took the change the bartender offered. He noticed the little slip of paper with a phone number written on it amongst the coins, and stuffed it all in the front pocket of his jeans. The woman held his gaze with blue eyes that sparkled flirtatiously. "My name's Michelle, by the way."

"I'll be sure to remember it." Griff winked and took his drinks, mentally putting Michelle in the *maybe later* column. She was definitely cute, and would no doubt make a fine Miss Right Now. But if things went south she had the power to do all manner of unhygienic things to his drinks, so Griff wasn't sure he should risk it. Switching his regular watering hole would be a bitch.

As Griff approached the booth, he let his gaze linger on the woman opposite his friend. She had a playboy bunny's body underneath those drab clothes. The fact that she didn't go out of her way to accentuate her obvious assets only made her more intriguing, like a wicked tease to Griff's vivid imagination. She might not be Griff's usual type, but damn could he have some fun with her.

Corey's crush, Griff. Corey's crush.

"Drinks all round," Griff announced and slid the beverages on the table between them. "White wine's your poison, isn't it?"

Red blinked at him, clearly surprised that he knew. Could she guess that Corey wasn't the only one who'd watched her with no small amount of interest over the past few months? Sure as bears shit in the woods, any guy with a dick was going to notice a rack like that, no matter how well it was concealed by a lace-trimmed blouse. Griff had simply been better at hiding his interest.

Until now.

Up close she wasn't merely pretty, as he'd judged her. She was beautiful in a manner that was soft, classic, like a fifties ingénue, with a body made for every modern-day sin Griff could imagine. And there were a lot of those. The way her mouth hung open in surprise had Griff's mind instantly turning down Bawdy Street. He saw the pink, wet flesh of her tongue resting beyond the plump outline of her lightly glossed lips and was filled with a raw, powerful need to suck it into his mouth.

"This is Erica—Erica Shannon."

Corey introduced them before Griff could make the hasty retreat he suddenly realized he needed to. She held out her hand, compelling Griff to take it. Her fingers slid into his, brushing against the flesh of his palm. "It's nice to meet you."

That whisper of contact electrified him, made him suck in a harsh breath. He swelled in his jeans, imagining that breathy voice rasping naughty nothings in his ear, picturing that lush mouth working its way over his chest and lower.

Oh crap. This has gotta mean trouble.

Griff couldn't very well walk around the pub in his suddenly uncomfortable condition. He hastily grabbed an unused chair from a table nearby, flipped it around and straddled it so neither Erica nor Corey could guess what had happened. He'd stay for a few minutes—one drink. He'd get himself under control, then he'd skedaddle and leave the lovebirds alone.

"Call me Griff," he managed to choke out. "Everyone does."

"I know."

She blushed and ducked her head, as though she'd just revealed a closely guarded secret. Realization stole through Griff—or was it wishful thinking? Either way he was beginning to wonder if Corey was the only one Erica Shannon had been studying these past few months.

The very possibility made his physical situation a whole lot worse, but he tried not to get ahead of himself. Erica did not look like the threesome type—and Griff could usually pick the type. He was pretty damn sure Corey had never even thought of doing anything like it—more's the pity. Straight down the line and unfailingly traditional, that was Corey. Griff's own preference for multiple-partner playtime was probably coloring his thoughts.

But a few minutes later, Griff looked over to find Erica eyeing him through her lashes, flicking him brief glances even as she appeared enthralled by Corey's small talk. In those moments Griff saw something fiery and reckless in her eyes, something that hinted at heat beneath the ice, wildness beneath the conservative exterior. That something called to him like a siren song, compelling him to keep turning the wicked ideas around in his head, no matter how he might be twisting things in his mind to suit his own tastes.

No matter how unlikely it was that Corey would agree to share the woman he was infatuated with.

Chapter Two

"You know Erica, you haven't said much about yourself."

Corey twirled his nearly empty beer glass—his second since he'd sat down with her—between his large hands. It made a swirling sound on the wood that Erica could hear even above the crowd noise and rock music. It was as though she was keenly attuned to everything about him, as though there were a physical connection instead of mere proximity between them. Watching his fingers slide up and down the glass made her picture with stark clarity the way his hands would move over her body.

It was becoming increasingly difficult to stick to small talk when all she wanted to do was beg him to touch her. "My life's not as interesting as yours." It was the truth, but not the real reason she hadn't revealed a lot of personal information. She simply didn't want to think or talk about herself right now. She wanted to be somebody else, somebody with the world beneath their feet, a whole life to look forward to. A woman who made a hobby out of flirting with men in bars.

In short, she wanted to be anyone but her.

Corey flashed her a smile that was equal parts shy and sexy. "I'm interested."

Mother superior would leave the convent for that smile. "I told you I'm a teacher."

Corey nodded. "History and English. Is that why you carry such a big book around with you?"

Erica detected an edge in the question, and she wondered if he thought her the biggest dork in the world. "I've always liked to read, my Aunt Claire's influence."

"Your aunt?"

His interest in her was obvious, and for once Erica decided to let down her shields a fraction. Whether it was the wine or the warmth of the man across from her, Erica didn't know. "She died earlier this year. She left me her house and her vast collection of leather-bound originals."

Aunt Claire had left her other things too, but Erica definitely did not want to discuss the details of that particular legacy.

"I'm sorry." The softness in his blue eyes told Erica it wasn't a meaningless platitude. "Were you close?"

"Yes." Erica's throat constricted around the word. "She raised me from the time I was twelve, when my mother died."

"What about your dad?"

Her father hadn't been able to handle Erica's needs, the panic attacks and separation anxiety she'd suffered after losing her mother to a long battle with cancer. He'd been tapped out after so many years dealing with his wife's illness. When he moved to the far north for work, Erica had moved in with Claire, who'd accepted the presence of her sister's sullen teenage daughter in her life with loving aplomb.

"He thought I was better off with my aunt," Erica said.

As though he sensed all she'd left unsaid, Griff offered bluntly, "He sounds like a prick."

Corey sent his friend a censuring look, but Erica smiled faintly. The days when she would have leapt to her father's defense were long behind her. She'd grown up and learned not to rely on a man to be there when the chips were down. "He lives in the Northern Territory now." With a whole new family, a less needy one. "We exchange Christmas cards but that's about it."

"Oh, Erica." Tugging on her fingertips, Corey coaxed her hand toward him. He held it turned upward on the tabletop, caressing her sensitive palm with his thumb while he looked into her eyes, more deeply than any man ever had.

Her heart was going to pump right out of her chest if he didn't stop staring at her like that, like he wanted nothing better than to hold her in his arms and make all the past hurts disappear. It would be so easy to fall for a man like Corey Wachawski.

But she wasn't here to start a relationship. She was in no position to fall for anyone. Erica extracted her hand because the contact seemed to be more about emotional connection than sexual stimulation, although the latter had certainly had its effect on her body. She shifted in her seat, trying to alleviate the ache. "What about you? Do you get on with your parents?"

Corey allowed her to steer the focus back onto him, even though this time Erica thought he was aware of her ploy. "My mother's great. Works as a secretary with a real estate company. My dad's a cop with thirty years on the job. He likes to rib me about becoming a fiery, says I broke his heart."

"Why didn't you go into police work?"

Griff chuckled. "He wanted to be in the beefcake calendar."

"Shut up." Corey rolled his eyes. "He's joking. That whole calendar thing's embarrassing."

"You see, Red, what you have here is the last of the noble men," Griff drawled. "He only posed for the firefighters calendar to raise money for the kids' burn unit—not for the chicks."

"What about you?"

Griff showed her a wide grin. "I did it for both reasons. And for a lark. I figure they were pretty desperate that year to ask a guy with a mug like mine to pose."

His self-deprecating statement had Erica studying the face in question. He wasn't handsome in the traditional, breath-stealing sense that Corey was. Griff's nose was a little crooked, his lips not as sinfully full as his friend's. But the lively sparkle that danced in his hazel eyes and the bold flash of his easy smile enhanced the appeal of his chiseled features, hard body and confident demeanor.

Corey said, "He's pretending to be modest. He knows he's in pretty good shape for an old bloke."

"Thirty-six is not old, you twenty-two-year-old shithead."

"Twenty-*five*."

"Close enough." Griff smiled. Erica sensed the age difference was an ongoing source of teasing between them. "I could still whip your butt in the gym, no matter how old you are."

"On the treadmill maybe. Not at the weight bench."

Erica listened, amused, as they continued their affectionate game of one-upmanship. So this was dick-measuring in action. She'd never had men do it for her benefit. Erica couldn't help but be a little flattered they might bother to try to impress her. Flattered and aroused.

She wanted them—both of them, like she'd never wanted before. But how on earth was she going to take the next step and make it happen?

"Can I buy you another drink?"

"Maybe a Coke," Erica replied to Corey's question. Her throat was suddenly parched.

Corey headed to the bar, leaving Griff and Erica alone. After the relatively easy banter they'd both shared with Corey, the sudden dearth of dialogue was as loud as the Nickelback hit playing in the background. Erica felt the weight of Griff's stare and the speculation in it.

Erica forced herself to meet his gaze and hold it. "I think one of my students would tell you to take a picture because it would last longer."

His lips quirked. "Just trying to figure it out."

"Figure what out?"

"Your angle." Griff placed his now-empty beer glass on the table and leaned his arms on the back of the turned-around chair he sat on. The change in posture brought his face mere inches from hers. His bald question was softly uttered, deceptively simple. "Do you want me?"

Erica found her mouth flapping open and shut uselessly for several wild thumps of her heart. "I can't believe you," she spluttered. "You're the bluntest person I've ever met."

"I like to know where I stand." He eyed her steadily for a tension-filled moment. "Are you going to answer?"

"What do you expect me to say?"

"That your nipples are so hard you have to keep crossing your arms to hide them. That you're so wet you can't stop squirming in your seat." The fact he'd noticed her discomfort made the heat in her body rise another few degrees. "Is that all for Corey? Or is there something in it for me?"

Erica glanced toward the bar to see Corey still waiting for the drinks. As though sensing her scrutiny, he turned and met her gaze. His smile was hot with promise, making Erica throb with awareness. Her mind raced with possibilities that Griff made more vivid with his rumbling words. "What do you think? Reckon he'll be willing to share you?"

"You know him best." Was that her voice sounding like Marilyn Munroe's? Was this *her*, staid, responsible Erica Shannon letting this virtual stranger know her deepest sexual desires? "You tell me."

"I'm not sure I know how it would sit with Corey." His soft admission told Erica Griff was rarely unsure of Corey. "Because I see the way he's looking at you, Red."

"How's that?"

"Like he wants to marry you a week from Sunday."

A chill raced through her, dampening some of her ardor. Long-term was not an option for her—now or possibly ever. "That's not going to happen. I can't have a relationship. But I want...I want..." *Damn my proper upbringing anyway. Why can't I just say it?*

"You want my hands on you." It was a statement, not a question, one that had Erica's insides puddling to mush while her every erogenous zone went on red alert. "Corey's hands too.

You want us both kissing you, touching you, making you come. You want us both loving you with everything we've got. Right?"

He'd outlined exactly what her body had craved for months, the sinful things she'd never really thought she'd have the temerity to admit she longed for. Here he was, offering them to her on a silver platter. Erica badly wanted to accept. More than anything else tonight, she wanted to *feel*, all the things she'd denied herself out of fear and modesty and her own reticence.

At length, Erica gave a wordless nod, the show of acquiescence making her skin prickle in anticipation. She was actually going to do this. Making the decision felt not unlike leaping off a cliff.

Griff closed his eyes briefly, as if he'd been hanging on her answer. When he opened them again there was devilish intent in their golden irises. "I can make it happen."

"Make what happen?"

Erica started guiltily when Corey reappeared, then chastised herself. She had nothing to feel guilty about. Corey was not her boyfriend, no matter how strangely familiar he might already seem to her. No matter how surprisingly human he was when she'd expected more arrogance from a man who looked like he did. She was a free woman and had every right to do as she pleased with Griff or any other man here.

"Give Erica a ride home," Griff replied. "You can both fit in with me."

"My car's in the shop," Corey explained ruefully. "It's kind of a rust bucket."

"Kind of?" Griff mocked.

"Griff was going to give me a lift." Corey ignored his friend's razzing. "Do you want to come with us?"

Did she want to *come* with them? She wanted to in every way that word could be interpreted.

Erica had taken the train straight here from work. If she hadn't, she would have been perfectly willing to lie about it and leave her car here overnight for the convenience of the local car

Sami Lee

thieves. "Yes," she said when she at last found her voice. "I'd like that."

I can make it happen, Griff had said. And he just had.

It was an awkward fit in the front of Griff's car, but as the Ute didn't have a backseat there wasn't much choice. Not that Corey minded. Once Erica was buckled into the middle space and he was wedged in beside her, he saw the benefits of having her so close. Her hair smelled like a spring garden and warmth emanated from her skin. Corey angled his body to the side to give her as much space as possible, and the soft curve of her shoulder pressed lightly into his chest.

Yep, there were definite advantages on his side.

Erica gave Griff her address and he pulled the vehicle out of the car park, having to reach between Erica's legs for the gearstick. Corey noticed the way Erica stiffened, and winced inwardly. She must think him the classiest guy ever for cramming her in the front seat of a car like a slice of cheese in a club sandwich.

"Erica?" Corey asked after they'd gone a few blocks and the tension in Erica's body didn't ease. "Are you comfortable?"

She turned toward him and smiled. Corey recognized irony in the gesture. "Not really."

"Would you rather sit on my lap?"

She made a tiny whimpering sound. Her face darkened in the dim light emanating from the dashboard instruments. "Do you make that offer to all the girls?"

"No." He'd sent Madison away, hadn't he? And thank God he had, or he wouldn't be here with Erica. "I've been waiting for you."

Erica quirked her brow in disbelief, apparently assuming, as most people did, that he never had to wait for any girl. Corey thought of telling her he hadn't been with as many women as she seemed to think, that he wasn't nearly as smooth as he wanted to be. A lot of the time his emotions ran away with him,

24

so he wasn't good at no-strings, casual sex. That was Griff's department. Corey didn't see the point of screwing some random woman whose name he could barely remember. Experiences like that left him cold.

Afraid Erica wouldn't believe him, he simply tried to be as honest as he could without getting into all that. "Erica, I really like being with you. I've seen you come into the Sovereign before and I wanted to meet you every time. I wish I'd done it sooner."

"You wanted to speak to me?" Her surprise was obvious. "Why didn't you?"

Corey shrugged. Across the car, Griff coughed into his hand meaningfully.

Erica glanced at Griff. "Pardon me?"

"You're not exactly the most approachable woman in the world," Griff said baldly. "You have a 'don't touch' look going on."

"Jeez, Griff." Corey groaned.

When Erica spoke her voice bordered on icy. "I see."

"There it is." Griff glanced toward her before returning his attention to the road. "The *look*."

"Erica." Corey tried for a soothing tone. "I think you're a stunner."

"But you also think I'm frigid, is that it?"

Corey could have sworn there was a smirk in Griff's voice. "I never said that."

"You're just a bit...daunting." Her eyes narrowed, and Corey hurried to fix the damage. "I mean to me. A bit. Because you seem really smart, and probably date doctors or lawyers, blokes with degrees, instead of guys like me."

Guys who barely finished high school and had to take the aptitude test twice before they'd let him become a fiery. Corey figured his verbal fumbling was only highlighting the notion he wasn't as intelligent as her or the men she was probably used to hanging out with. His heart felt heavy as he finished. "I thought you might tell me to take a walk."

Her anger seethed in the silence for a few moments during which Corey was certain he'd blown it completely. Why did Griff have to open his big mouth?

Then abruptly, Erica spoke, her words coming out in a staccato rhythm. "The last man I dated was a history professor. His name was Doug. We dated for over two years. We had plenty to talk about, but he was hardly interested in touching me. I want someone who's interested in touching me."

Corey was so stunned by the idea that Erica's ex-boyfriend hadn't been all over her every minute of every day that he didn't speak for a moment. Into the silence, Griff's laugh danced. His voice was warm and raspy. "I think you can stop looking, Red."

Corey watched in astonishment as Griff reached up and smoothed a hand over Erica's hair. It was a gesture filled with surprising affection, with tacit apology for his frankness. It was also a liberty taken that Corey was amazed Erica allowed. But she didn't upbraid Griff or wrench away. Instead she closed her eyes on a sigh, as though his touch contented her, made her...

No way. No way is Griff turning her on.

Corey curled a hand around Erica's nape. Her skin was supple and soft, the dark discs of her eyes like pools of melted chocolate. Shallow breaths puffed out of her, as though she was excited.

Because of Griff or him?

"Erica." Corey hardly recognized the steely determination in his voice. "*I* want to touch you."

The simple declaration didn't cover it, not when every muscle in his body strained from the effort of not mauling her where she sat. Corey fought to moderate his actions as he pulled her to him, covering her mouth with his. He had often imagined kissing Erica. In those dreams he'd always seduced her slowly, with patience and skill, turning her into putty and making her plead for more.

As much as he wanted to live up to those intentions, reality wasn't like that. Whatever finesse he possessed was obliterated by the plush invitation of her open lips, by the intoxicating mix of wine and sweet soda on her tongue. Her kiss drugged him, made him thirst for too much, too fast. He fed on her, devoured her.

She responded with enthusiasm, allowing him to take what he needed. Her keen little moans, the way she grabbed his shirt in frantic fistfuls as though she wanted to rip it off, lit a fire inside Corey. He'd been kissed with gusto before, but never quite like this. It was as though the first touch of his lips had released her from some unseen bondage, ties that kept her deep within herself. Once they got started it seemed like Erica drove the kiss, but it wasn't about her taking control. It was about her losing it.

It made Corey think she needed protecting. She was different from most other women he met. Erica was shy and soft and sweet, with a passionate center that electrified his senses. Their lips and their bodies fit together like a hand fit a glove. He *would* take care of her, give her whatever she needed.

Erica would be his. *All his.*

Her grip on his T-shirt tightened. She dragged the material upward and touched a hand to the bared skin of his torso. Corey's abs, along with everything else in the vicinity, went as hard as forged iron. "Erica." He wrenched his mouth away from hers and tried to catch his breath. "Slow down."

"Why?"

Right, Wachawski. Why? When she moved her touch downward and her fingers brushed his full-blown erection, Corey remembered. He winced and grabbed her wrist to keep her from exploring further. Aware that Griff was so close, Corey lowered his voice to a whisper. "I might come in my pants if you touch me there."

Erica flagrantly disobeyed him, settling her hand over his fly. Corey closed his eyes on a groan. It was as if her fingers were made to curl around him. He wondered how well they'd fit together everywhere else. Intuitively, he knew. *Perfectly.*

"Touch me, Corey."

Corey could have kicked himself for making her ask it in that heartrending voice. He was holding back to keep from making a fool of himself, not because he didn't want to put his hands all over her. How could she not know that?

Stupid professor dude.

He dipped his head and kissed her again, until she melted against him. Then he gently cupped a breast in his hand and squeezed. She was full and round, a bounty of soft womanly flesh. Through the filmy blouse she wore, her nipple thrust against his palm.

Corey rubbed his hand back and forth until her breath caught. "Is that how you want to be touched?"

"Yes, please."

Erica's hand flexed, lightly squeezing his cock. Corey couldn't prevent his hips from rocking into her grip. The thick denim was the only thing saving him from losing it completely. That'd be great, unloading prematurely while Griff was driving them home. Corey would never hear the end of it.

Glancing across the space that separated them, Corey thought he saw the ghost of a smirk on the other man's face and knew he was right. He also wondered if Griff's silence wasn't a tacit invitation for he and Erica to continue what they were doing as though he wasn't there.

Corey murmured, "Erica, how far away is your place?"

"I'm not sure." Erica blinked dazedly and glanced beyond him to the cityscape whizzing by.

"Five more minutes." Griff's voice was a thick husk, tinged with impatience rather than the amusement Corey would have expected. He gestured to the car in front. "Ten if this guy doesn't get a wriggle on."

Corey wondered if Griff was pissed off at him. "Are we bugging you, Griff?"

Griff flicked a glance his way. In the red-tinged glow from the traffic light, his eyes burned like lava. His jaw was set in a tense line that belied the lopsided grin he offered. "Not bothering me at all."

Something hot and prickly chased itself over Corey's already sensitive flesh. Griff was tense, but anger wasn't the cause. Was it possible...?

Erica settled her face into the curve of Corey's neck and swirled her tongue over his skin. As the car eased through the suburbs, Corey was now peripherally aware of his friend's presence. Of his friend's interest. He wondered if Erica was. If so, it did nothing to subdue her wild responses to his kisses. Neither did she stop him touching her breasts. And if Griff wasn't forced to concentrate on driving, he'd be able to see everything they were doing to each other.

Sure as anything, he could hear it.

"Corey, I want your hands on my skin."

God, he wanted that too. Corey wondered if she'd let him undo her blouse. If she'd let him part the fabric and unhook her bra right here in the car with Griff beside them.

The idea didn't horrify Corey. He could barely speak over the shock constricting his throat. "Now, Erica?"

"Yes, now."

The ugly sound of grinding gears punctuated Erica's plea. Griff was always so careful with his precious car that realization hit Corey. He wanted this. Griff wanted Erica too, so much so he was driving like someone on their learner's permit.

After Griff maneuvered into the correct gear he moved his hand off the shift...and settled it on Erica's leg.

Erica didn't object when Griff gave her thigh a squeeze. Corey stared at the sight and wondered why he didn't object, either. When Griff started slowly stroking his hand up and down, Erica caught her breath and glanced over at Griff.

Griff met her gaze. "Sure this is okay?"

Erica nodded, gasped again when Griff trailed his touch higher on her thigh. As Griff steered them through the maze of Friday-night traffic, Corey's gaze remained fixed on the sight of his friend's hand massaging Erica's leg, shifting her skirt upward, exposing the pale column of her thigh. Griff slipped beneath the shroud of grey material.

Erica said, "Oh *God*."

Inwardly, Corey echoed the sentiment. Griff was touching Erica's most intimate place. Stroking her and making her hips rock in helpless response.

Corey wondered why he didn't stop this, why he wasn't angry. Erica was shocked but not surprised by Griff's advances, giving Corey the distinct impression they'd hatched this plot together. He'd wanted to make Erica his, but at some point Corey's plan had been snatched out from under him. He should be seriously pissed at Griff for intruding on the intimacy he wanted to create with Erica.

Yet he wasn't. He was too turned on to think, so caught up in the unexpected, dirty beauty of watching Griff finger Erica that objection was the last thing on his mind. Perhaps he was in shock, or so swamped by arousal nothing else could penetrate his lust-fogged mind. All Corey knew was that he wanted to watch Erica come. This way, he'd be free to see every beautiful expression on her face while she lost herself at Griff's hand.

Jesus. He was thinking threesome and he'd never done anything like it before. Corey knew Griff had—with two women. Had he ever done it in this combination?

Griff's apparent self-assurance told Corey the answer was most likely yes. But Corey had no clue how something like this was supposed to play out. Suddenly, he felt as unsure as a virgin.

"Number eighteen, right?" Griff asked.

At Erica's nod, he swung the car to the left, into the driveway of a Queenslander-style house. He had to release Erica to power down the car. Completing the task in record time, Griff unsnapped his seat belt and turned.

In the dim light from the dash instruments Griff had left on, Corey recognized the heated glint of pure lust in his eyes.

He reminded Corey of a tiger. The shadows slanted across his face, dissecting the amber coloring of his hair and the topaz glimmer of his eyes. He all but growled, "It's too bloody late to tell me to stop, Cor. I have to make your girl come now."

Corey closed his eyes on a groan. Despite what Griff said, it wasn't too late. Griff would back off if Corey asked him to.

Beside him, Erica squirmed. "Please, Griff."

Hearing her utter another man's name like that stung. But lust acted like a buffer, protecting him from the worst of it. Corey wanted to see Griff make Erica come more than he wanted her to himself. He clung to Griff's words, how he'd referred to Erica as *your girl*. When this was all over Corey swore he'd make that happen, he'd make Erica his. Somehow.

Right now, she was *theirs*.

Chapter Three

With a minimum of preamble, Griff slipped his hand back beneath Erica's skirt to touch silken skin. She had one foot on each side of the gearstick already, but her thighs fell apart farther when he traced the edge of her cotton underwear.

She was all sultry heat and yielding softness, the embodiment of feminine temptation. Burying his face in the sweet-smelling curtain of her hair, Griff pushed his finger inside her slick channel and groaned at the ease of his entry. "You're so wet, Red. Tight and soft, just how I want you."

Her words were a breathless accusation. "You made me this way."

Griff chuckled and brushed his lips over Erica's earlobe. "Corey started it, but you liked knowing I could hear everything that was going on. It made you hotter, didn't it? It made you all slippery and ready for my touch."

When she didn't immediately respond, Griff gave her earlobe a sharp little nip. She gasped and thrust her hips into the steady motion of his hand. "Yes," she admitted. "It turned me on. I like you being here too."

Corey emitted a guttural noise. There was helpless arousal in the sound, with an underpinning discontent Griff couldn't deny. Corey had wanted Erica to himself tonight, but here she was wedged between the two of them because Griff had been— *face it*—a bit of a selfish prick. He'd made sure he got what *he* wanted, no matter that it usurped Corey's plans. The fact that Erica wanted this too didn't nullify what it cost Corey to give up the alone time with Erica he'd been aching for.

Griff had no intention of stealing Erica out from under his friend, even if she was turning out to be a sexual firecracker, a forceful woman capable of ensuring her needs were met. In other words, much more Griff's type than he'd realized.

He pushed aside the inkling of regret that surfaced at the idea of giving Erica up after only one night. "Corey." Griff waited until Corey tore his eyes off Erica's face to meet his gaze. "It'll be all right. It's like a treat for her, both of us wanting her so bad, making her feel good. Just this once."

"Yeah, I get it." Despite the words, uncertainty remained in Corey's expression. He licked his lips in a nervous gesture. "What do I do?"

Oh fuck. A thousand possibilities flitted through Griff's mind, at least half of them things that were definitely not on the menu. His cock jerked inside his jeans. His heart became a wild, hammering thing in his chest.

All because Corey Wachawski had licked his lips and asked for instructions.

Holy shit.

Erica whimpered in disappointment, making Griff realize he'd stilled the motion of his finger. He returned his attention to her, trying to wrestle his unwelcome Corey-related urges back into the lockbox they'd been stuffed in for going on five years now. Firmly reminding himself that they belonged there, always, because Corey's sexuality was not a malleable thing, the way his was.

"How about it, Red?" His voice was thick, his query slow in coming. Desire seemed to have swollen his tongue. "Do you want Corey to kiss those pretty tits of yours?"

"*Yes.*"

Corey was working at the buttons of her blouse before the word was out of Erica's mouth. Griff saw the other man's fingers trembling as he parted Erica's blouse and shifted her bra cups aside, exposing her breasts. The full globes were just visible in the scant light from the dash instruments, but Griff's breath caught.

Corey sighed. "Erica, you're perfect." Then he bent his head to her.

The soft sucking sounds Corey made as he gave Erica's breasts their due attention made Griff's cock buck and weep inside his Levis. "That's it, Cor, suck those tasty nipples. Make her squirm." Griff wasn't even sure Corey heard him because his voice was so raspy. He whispered in Erica's ear. "You like it, Red? You just about ready to come?"

Her incoherent moan wasn't clear, but the hot spill of her feminine juice on his fingers screamed yes. She was close to losing it. Hell, Griff was close to losing it himself, merely from the sound and smell of her—of both of them.

The metallic noise of Corey's zipper being lowered rent the claustrophobic space of his car's interior. Griff squeezed his eyes shut, as though that could somehow lessen the impact of the knowledge that Erica was blindly reaching into Corey's open jeans and fondling his cock.

"Erica, I can wait."

"No," Griff found himself saying. He nipped at the tender flesh of Erica's earlobe and touched his thumb to the swollen nub of her clit. "Do it, Red. Take Corey's hard cock out and stroke it. Get him off while I'm finger-fucking this tight, juicy cunt of yours. I want to see you both come."

Corey offered a weak protest, but Erica followed Griff's commands without question. Griff heard the telltale sound of her hand working on the stiff flesh of Corey's hard-on. It mingled with Corey's groan of delight as he all but fell back against the passenger door and let her pleasure him.

Griff kept nipping at Erica's throat, kept thrusting into her with his finger and circling her clit with his thumb. He didn't look at what she was doing to Corey. He couldn't look and maintain any semblance of restraint.

Christ, he thought he could have an uncomplicated three-way with these two without wishing it could be more. Without wishing Erica wasn't the only one making Corey come. Without wishing Corey was the type to let him go that far.

Apparently not. Damn it all, he wanted Corey too.

Griff tried to tune out those desires, rasping into Erica's ear. "How does that feel? Good?"

She nodded. "Yes. So good."

Her obvious need egged him on. "How about Corey's dick? How does it feel to hold him in your hand?"

"Oh, he's so..."

"*Tell me.*"

"So big."

Shit. He so did not need to know that.

"Erica." Her name was a tortured moan on Corey's lips. "I'm going to lose it if you don't stop."

"Don't stop, Red," Griff said. "Make him come. *Now.*"

"*Griff.*"

Corey stared at him, his expression tense. His lips were parted, his breath falling out in rapid pants. "Erica." Corey spoke her name but didn't take his eyes off Griff. "I can't stop, I'm going to come."

Griff swallowed a curse, helpless to do anything but watch as Corey arched his hips, blowing all over Erica's proper-looking skirt and blouse. He almost lost it himself but held back with all he had in him, concentrating instead on adding pressure to Erica's clit, shafting her as deep as he could with his finger. He tongued the shell of her ear and murmured, "Your turn, gorgeous. Come for us now."

A sob choked out of her and she convulsed around him. She tried to slam her legs together but couldn't because of the gearstick, so Griff kept the pressure on to help her ride it out, talking her through it with gently cooed words until her writhing body sagged against the seat, spent.

"Erica, I am so sorry."

Regret and embarrassment mingled in Corey's apology, but Erica's response was nothing but dreamy awe. "Don't be. Nothing like that's ever happened to me before."

"Oh, baby."

35

Griff withdrew from Erica's body, turning away, as the two of them kissed. He ran a hand through his hair, only to realize it was shaking. The need for air had him yanking on the door handle and all but stumbling into the darkness.

The suburban street was quiet. A half-moon formed a white semi-circle in the black sky, a smattering of stars twinkled like shattered glass. Griff stared up at the universe, willing his heart to slow and his body to cool.

He should not have started this. He was at risk of repeating past mistakes, and Griff really wanted to be too smart for that. Yet right now he felt as stupid as he had years ago when he'd first realized his lovers, Anna and Jack, saw him as an add-on to their life, not an integral part of it.

"Griff."

Griff turned to find Erica studying him, her dark eyes fathomless in the moonlight. Her lips were swollen and still wet from Corey's kisses, which only reminded Griff he hadn't even tasted them. Kisses weren't for him, because he wasn't part of the main couple. He was the third wheel—again—which granted him access only to what was left over.

Which, he reminded himself, could amount to a hell of a good time.

Having a good time here, that's all.

Griff reached up to trail his knuckles over Erica's cheek. "How are you holding up there, cute stuff?"

She lowered her head, a show of discomfiture. "I didn't even say thank you."

"Jesus, you never have to thank a guy for *that*." He wondered if her limp-dick professor had made her think she was some kind of tedious responsibility, and figured he'd smack the guy's face with relish should the two of them ever meet.

Corey emerged from the dark to stand behind Erica. He slid his arm around her waist and drew her back against him. As though she were his, and only his.

Dale Griffin, you need to get back in your car and drive away, as fast as you can.

Griff didn't listen to the sensible inner voice but instead did the least sensible thing possible. He stepped forward and took Erica's face in his hands, drawing her mouth to his.

Sealing his lips over hers had a predictable effect on his libido. His cock stretched even more painfully, his blood pumped with renewed impatience through his veins. Less predictable was the way her soft lips and luxurious sigh made his gut clench. There was a vulnerability in her kiss that contradicted the boldness with which she threaded her fingers through his hair and offered herself. The sweetness of her belied the wanton way she arched into him, pressing her breasts to his chest.

Her blouse was still open from their activities in the car. Griff could feel the heat of her flesh permeating the fabric of his shirt. He also felt Corey holding her more tightly to him, brushing his lips over her temple as Griff played with her mouth.

It would be so easy to lift his head and pull Corey in too. To kiss that fucking sexy mouth of his while one of them—both of them—reached up and caressed the body between them, toying and teasing and tweaking until all three of them were reckless with lust once more.

Griff wrenched his mouth away from Erica's before he did something *really* stupid. Her aloof veneer had been completely stripped away, leaving an expression of raw need and tender fragility. That expression caught him in the chest and held tight. Corey's girl had a powerful effect on him, not all of it sexual. He *should* leave. But he couldn't, no matter what he risked by staying.

"Let's get you inside, Red," he said, "Before I do something nasty to you on the hood of this car."

Erica's bathroom was redolent with the aroma of lavender. When Griff turned on the shower taps, steam billowed out of the long, narrow stall like sweet-scented smoke. It wrapped around the three of them, shrouding them in a sultry mist.

Griff threaded his fingers through Erica's hair and gently tipped her head back so he could place a trail of wet kisses along her throat. "Corey made you all sticky, didn't he, gorgeous? We're going to wash you off now."

Corey felt his cheeks heat at Griff's words. If he'd made her "sticky" it was at least half Griff's fault. He'd egged Erica on. And he'd stared at Corey the whole time, with such a searing, hot expression that Corey had been unable to temper his response. He'd come, forcefully, without ever tearing his gaze from his best friend's.

At the time it hadn't seemed like a monumental thing. Now, as Erica helped Griff out of his T-shirt, Corey's heart thundered in his chest. Anticipation dried his mouth as Griff's golden skin was revealed, inch by inch—his ripped abs, his taut chest, and the armband tattoo that encircled his left biceps.

Erica trailed her fingernails over it, clearly fascinated. Griff smiled. "Not the kind of girl who dates guys with tattoos, are you, Red?"

"No," Erica admitted, almost bitterly. "I'm the boring, cautious type."

"Not from where I'm standing." Griff reached up and tweaked her nipple through the thin silk of her bra to make his point. "Nothing boring about you. Right, Cor?"

Griff turned Erica in his arms so her back was pressed to his chest. Then he unhooked her bra and let it fall to the tiled floor. In the scant light of the car, Erica had taken Corey's breath away. Now, he thought he might have a heart attack. "You're very exciting, Erica," he croaked.

"He's been eyeing you from across that pub for months, trying to find a way to talk to you. You've got her now, mate," Griff pointed out. "So come and play with her."

Heat scorched Corey's face as he realized he stood in the doorway like a dolt, doing nothing to participate. In one hurried motion, he hauled his shirt over his head and strode toward

Erica. Griff held her out to him like a gift, and Corey took her into his arms, kissing her lush mouth, eating up her excited little moans like each one was a sweet, long-hungered-for morsel. Her breasts skimmed his chest, their taut crests scraping his skin in a delicious friction that made his jeans way too tight.

He was going to blow prematurely—*again*—if he wasn't careful.

Erica gasped into Corey's mouth when Griff parted the zipper of her skirt, causing the garment to go the way of her blouse and bra. Corey slid his grip downward and cupped her ass through the dainty panties she wore, bringing her into closer contact with his raging erection.

"God, what an ass," Griff rumbled. "Strip those panties off her."

Corey's excitement spiked, his fingers working immediately to do Griff's bidding. He took Griff's orders all the time. Griff was a senior firefighter, above Corey's pay grade and miles beyond him in work experience. Griff had never given him instructions in a personal setting before, but following them felt entirely natural and somehow strangely thrilling at the same time.

Being told what to do by Griff was *hot*.

"Oh yeah." Griff ran his hands over Erica's bared ass cheeks, his fingers brushing against Corey's in the process. Corey's pulse leapt. His arms were full of warm, willing woman, and the sinuous movement of her feminine body aroused him unbearably. But there was something else going on, something blazing in the air between him and Griff that added an edge to his desire, that nudged a boundary Corey wanted to push wider even as the thought of it scared him.

What the hell was happening?

"Get her in the shower. She's going to run out of hot water at this rate."

Griff's easy humor dispelled some of the tension. Corey chuckled as he guided Erica into the stall, hanging back long enough to step out of his jeans before following her in. "I don't know about you," he began when he had her in his arms again. He lowered his voice so only she could hear him above the patter of water on tile. "But I'm a little nervous."

The laugh Erica released tremored. "Me too."

"I won't hurt you." It was an easy assurance to give—he meant it with every fiber in him. "Neither will Griff. He's a good guy."

She smiled softly. "I know."

Corey smiled too, delighted that she'd seen past Griff's sometimes-brusque exterior to the decent man beneath. It made his emotions open more to her, strengthened the kinship he felt already existed between them. "You're a special woman, you know that, Erica?"

From the way she almost blanched at his praise and ducked her head, Corey figured she had no idea. Heck, it didn't make any logical sense that he was so sure of it. But somehow he was.

He wanted to make her sure of it too.

When Griff stepped into the shower with them, he dropped a couple of foil packets into the soap dish. Then he plucked a bottle of shower gel from where it rested on a glass shelf and squirted a generous amount over Erica's back.

"I can tell you've never done anything like this before, Erica." It was the first time Griff had called her by her Christian name, and his voice gentled as he spoke it. He rubbed the shower gel in slow circles over her shoulders until it lathered and made her skin slick and fragrant. "So we'll take it slow. We'll be gentle—if you want it rough you'll have to tell us, okay?"

He waited until Erica nodded, surprise in her eyes. Corey doubted she'd ever asked for anything rough in her life.

"And we'll make it easy on you. I'm going to tell Corey what to do to you." Against Erica's soft stomach, Corey's hardness jerked. "All you have to worry about is enjoying everything. Okay?"

"O-okay."

"You can trust me. Corey too. You know that, don't you?"

Corey was gratified by Erica's unequivocal nod. That trust was important to him.

"Get down on your knees, Cor," Griff told him in that gravelly, lust-thickened voice. "I want to watch you eat Erica's tasty-looking cunt."

God. Like before, Corey didn't hesitate. He eased Erica back against the tiled wall, out of the direct line of the shower spray. Then he lowered before her.

Using both thumbs, Corey gently parted her lips and ran his tongue along the inner edge of them, narrowly avoiding her most sensitive place. Erica writhed against the slippery tiles at her back, thrusting her pussy at Corey's face. Corey kept teasing her with his tongue, knowing her eventual release would be more intense if he took his time. She'd already climaxed in the car, and he wanted the second time to be equally as good.

"That's it, Cor. Like that."

Griff was standing beside Erica, playing with her eager tits, his gaze alternating between watching her and fixing on Corey, on what he was doing between Erica's legs.

And there, right beside Corey's head, was Griff's cock. It was long and large, the smooth skin covering it flushed red with arousal. His balls were full and tight. Griff was the only person who hadn't come yet, and it was obvious he badly needed to.

Corey was fascinated, excited and...tempted. By what?

Griff's cock. He was tempted to transfer his tongue from Erica's pussy to the throbbing head of Griff's hard-on and taste it, tease it, please it. Until Griff lost control for once in his life.

Holy fuck.

Corey's gaze slammed into Griff's as the impact of his thoughts hit full force. He was wondering what it would be like

41

to give his best friend a blow job. Griff's eyes were knowing, tortured, as if he sensed Corey's state of mind.

As if he wanted the same thing and was tormented by his inability to ask for it.

"She needs to come." Griff could just as easily have been talking about himself. "Suck her clit. Don't stop until she screams your name."

Turning away from those other, confusing urges, Corey bent his head to Erica again, taking her sweet bud into his mouth.

Chapter Four

"You like the way that feels, don't you, Erica?"

Griff's rasped query made Erica tear her gaze away from the sight of Corey's dark head moving at the juncture of her thighs. Griff's eyes glittered like shards of polished topaz fanning out from the dark spots of his pupils. His excitement was a thick aura radiating from him, a mixture of potent male pheromones that could so easily have threatened her.

Yet Erica wasn't frightened of Griff, any more than she was of Corey.

He traced circles around her areola with his wet, gel-slicked fingers. "Christ, you have a body on you. I can't wait to sink my hard dick inside it."

Erica's hips bucked in an involuntary response. Corey's grip on her thighs tightened, maintaining control of what he was doing. No fantasy she'd ever had could measure up to the reality of having Corey's insistent tongue between her legs and Griff's adroit hands stroking her breasts.

"Yeah, that's it, Erica. I like it when you lose control." To Corey he said, "Finger her hot cunt while you're doing that. Find that G-spot and tickle it."

Against her pussy Corey's groan vibrated. Her inner walls contracted even before Corey drove his finger inside her, searching for a special place Erica had always thought a myth. She soon changed her mind as Corey fluttered his middle finger far inside her core, sending out delicious ripples of ecstasy. "Oh God!"

"That's it. Don't stop," Griff commanded. "Suck her clit nice and hard."

Corey did as Griff demanded, taking Erica's eager button into his mouth and suckling. He kept moving his finger inside her while Griff pinched her nipples repeatedly. The intense pleasure of it all unraveled Erica. She climaxed violently, spilling wetness on Corey's tongue that he eagerly lapped up.

"Christ, Red." Griff turned her face toward him so he could claim her mouth in a marauding kiss. The hand with which he cupped her cheek trembled, bespeaking his own as-yet-unfulfilled needs.

Erica wanted to satisfy him—both of them. So when Griff made his next husky demand she didn't bother summoning the energy to question it. "Turn around and face the wall."

She put her back to the men, staring at the cheerful yellow and white tiles through the billowing steam in the stall.

"Put your hands flat on the tiles."

Her heart thundering, Erica did as Griff said.

"Corey, what do you want her to do?"

Corey's thick, excited voice answered, "Spread your legs apart, baby."

Erica's womb throbbed as she did what she was told. She was not a submissive woman, but there was something so darkly thrilling in following their instructions, not quite knowing where it would lead.

"Oh yeah," Griff said. "Push your ass back as far as you can."

Erica whimpered as she did it, curving her spine. On the wall beside her, Erica saw two hands reach for the foil packets Griff had placed in the soap dish earlier. Anticipation was like a hot spike in her womb as Griff announced, "Corey and I are going to take turns fucking you now, Red. Does that sound okay?"

Erica was so light-headed she could barely nod. "Yes."

Mere seconds later her entrance was prodded by something hard and hot. Erica didn't know which of the men was positioned there and for some reason the idea delighted her.

She closed her eyes, prolonging the moment of mystery, the absolute wickedness of having her private parts breached and of having no certainty of who was doing it.

Her pussy walls rippled over the invading cock as it moved within her. She moaned her satisfaction as it filled her completely. Behind her she heard the soft sound of Corey's swearing and thought it must be him inside her. But a moment later, she registered the callused grip that held her hips in place and knew it was Griff.

She knew the difference in the way they used their hands, the subtle variety in the texture of their skin. Already, she knew. It was astonishing.

Opening her eyes, Erica glanced over her shoulder. She saw Corey standing a little to the left, staring at the place where Griff's cock pushed inside her in smooth strokes. Griff pulled her ass cheeks apart, and Erica knew he did it to improve Corey's view.

Griff asked, "You like watching?"

Corey merely nodded in response to Griff's question.

"I like it too."

Griff pulled out of her then, making an incoherent wail of protest burst from Erica's mouth. But she wasn't abandoned for long. Corey was soon positioned between her spread thighs, the broad head of his cock dipping into her wetness. He grasped her hips and pushed inside.

Erica gasped. She knew enough not to say so, but Corey was bigger than Griff. His girth stretched her, made her muscles get some serious exercise as he started plunging in and out.

She sensed Griff watching the show with as much rapt interest as Corey had. The sexual escapades of her fantasy life had been all about her pleasure, they'd never included this level of voyeurism. They were watching each other have sex with her. It should have made her feel used, violated. Instead it made her feel like a treasure they shared.

"Erica, baby," Corey panted. "You're incredible. So tight and hot."

Moving close to her ear, Griff murmured, "Tighter for him than it was for me." Erica turned wide eyes toward him but he merely chuckled. "Fucking huge, isn't he?"

Erica managed a rueful smile while her body jerked with each plunge of Corey's massive member. "Oh my God, yes."

Griff pressed his smiling lips to her temple. "You're very sweet to try and protect my ego that way, cute stuff. But I'm just glad we're showing you a good time."

He reached over her head for something. A moment later there was the cool trickle of shower gel on her lower back. Griff turned it to lather with his hand, then spread it downward to coat her ass. "Slow down for a sec, Cor."

The way Corey clutched her hips told Erica it cost him dearly, but he slowed his pace. Then Griff's hand slid into the cleft of her ass, his finger inching toward her back entrance.

When he first probed the opening, Erica flinched. "I won't do anything you don't like." Griff said. "I promise."

It wasn't logical, the trust Erica had so swiftly placed in them. Yet it was there, as real as the water cascading all around. "It's okay."

Griff dipped one digit into the tightness of her asshole. Her muscles clenched around him, a pleasant contraction that made her vagina spasm around Corey's cock. When Griff slowly sank his finger in deeper, she moaned. Corey swore graphically, the motion of his thrusting cock stilling completely.

"You like how that looks?" Griff asked him.

"Jesus... Holy shit, Griff."

Griff continued manipulating her hole with teasing strokes of his gel-coated finger. "Thinking about stuffing your huge dick in there?"

Even as Erica gasped, both thrilled and apprehensive, Corey hesitated. "I've never done that to anyone. I don't want to hurt her."

"Show off," Griff drawled. He murmured in Erica's ear. "Have you ever had anyone in your ass before?"

Erica shook her head. "But I have..." she stumbled over the humiliating confession, "...toys."

Pulling back, Griff stared at her. This time when he laughed it was a sound full of admiration. "Erica Shannon, you are my kind of woman. You want me to fuck this beautiful, tight ass of yours, don't you? You naughty little tart."

Erica blushed at his teasing, at the unexpected deliciousness of being called a tart when she'd never been anything but prim and ladylike. At least never before tonight.

With a groan of tortured disappointment, Corey withdrew from her body to give Griff room. Griff's lightly haired thighs pressed against the back of hers as he nudged at her back entrance with the head of his penis.

The first press of his shaft into her body made Erica still. "Relax," he told her, and with a long release of breath she did. Her body grew more pliant, allowing her to accept Griff's careful entry.

Erica lost her breath, so stunned was she by the shock of sensations. There was a level of discomfort she could never have been entirely prepared for, no matter how many times her toys had been put to use. Griff remained motionless, letting her grow accustomed to having him seated so deep inside her. She felt the ragged draw and exhale of his breath on her back and knew he wanted to move faster, but he refrained. For her sake.

He snaked a hand around her body, finding the thatch of springy wet curls at her front. He flicked a finger over the flowering bud of nerves buried within. The spike of pleasure was intense. She rocked back against him in reaction. Then he began to move his cock in her ass with confident strokes while he increased the pressure on her clit with his finger.

The urge to hurtle at high speed to the end welled inside her. "Oh God, Griff. Griff..."

"Easy." He moved his hand away from her mound and shortened the length of his thrusts. "It gets better."

Better? Any better and she might shatter. Yet she knew he was right when he removed her hands from the wall, holding her steady with his sturdy body while Corey stepped around to stand before her.

He was so big. His chest was smooth, the lightly tanned skin packed full of strong, well-defined muscles. His penis was beautiful, sprouting from the patch of thick dark hair between his legs like a promise.

"God, Erica." Corey stepped forward, but Griff put a hand on his chest to stop him from grabbing her and stuffing her full of his cock in one desperate plunge.

Griff's hand remained on Corey's chest, the tanned fingers splayed over his pectoral. Corey looked over her shoulder at Griff, something passing between them in the eye contact. A secret, a mystery Erica wasn't sure she should be privy to. If there was more to Griff and Corey's relationship than met the eye, now wasn't the time to figure it out. Right now she was willing to be selfish and concentrate on her own pleasure. Closing her eyes, she let her head drop back on Griff's shoulder.

Griff withdrew from her body slowly, making Erica yelp in protest. But a moment later he held her by the legs and lifted her up, opening her wide so Corey could step into the V made by her thighs.

His hard chest brushed the sensitive tips of her breasts. The need for release was so thinly stretched that her feminine muscles clenched at the scant contact. Corey's chest vibrated with the rumbling noise he made, as though he shared the precipice on which she teetered.

"Wrap your legs around him, Erica."

She did as Griff instructed, and the instant her feet met at the base of Corey's spine his cock cleaved a path all the way to the door of her cervix.

Erica clutched Corey's shoulders, her fingernails digging deep into the flesh. His face was a mask of ecstasy and restraint as he moved inside her. He filled her utterly, crowding into her feminine spaces and bringing her to life.

Into her ear, Griff murmured, "I'm going to come back inside you now."

Corey withdrew enough to allow Griff entry. Griff groaned as he sank his cock into her in one gliding motion. Corey supported her with his strong frame while Griff pumped into her ass a few frantic times. Then he slowed once more, allowing Corey to ease her pussy over his erection.

They were both inside her, filling and extending her body to its outer limits.

"God, God, God." She buried her face in Corey's neck and held him so tight her arms shook.

"Is it okay?" Corey asked.

She wriggled between them, her flesh sliding between Corey's chest and Griff's back. "It's unbelievable. Please, I want you to move."

"You want us to fuck you," Griff murmured in her ear. "Say it like that. I want to hear those dirty words coming out of your prim, schoolteacher mouth."

Griff punctuated his statement with a slow rotation of his hips. "Oh God, yes." Erica relented. "Fuck me, please. I want you both to fuck me."

They began taking turns inside her depths, working together like alternating pistons. Corey would drive his cock all the way home, right to her G-spot. Then as he pulled back, Griff would slide into her ass. It was slow at first while the men got used to each other's rhythm. Soon enough they started moving with almost mechanical precision.

But they weren't machines, they were men. Hot, healthy and full of passion. Their breathing was ragged, their moans tortured. They both needed to climax, as much as she did, and were hanging on to their control by the tips of their fingers.

Corey bent his head, his teeth nipping at her neck while his hands moved up to cover her breasts. "It's incredible," he said. "I can feel..."

"We can feel each other, Erica," Griff finished Corey's thought. "Through that thin wall of tissue you have inside you. I can feel Corey's cock sliding against mine."

The cadence of Corey's thrusts increased as though he could no longer exert mastery over the pace. "I'm going to lose it."

Griff slid his hand between Erica's legs. His knuckles brushed Corey's stomach as he did so and Erica felt Corey's recoil, heard the sharp gasp that fell out of him at the contact. "Griff...oh shit."

Griff located Erica's clitoris just as Corey jerked his release inside her. With fast-circling fingers, Griff pushed her toward her own climax. The sensations came at her from so many directions Erica hardly knew where or when her orgasm began. It was simply there, all around her like a rainstorm, inside her like a thousand tiny sparks of lightning.

Then Griff's thrusts grew savage in her ass. Erica's pussy clenched the remnants of her orgasm around Corey's still-hard cock as Griff let out an all-mighty roar, his organ pulsing inside her with the fury of his release.

Corey leaned back against the shower wall, his arms banding Erica tight to him. Griff all but collapsed on her back, wedging her between them. She felt as heavy and immovable as a bag of wet sand, replete in a way she had never been before.

If these were her last moments on earth, she'd die a happy woman.

The thought gripped her in its icy fingers. A chill chased its way over her body.

"Baby, are you cold?"

Cold didn't cover it. The steam still billowing around them was hot, but Erica was suddenly frozen inside. Reality had returned with the brutal force of an ice storm.

She'd die a happy woman.

But she didn't want to die. She wanted to live.

"Hey, Red. What's up?"

Griff pulled out of her body, his voice a soothing timbre. Erica levered away from Corey's chest until he too released her. With shaking hands, Erica opened the shower door and grabbed her towel, wrapping it around herself.

It didn't do any good. The chill was on the inside.

Someone shut off the water. Erica glanced back to see Corey and Griff stepping out of the stall, concerned looks on their faces. They were big, naked and wet. The reckless impulse that had compelled her to seek out this encounter made little sense to her now. She'd just let two men she barely knew inside her body. She'd let them *fuck* her, begged them to.

In her aunt's shower—her conservative spinster aunt who would never have approved of this kind of behavior.

What on earth had she been thinking?

"I...I'm sorry." She had no idea what she was apologizing for, but Erica was beyond cogent thought. Now that the whirlwind of crazy passion had died down, she was appalled at herself.

Without another word, Erica dashed out of the bathroom. She made her way to the bedroom across the hall, the one that had been hers since that summer she was twelve and life as she knew it changed irrevocably. She pulled her robe from its hanger and slipped it on.

"Erica?"

She turned to see Corey standing in the doorway to her bedroom wearing only his jeans and an expression of deep remorse. "Did we hurt you?"

Erica shook her head. She couldn't let him think that.

"You're upset." He stepped into the room and put his hands on her shoulders. "Why?"

"I...I don't know." She offered the lie because she knew she couldn't spill the entire truth to Corey. He was a nice guy—a *wonderful* guy. He would probably feel obligated to comfort her if he knew...

Erica crossed her arms over her chest, trying to warm her suddenly chilled fingers. She brushed the spot on the side of her left breast where it was.

The lump.

Erica trembled, horrified anew at the implications of it. The same implications that it had held for Aunt Claire a year ago, for her mother over two decades before that.

Oh God.

"Erica, you're scaring me."

Erica had been scared for as long as she could remember. That's the person she was, timid, fearful. Not the bold, adventurous woman Griff and Corey had seen tonight. She'd wanted to remind herself she was alive, to live fearlessly, recklessly and completely, even for just a moment.

But that moment was over. Now, she had to face reality. She had to do what she should have done from the first. Make an appointment with her doctor and prepare for the worst.

Because the worst could be here sooner than she'd expected.

"I'm all right."

From the hallway Griff heard Erica's words and recognized the patent untruth. He zipped his jeans and headed for the bedroom.

Apparently Corey was as unconvinced by Erica's assurance as Griff. "Tell me, baby. Are you upset because of what I…because you thought I was interested in Griff?"

Griff halted his strides, freezing in the bedroom doorway. His heart seized in his chest as he stared at Corey's broad, bare back. Moonlight shining through the window and the light from the hall provided soft illumination. Griff could just make out the way Erica's head shifted from side to side.

"I suspected you were. It doesn't bother me."

Erica suspected it? Griff had been sure he'd imagined those few hot looks Corey sent his way, the crackling awareness that had popped up between them. He'd figured it was all a product of his own wishful imagination.

But Erica had seen something too. Not only that, it didn't faze her. Had Griff really thought she'd be the closed-minded, judgmental type? From her sexy performance in the shower and now this, Griff realized he'd been dead wrong about her.

She was in fact the perfect woman.

And Corey, Griff's perfect man, his dirty little infatuation, was *interested* in him.

Holy fuck.

"Whatever else happened, it doesn't change what I feel about you," Corey was saying. "I care about you, Erica. I know you must think I do this sort of thing all the time, but I don't. You're special to me."

"You're special to both of us."

The two of them turned, making Griff understand he'd said the words aloud. His palms started to sweat. He didn't tell his one-night-women they were special because he wasn't the lying kind. But the truth rang in his words, bringing a sense of déjà vu.

He'd been this quick with Anna and Jack. One night and he was a goner. Oh man was he in trouble.

Their declarations had the opposite effect on Erica than the one they'd intended. She stepped away from Corey, her face setting in grim lines. "You don't have to say that. It was very nice of you both to bring me home and... Well, it was nice. Thank you, but I'm fine."

Thank you? What was with this woman and all the gratitude? They ought to be thanking her, not the other way around.

"It was nice?" Corey's tone was incredulous. "That doesn't do it justice. Erica, come on. You're not trying to say you want us to leave now. Are you?"

Even before she responded, Griff could see that was exactly what Erica was trying to say, in her too-well-bred-to-be-that-blunt manner. She wanted them gone, not five minutes after they'd shared their bodies. The swiftness of her dismissal stabbed at Griff's gut.

Tonight Griff had gotten a glimpse of perfection. A sensuous, giving woman willing to push her sexual boundaries and a man who—God help him—he'd been quietly in love with for years reacting to him as more than a mate for the first time. The potential for the ultimate satisfaction was there, but it was out of reach if Erica wasn't willing to explore it.

"I think it's best if you go."

Erica's quiet statement confirmed it. She was kicking the both of them out of bed before they ever got in it.

"How can you say that, Erica? I thought we'd spend the night together. Don't you want to?"

"Corey, I can't."

"We don't have to do anything. We can just talk or sleep. Whatever you want."

Griff felt his skin prickle. Wachawski was on the verge of making a huge fool of himself.

"Corey, please. I didn't expect you to stay after we had sex."

Corey took a step backward as though she'd punched him. Instinctively, Griff strode toward him, clapping him on the shoulder in case he needed the steadying hand. "Come on, Cor. Time to head off."

"What? No." Corey shook his head and implored Erica. "It was more than sex. You felt it too, I know it."

"Corey, don't." Griff needed to do a little imploring of his own. He couldn't stand to see Corey get snubbed like this and have the guy reduced to begging. Griff understood what he was going through. He also wished like hell tonight had lasted longer than this, but what could they do?

Not stay where they weren't wanted, that was for damn sure. That was something Griff had promised himself he'd never do again.

Griff tightened his grip on Corey's shoulder and urged him toward the door. Erica watched them move away, an unreadable expression on her face. It was as though she'd disappeared inside herself, throwing up a solid wall between her and the outside world. A barrier between her and them.

Instinct told Griff that barrier wasn't coming down anytime soon.

Snagging their shirts from the floor on the way, Griff guided a stunned Corey out of Erica's house. They didn't say anything as they got into Griff's car and he pulled out into the street. Corey remained silent for so long Griff felt the need to break the tension. "Rejection's supposed to build character, you know."

Corey snorted softly. "Jerk."

Griff smiled to himself and kept driving. They made it to the street in front of Corey's apartment complex before either of them spoke again.

Sounding resigned, Corey said, "I still really like her."

Griff thought of Erica's silly habit of thanking him for getting her off, of her blushing admission that she owned sex toys. He sighed weightily. "I like her too."

"I think there's something wrong. Something must have upset her to make her do...what we all just did."

Corey's words echoed Griff's thoughts. From the start he hadn't picked Erica Shannon as the threesome type. "Maybe, but that's none of our business."

He felt Corey's gaze on his profile, sensed the myriad questions he considered asking. He wanted to broach the subject of what happened in the shower, or what *might* have happened between the two of them if they'd spent any more time in three-way heaven. He was wondering where they went from here, now that it seemed they both had an equal stake in the whole Erica situation.

"I won't do anything about her. She's yours if you want to give her a call, check up on her." The offer tightened Griff's chest. *She's only a woman, Griffin. Plenty of those around.* "Just because she couldn't handle two on one, doesn't mean she wouldn't be interested in hearing from you."

"I don't know. Maybe."

"Go on." Griff forced a smile. "It'll be a change-up, you having to pursue a girl for once. Usually they fall in your lap and beg you to fuck 'em. You've gotten lazy."

Corey flipped him the bird, a grin playing on his lips.

Griff let out a quiet sigh of relief. If there was a dose of regret mingled in with it, so be it. He'd done what he should have done from the first—stepped aside and left the lovebirds alone. He knew he was cutting off any possibility that he'd get to explore Corey's interest in *him*, too. Griff would never forget tonight though, or those brief moments where Corey had looked at him like he wanted to go down that road.

He had a bad feeling it wasn't going to be so easy to forget about Erica Shannon either.

Chapter Five

"Are you going to the Sovereign tonight?"

Erica managed to hide her inner wince at Pam Spencer's question. She even managed to answer in a normal voice, one that didn't give away the truth. *I had sex with two of those hunks the girls are always talking about and now I can't ever go back there.* "Not tonight."

"Oh come on, it's Julie's birthday."

"I'll have to owe her a drink another time."

Erica felt her colleague's assessing gaze on her face. Suddenly she asked, "Erica, are you all right?"

The direct question surprised Erica enough that her façade of calm slipped. She choked on her answer, making it appear like the lie it was. "Sure I am."

"No you're not," Pam concluded. "All day you've been so distracted and pale. You're not sick, are you?"

The stress of the last few days seemed to fall on Erica's shoulders all at once, and she trembled under the weight of it. Her voice quavered. "I hope not."

Something lit in Pam's hazel eyes, a flare of determination. "Come on. I'll buy you a coffee."

"Weren't you going to the Sovereign?"

Pam waved a hand and twisted her lips. "I've never liked Julie that much."

Astoundingly, Erica laughed. It released the pressure from her chest and made the sting of suppressed emotion moisten her eyes. "Neither have I."

"We have more in common than I thought."

They left the school grounds on foot, walking the two blocks to a small shopping complex that comprised a movie-rental place, several takeaway food outlets and a friendly neighborhood coffee shop the teachers at Ashton Heights often frequented. Now, the place was sparsely populated and none of the patrons were Erica's fellow teachers. She and Pam took a booth table at the back and ordered a latte each.

After a couple of minutes of small talk about their respective classes, Pam said, "Listen, Erica, we don't usually spend a lot of time together outside of work, but I know you've been through a lot this past year." Everyone at the school was aware Erica had taken carer's leave, and she'd been sent a lovely arrangement of flowers from the English department when Aunt Claire had passed. "And you only transferred to Ashton Heights in February. It had to have been hard to make friends with all that was going on. I just want you to know that if you need someone to talk to, I'm here."

Pam was an attractive, freckle-faced blonde with light hazel eyes and a fondness for wearing zany earrings. Today a pair of colorful parrots dangled from her lobes. Erica had always thought Pam a nice person. And it *had* been difficult to form meaningful friendships at Ashton Heights when her year had been spent wrapped up in Aunt Claire's medical issues.

Or perhaps her lack of deep relationships had more to do with her innate reticence than circumstance. She could have reached out to Pam at any time. Erica had always known she was a woman willing to lend a sympathetic ear.

"You're right, I have been stressed about something." Erica took a sip of her coffee without tasting it. Her heart started to pound. *Just say it. She's a woman, she'll understand.* "I found a lump in my breast."

It was the first time she'd said it out loud. Erica was both terrified to have the words vocalized and relieved that the truth was out there.

Immediately, Pam reached across the table and touched Erica's arm. "Oh, Erica. I kind of sensed it wasn't the flu but I had no idea. How are you holding up?"

"I'm fine." The answer was automatic, but Erica found herself annoyed by her own lie. Would it kill her to admit she wasn't as strong as she wanted to be? "Actually I'm not fine. I found it last Friday morning, in the shower. I went to work for some crazy reason, and I felt like I was in a daze. Then I..."

Erica pulled back on offering the details of what she'd done Friday night. That was not something she was comfortable sharing with anyone. "I spent the weekend trying to sort it out in my head. I didn't want to face it but I had to. Calling my doctor was one of the hardest things I've ever done. I don't know what I was waiting for, I have a family history. I can't afford to waste time."

"Your aunt," Pam concluded softly. "It was breast cancer, wasn't it?"

Erica nodded, feeling the familiar painful pang that reminders of Aunt Claire's last weeks still engendered. "Inoperable by the time they found it. We only had a few more months together."

"I'm so sorry. That makes this worse, doesn't it? You having a family history."

"Yes. Sometimes I feel like searching for lumps has become an unhealthy obsession." Erica tried for a smile. "But what choice do I have? I have a mutation on the BCRA1 gene—I went to genetic counseling last year, had the test when Aunt Claire was diagnosed. My chances of living to a ripe old age *without* contracting cancer are pretty slim."

"Oh bugger." A crimson flush infused Pam's face. "I feel awful. Here I was all day feeling sorry for myself because I went on a blind date the other night with a guy who started picking his teeth with his fingernail at the dinner table."

Once again Pam made Erica laugh when she was least expecting it. She wiped moisture from the corners of her eyes. "With his *fingernail*? That is terrible."

They shared a laugh over the ludicrousness of it. Then Pam sobered. "Good Lord, it must make dating a nightmare for you."

"I haven't done much of that lately." What happened last Friday with Corey and Griff did *not* constitute dating. "I was going out with a man a while back, but once he found all this out he couldn't get away fast enough."

"What a loser."

Pam's vehement statement sounded good to Erica. It was true—Doug had not been a winner, or even a nice man. Neither had he been a very capable lover. Recent experience had turned a glaring spotlight on that fact. Erica had no idea why she'd waited for him to break up with *her*.

Except that, given her situation, she'd never really thought she could do better.

"Never mind. There are plenty of men out there who wouldn't care about your medical problems."

"I doubt it." The gene mutation she carried also made her susceptible to other forms of cancer, most notably ovarian cancer. Even if this lump turned out to be a harmless cyst, or if it was malignant and she managed to survive the necessary treatment, she would always be at risk. Chemotherapy could make her sterile or her ovaries might have to be removed before she could have children.

What man would be willing to accept such a long list of negatives in his potential mate?

"It'll work out, you'll see," Pam announced brightly. "This lump will turn out to be nothing, and you'll find someone to support you through whatever else life brings. That's what'll happen, mark my words."

Erica offered a wry smile. "You've decided this, have you?"

"You bet." Pam grinned. "I like to plan my friends' lives for them."

"That's good to know." Despite Erica's droll response, Pam's words warmed her and chased away some of the ice-cold anxiety. No matter the outcome, she sensed Pam wouldn't bolt if things got ugly. That their acquaintance had begun to turn into a real friendship.

And Erica was finally willing to admit that soldiering on alone was not the best way to handle her situation. She needed all the friends she could get.

Erica and Pam didn't leave the café until the barista started stacking chairs on top of tables all around them. Erica begged off Pam's suggestion of continuing on to dinner. She had slept only fitfully for the past few nights. She was exhausted.

Deciding to fix herself something light, Erica bought fresh salad ingredients and a portion of barramundi. She might not feel much like eating, but she needed to keep her strength up.

She was in her kitchen adding spices to the fish when her phone rang. Her hands were covered in chopped coriander and garlic, so Erica decided to let the machine get it.

"Hi, Erica, it's Corey." In the subsequent pause Erica's heart refused to beat. He cleared his throat and added, "Corey Wachawski."

As if she was always bringing Coreys home and letting them strip her bare for the enjoyment of their friends. Erica's knees buckled. She dropped the fish into the baking dish and stood motionless, listening to every word in stunned silence.

"Don't be creeped out that I looked up your number, it's in the white pages. I had to call because...I've been thinking about you, Erica."

His admission made Erica slump against the kitchen counter with a shocked gasp.

"I know you told me—us—to leave but I can't help thinking we shouldn't have, no matter what you or Griff said. I can't shake the feeling something was really wrong the other night, and I need to know if you're all right. *Are* you all right? If you're there, will you please pick up?"

Erica glanced down at her sticky hands and hesitated. But deep inside she knew it wasn't fish oil and herbs keeping her from racing to the phone. She simply had no idea what to say to Corey.

I'm sorry I kicked you out the other night, but I didn't quite know what the post-coital protocol was in a situation like that. Oh and by the way, I only had sex with you and Griff because I might have cancer and the shock of it made me uncharacteristically rash.

"Okay, I guess you're out." Disappointment was clear in Corey's sigh. "Tell you what, I'm going to give you my numbers. I really hope you call me. Because if you don't I'll have to call you again to make sure you got this message, and I might start sounding desperate. You wouldn't want to make me sound desperate, would you, Erica?"

He finished by rattling off his home and mobile numbers, twice. Only then did Erica wash her hands and hurry to the phone. She replayed Corey's message, trying to understand why he'd bothered to call her at all.

She'd brought them both home, let them have their wicked way with her and then she'd quite abruptly asked them to leave. Why would Corey want anything more to do with her?

And what about Griff? Even as the mere sound of Corey's voice made her heart race, it also prompted Erica to think of Griff, how sexy and skilled he'd been, how he'd taken the lead for both her and Corey and brought her to orgasm over and over.

She couldn't help but wonder if Griff had thought about her too.

God, what was wrong with her? Little more than an hour ago, she'd lamented to Pam that few men would willingly take her and her problems on. Now she was contemplating the nuances of an affair with *two*.

It wasn't going to happen. Corey was probably only being the nice, responsible guy he was. After all, he hadn't asked her out. He wanted to assure himself she wasn't a mental case, that was all. And Griff hadn't phoned at all.

Erica went back to preparing her dinner, whatever minimal enthusiasm she'd managed to muster for food now completely gone.

Wednesday dragged on and on, as though every hour lasted ninety minutes instead of sixty. The students seemed particularly contrary, and the temperature spiked higher than usual for early spring, a harbinger telling of a particularly humid Queensland summer ahead.

Her doctor's appointment was set for after school, and Erica drove herself to the medical center. Dr. Mariana Singh had seen Erica's Aunt Claire through her own diagnosis and didn't take Erica's discovery lightly. She performed the physical exam and confirmed Erica's fears with her quiet comment, "Yes, there is something there. We should take a look at that as soon as possible."

After that, the doctor picked up the phone and proceeded to call a specialist. She'd managed to get Erica in to have a needle biopsy the very next day.

By the time she headed home, it was approaching dinnertime. As none of the takeaway options available appealed to Erica, she decided to skip dinner altogether in favor of a cool shower and some mindless television.

She had just stepped out of the shower when the phone rang. Her heart skipped even as her sensible mind told her it couldn't be him, not again. She hadn't called him back. No doubt he'd taken the hint that she didn't have anything to say.

Apparently not.

"You see, Erica," Corey began after the electronic beep. "I don't want to give up just yet because I have a feeling this is too important. I've always thought so, ever since that first night I saw you walk into the Sovereign with your workmates. There was something about you that caught my attention. I could hardly stop looking at you."

Dripping wet and wearing only a towel, Erica raced into the living room where she could listen to his words more closely. Her heart thundered, picking up speed and strength with every word spoken.

"I hung back because I was scared. Scared that I'd use some dumb line on you and you'd dismiss me. Scared that you were involved with someone or that you flat out wouldn't be interested. I thought it was better to hold on to the fantasy of one day being with you than to mess it up and know it would never happen."

Before she was fully aware of what she was doing, Erica lifted the receiver. "Corey, this is crazy."

"Erica, hey." She heard the relieved smile in his voice and melted inside. "What's crazy?"

"You expect me to believe someone who looks like you was nervous about approaching *me*."

"Why not? You're pretty. You're smart. Smart girls don't usually take me too seriously."

Erica scoffed. "More than likely they never thought they'd have a shot with you."

"I don't know." Erica fancied she could hear his shrug on the other end of the line. "I was always big for my age, which made me self-conscious back in school. I was tongue-tied around most people, especially girls, and I guess they figured I was stupid because of that. My grades didn't exactly shine," he added wryly. "I haven't been as lucky with women as you think."

Erica doubted Corey needed much luck. "I don't think you're stupid, not at all."

Doug, with all his degrees and publishing credits, didn't have an ounce of emotional sensitivity. Corey had that in spades. As far as Erica could see, there were different kinds of intelligence.

Erica was also very well aware of how difficult high school could be for someone who didn't quite fit in. She'd been quiet, with shocking red hair and an almost obsessive interest in books. She hadn't exactly been a popularity queen herself.

"You're a nice person, Erica. I want to get to know you better."

"I'm not so nice." Erica thought of the way she'd used Corey and Griff to assuage her own fears the other night, then kicked them both out *sans* explanation.

Misconstruing her meaning, Corey murmured. "If you're naughty, it's only in the good way."

If he'd poured simmering honey all over her, Erica couldn't have felt more cocooned in sweet warmth. Knees weakening, Erica sank into the couch with a sigh. She couldn't quite keep the smile out of her voice. "You're teasing me."

"It's my revenge. Thoughts of you have been teasing me for days. I can't stop thinking about you."

"Oh, Corey," she sighed. "I'm not in a position to start anything. I'm not a good bet right now."

It was so close to what Doug had said to her before he'd left for the last time that Erica shivered. She hated to think she'd bought into Doug's low opinion of her "prospects", but it was true. She was in no position to offer Corey any kind of hope, not when she was hanging on to every last shred of it for herself.

"I don't believe that," Corey countered. "I think you're exactly who I want to take my chances with. Have dinner with me, or we'll go to a movie. Go roller blading in the park if you want."

Erica released a faint chuckle. "I'm not much of a roller blader."

"Phew. Me neither. Roller blading is so out."

Erica closed her eyes as disappointment sank like lead to the pit of her stomach. "Everything is out, Corey. I told you, now is not a good time for me to get involved with anyone."

There was a pause on the other end of the line. Erica sensed Corey mulling something over in his mind. Then he asked, "What about Griff?"

Erica's heart skipped. "What about him?"

"Maybe you'd relax your rules for Griff. Did you like him better than me?"

It was a fair-enough question, under the circumstances, yet Erica was gobsmacked. It was like comparing the exceptional to the extraordinary and asking which had more value. "That's not what this is about."

"Are you sure? Because if you want things the way they were last time, all three of us together, it's okay." Corey's voice went threadbare, as if imagining the setup tightened his vocal cords. "Because I want it that way again too."

Chapter Six

Suddenly Erica was achingly aware of her almost naked state. She was dripping water from the shower all over the hardwood floors and leaking another kind of moisture onto her thighs. The mere suggestion of indulging in another night like the one she'd had with Corey and Griff aroused her unbearably.

How could she feel like this when there was every possibility a dreadful disease was decaying her insides?

At last she stammered, "I don't know what to say."

"Say you'll come to the Sovereign tomorrow night and meet us for a drink."

"I *can't.*"

"Somewhere else is fine, anywhere you want."

"Corey...does Griff know you're asking me this?"

His admission was slow in coming. "No. But he likes you, Erica. He likes you a lot."

Her heart hammered like a schoolgirl's with her very first crush. "He does?"

Corey chuckled softly. "What did you think?"

"I don't know. That maybe he liked *you.*" By the stunned silence on the other end of the phone, Erica realized she'd put her foot in it. "I'm sorry, but you did tell me the other night you were interested. I thought it was mutual."

"I didn't say I was interested exactly. I've never done anything..." He trailed off. Then he asked, with a pretense of casual interest, "You thought it was mutual?"

Gathering the towel closer around her body, Erica sat on the couch. "I figured maybe the two of you had a history."

"Not that kind of history," Corey clarified emphatically. "I've known Griff since I started in the fire service. In fact, he helped me get in. Gave me a recommendation because I'd put in volunteer hours, and helped me pass the written stuff. He'd give you his last twenty bucks if you needed it, he's that kind of bloke. The best one I know."

Quietly, Erica said, "You love him."

"He's my *mate*." Corey let out a long heartfelt sigh. "At least that's what I always thought."

"Corey, he's the one you should be calling, not me."

"You're wrong, Erica. I haven't been able to stop thinking about you, and whatever else is going on with Griff, it doesn't change that." His tone dropped several octaves. "I've been semi-hard since you picked up the phone."

Her body responded in kind to his suggestive words. Beneath the towel her nipples grew stiff, and between her legs the dull throbbing became more insistent.

"Corey." She'd meant to speak his name in a warning tone but ended up sounding breathless.

"Please tell me I affect you the same way so I know I'm not alone here."

Erica closed her eyes, praying for the strength to lie to him. It didn't come. At length she let out a breathy sigh. "Yes, Corey. You affect me."

It was quite the understatement.

"This stuff with Griff, I'm a bit confused about it." He scoffed softly, as though he'd made an understatement of his own. "Does it put you off?"

"I think people ought to take happiness where they can get it. It doesn't worry me how they make it happen."

"Does that go for you too? Aren't you entitled to get what you want?"

Closing her eyes, Erica thought of all she wanted. For this lump to be benign, to not be burdened with this horrid gene mutation. The first there was still a chance for, but the second wish could never be granted. The gene was in her, implanted before she was born. All she could do was deal with it.

The other things she wanted had nothing to do with cancer. Someone to care about her, someone to love. A family, if that was possible. If her ovaries went the distance.

And yes, she wanted sex like she'd had the other night. Sex with Corey *and* Griff, even when one of them would surely have sufficed for any red-blooded woman. But what they'd done last Friday had imprinted the two men in her mind as a duo. Although Corey had caught her initial interest, Erica could no longer think of him without thinking of Griff.

But what kind of greedy, deluded individual asked for the attention of *two* men, when she hadn't even been able to keep her last serious boyfriend around?

"I don't know," Erica eventually replied. "I'd like to think so."

"Then think it. I want to give you everything you've dreamed of, baby. You only need to tell me what that is."

"Are you talking about...sexual things?"

"I'm talking about everything, but we can start there."

His expectant silence made her heart pound. "Now?"

"Yes, now. I'm not hanging up. Are you?"

The challenge sounded cocky but there was a hint of vulnerability beneath the outward confidence that made Erica weaken further. She should never have picked up the phone. Corey Wachawski was proving impossible to hang up on. "No. But you might need to hold on while I get dressed."

In the heartbeat of silence that followed, Erica comprehended she'd once again said too much. "*What?*"

Erica tried to explain. "I was in the shower when you called."

"God," Corey groaned. "Don't make me picture you like that. I can barely take a shower anymore without..." He chuckled ruefully. "Unloading."

The thought of Corey doing that while thinking about her, while thinking about Griff, made Erica's clit pulse. Putting clothes on suddenly seemed unappealing. Her skin was flushed hot, so that even the towel wrapped around her was too stifling.

Helpless to control her actions, Erica slipped a hand between her thighs and pressed it against her throbbing flesh. It didn't alleviate the building ache.

"Does it turn you on, Erica? Remembering how it was when Griff and I were with you in the shower, how we took turns fucking you from behind?"

Erica released a strangled sound and admitted it. "Yes."

"I think about it all the time. I think about all the stuff we didn't get to try, things I want to do with you."

Erica swallowed, both nervous and excited by where this was heading. "Like?"

"Like sex in a bed, for a start." There was a smile in his voice. "Right now I'm picturing you on your knees, wrapped only in a towel like you are, slowly licking my cock."

Between her legs, Erica's hand flexed. Her flesh responded with an eager quiver, making it impossible for her to keep from moving her hand up and down in rhythmic strokes. Her tortured moan traveled down the telephone wire.

"It excites you, doesn't it? The idea of me using your mouth like that?"

"Yes."

"What about Griff? Would you let him do the same thing?"

There was something deliciously submissive about the mental picture that formed, of those two gorgeous men forcing her to service them. But Erica found herself admitting a fear she wouldn't normally express. It seemed Corey was always compelling her to make unexpected admissions. "I would but I don't think I'm very skilled at, um, oral sex."

Annoyance laced Corey's query. "Who told you that? The idiot who wasn't interested in touching you?"

Doug hadn't actually complained about her technique, but his patent lack of enthusiasm for the act had eventually made Erica stop trying. "There's a chance I'm actually *not* good at it, you know."

"Listen to me here, Erica. Any man who complains about any effort you make in that department does not deserve you. Not a minute of your time, you hear me?"

His staunch defense made her heart warm, made the awkward insecurities she'd experienced with Doug slip away. "Thank you, that's sweet."

"Sweet nothing, I'm serious. You'd only have to run your tongue over me once and I'd be thanking *you*. I'd be begging for more and praising my luck that you were willing to go there."

Erica smiled. "Okay, I get it."

"You sure? If you want I can drive over there and prove it to you."

It was a flippant offer with serious undertones that Erica so wanted to take him up on. But she replied, "I'm happy like this."

Strange as it seemed, she was. Right now, talking to Corey about surprisingly intimate things, Erica *was* happy. She wasn't thinking about tomorrow or next week or anything but this moment.

"I figured you'd say that." Corey groaned. "Never mind that my dick resembles a telegraph pole right now. Shit, listen to me. I sound like Griff."

"That's okay. I love the way he talks."

"I was raised to be more polite, but damn, you bring something out in me. You make me more like him."

"Is that bad?"

"No. I've always admired the way Griff can say whatever he wants and somehow get away with it."

"What do you want to say right now?"

"That I'm so hard I'm not going to be able to sleep unless I... Can you guess what I'm doing right now, Erica?"

Erica closed her eyes. "Yes."

"Because you're doing it too. Touching yourself because you can't help it. I can hear those soft little moans you're making. They're driving me crazy."

"Oh, Corey." Between her legs, her hand began to move faster.

"Can you guess what I'm picturing while I'm stroking my hard-on, or do you want me to tell you?"

"Tell me."

His sigh was shaky. "I'm imagining you licking and sucking my dick, and you are so damn good at it that I want to come every time you close your lips around me. But I don't let myself have an orgasm like that. You need me hard because you get so horny from sucking me, you have to have me inside you. Griff is there too, telling you to get on the floor, on your hands and knees. I slip into you from behind, so hard and tight you cry out. Griff puts his cock in your open mouth, pushing it all the way in. Every time I come back inside you, it forces you onto Griff's cock, makes you take him to the back of your throat."

The idea of being caught between them like that, of being shamelessly used for the pleasure of those two men made Erica's arousal spiral out of control. The couch springs creaked as she rocked her hips with increasing vigor. No longer keeping up even a pretense of modesty, Erica spread her thighs and plunged two fingers into her aching, empty pussy, imagining it was Corey there instead. With her other hand she held on to the phone like she was making an emergency call. "Corey. Oh God. I'm going to... "

"Jeez, so am I. I'm going to have an orgasm thinking about how sexy you'd look taking it from both of us like that."

"Yes, Corey. Oh, *yes.*"

"That's it, Erica. Come for me like I'm coming for you."

The orgasm shot Erica into the glorious state of sexual free fall she usually explored on her own. As had been the case last week, sharing it made the rapture more intense. On the other end of the line, she heard Corey's guttural groan and knew he'd reached his own peak.

Erica pictured the pearlescent evidence of his climax landing in creamy spurts on his tight abs. The mental image made her orgasm purl on and on in ripples. When the furor finally died down, she was left trembling and alone, almost as shocked as she'd been a week ago when Corey and Griff had both been with her.

Once again the realization of what she'd done was stunning. Phone sex was something she'd only heard about. She'd never imagined *doing* anything so brazen. Embarrassment niggled but was outweighed by a sense of euphoria and perverse pride. Maybe she wasn't so boring and straightlaced after all. Perhaps she was even sexy.

What a time to work that out.

"Erica." Corey rasped her name in astonishment. "I didn't mean to do that."

Erica could hardly speak. "I've never, ever…"

"Me neither." His laugh tremored. "I told you I haven't been as lucky with women as people think. I feel pretty damn fortunate right now though, Erica. You blow me away."

"Corey Wachawski, you are the sweetest, sexiest man I've ever met."

He sighed. "We're going to see each other again, baby. We have to."

Reality was a dark, heavy thing that smothered her fledgling sense of elation. Phone calls were one thing, actually seeing him was impossible. He'd think she was offering more than she had to give.

As though sensing her hesitation, Corey didn't press her to commit to anything. "Will you stay on the line? I'd like to talk for a while. That's all, just talk."

Erica closed her eyes. How could she say no to him when he asked for something so simple in that sweet baritone voice?

"Okay," she agreed. "Let's talk."

"You're up, Wachawski."

Corey tore his gaze away from the Sovereign's entry doors to see Steve Waller handing him a set of darts. "How'd you do?"

Steve laughed. "A twenty-five and two bull's-eyes. Thanks for paying so much attention to my stellar performance."

"He's been staring at those front doors all night," one of the other firefighters, Mitch West, chipped in. "I figure he's waiting on a girl."

Steve, Mitch and another guy everyone called Curly put their heads together, fluttered their eyelashes and crooned in unison. "Oooh, a girl."

"Very funny." Corey snatched the darts off Steve and moved to the starting mark. He forced himself to focus as he took aim. The first dart hit the outer rim of the board; the second netted him ten points. By the time the third sailed into the backboard, the guys were razzing him soundly about his unsteady hands and speculating on how they'd become that way.

"So who is she?" Steve asked point-blank when Curly took his turn at the mark and hit a fifty-pointer first try.

"No one you know."

"Nobody you *want* me to know." Steve grinned at his brilliant deduction. "Afraid she'll change her mind about you once she gets an eyeful of the trademark Waller smile?"

"Sure, that's it."

Corey couldn't help but grin at Steve's outlandish teasing. He wasn't worried about competing with Steve Waller for Erica's attention. All he was afraid of was her not showing up at the Sovereign ever again. He was a little scared she'd meant it when she said a relationship wasn't on the table, because that would mean last night's phone conversation hadn't meant nearly as much to her as it had to him.

He thought of going around there, but he wanted to give her a chance to come to him. Corey sensed pressuring Erica right now would have the opposite effect than the one he wanted. And what he wanted was exactly what he'd told Erica— for her and Griff and him to be together once more. Okay, maybe more than once more.

His gaze strayed to the bar where Griff was having a long conversation with the bartender. The blonde woman was cute and obviously into Griff, if the way she smiled and leaned on the counter to best display her cleavage was any indication. Corey wondered if Griff would take her home, if sex with a random woman—and only a woman—would be enough to satisfy him tonight.

"Are we going to see this bird in here some time?" Curly asked as he returned to the table and picked up his beer.

"I don't want any of you jokers setting your eyes on any girl of mine." The remark popped out before Corey could think better of saying something that sounded so possessive. The subsequent round of teasing jeers made him cringe.

"You lot sound like a pack of galahs."

Griff's mocking observation subdued the commotion. Steve took one of the beers Griff slid on the table and turned his attention to Griff's love life instead of Corey's. He tilted his head toward the bar. "You on the pull tonight?"

"When am I not?" Griff smirked. "Who's winning this epic contest?"

As Steve updated him on the game, Griff's gaze slid over the four of them as a group without landing on any particular man. Specifically not landing on him, Corey couldn't help but think. It had been that way for days, since their night with Erica. It was as though the other man wanted to pretend Corey didn't exist, that their friendship had never been. It cut Corey to the quick, and made him mad as hell at the same time.

Never in his life had Corey considered his sexual preferences mutable, but evidently they were. Nothing between him and Griff was the same, and while Griff's cool attitude was partly to blame, Corey couldn't discount his own part in the chasm that had opened up between them. He couldn't be in the same room with Griff anymore without remembering what the man looked like naked, and the recollection never failed to cause a spike in his heart rate.

Did Griff sense that in him? Is that why he'd avoided Corey all week? Perhaps he'd read the situation wrong, and Griff was one hundred percent straight, so straight he was disgusted, not tempted, by Corey's newfound interest.

The sound of a woman's voice nearby made Corey's ears prick up. He caught a snatch of conversation, something about "students" and "homework", and his gaze snagged on a mane of red hair shining around a pair of creamy pale shoulders. His heart flat out stopped beating, trapping the air in his lungs.

He'd told Erica he'd swing by the Sovereign tonight, so that if she felt like dropping by—not like a date or anything that presaged a *relationship*—she could, no strings attached. He was halfway to standing before the woman turned and he saw her face. The disappointment was momentarily crushing.

It wasn't her.

His companions were too busy discussing the latest rugby-league results to notice Corey's reaction. All of them except Griff. Their gazes met and held. Corey saw comprehension in Griff's hazel irises, understanding and something else that looked a lot like discontent.

Griff was the first to break eye contact. Taking one last swig of his beer, he put the half-empty glass on the table. "I'm going to love you lot and leave you. I'm stuffed."

"Sure, mate." Steve winked. "Get a better offer, did ya?"

Griff offered an enigmatic smile that didn't reach his eyes. Without further explanation, he lifted two fingers in a nonchalant salute and turned on his heel, striding out of the pub without a backward glance.

Corey watched him leave, his emotions running riot. The bartender noticed Griff's abrupt departure as well, dejection clear on her face. Griff obviously hadn't made a date with her. Why had he let everyone think he had?

Because he wanted Corey to believe that night with Erica meant nothing to him, that Erica meant so little to him she could be easily replaced with the closest piece of flesh.

He's lying.

Corey wasn't sure how he knew. He simply did.

"I'll see you guys later." Corey left the rest of his own beer and departed with no explanation. He felt the surprised stares of his colleagues on his back as he followed the path Griff had taken to the pub's frosted-glass exit doors.

Corey stepped out into the warm spring night. He scanned the car park for the familiar red Ute and saw Griff standing beside it, digging in his jeans pocket for the keys. Corey headed that way. "You looked at her too."

Griff turned, surprised. "What?"

"The redhead inside. You looked at her."

"So?"

"When you thought for that split second it was Erica, did you want it to be her?"

His expression was carefully neutral. "I didn't care one way or the other."

"Bullshit. I know you meant it when you said you liked her."

"I liked fucking her, that's for sure. She was a hot piece of ass beneath that schoolmarm look."

The urge to grab Griff and shove him up against the car in anger was swift and surprising. Corey might have done it if he hadn't guessed Griff was being deliberately vulgar to deflect attention from the real issue. "She wasn't just a piece of ass, not to me. I don't think she was to you either. I saw the way you changed when you were with her, the way you smiled at her and took care of her. You told her she was special."

"I say that to all the girls. Women like to hear certain things from a man after she's let him screw her senseless. I give them what they want, that's all."

"Why are you being like this?" Corey asked, dropping the subject of Erica for now because he saw he wasn't going to get anywhere. "Why has everything changed between us?"

"Fuck off. Everything's exactly the same."

"You won't look at me." Corey hated the way his voice caught, giving away how much Griff's attitude of late had stung. "You treated me like shit on your shoe this week."

"Didn't mean to." Genuine regret laced Griff's sigh. "I want you to be happy, Cor. You seem to think Erica does that for you, so go for it. Why are you giving me a moment's thought?"

There were so many truths he could have uttered but fear stopped him giving everything away. "Because Erica wants us both again."

"She *what*?" Griff's astonishment pulled the veil from his expression. "How do you know that?"

"I called her. We talked for hours. She's...amazing." Thinking about her and all the confidences they'd shared made Corey's heart gallop, made a goofy smile curve his lips. She'd been lonely growing up, and Corey identified with that because despite being generally well liked he'd never felt understood. She was sweet and generous even after going through the hardship of losing her mother so young, and her aunt so recently. Her Aunt Claire had longed to spend her final days at home, and Erica had taken leave from work to care for her until her dying day.

She carried so much sadness within her, and Corey wanted nothing more than to lift it for her. Well, that and to explore the chemistry between them...between all three of them.

"That's great, Cor. Go, be amazed."

The edge to Griff's words made Corey's ears prick up. "Are you jealous?"

"Of a phone call? You're putting an awful lot of stock in it if you think it means she wants us both again."

"We didn't just talk." Recalling the explosive orgasm they'd shared made Corey flush hot. "We *really* talked, if you know what I mean."

Griff seemed to get the implication. "And you discussed *me?*"

"Yeah."

"*Fuck.*" Abruptly, Griff turned away and grabbed the door handle of his car. Realizing it was still locked, he swore again and reached for the keys he'd shoved back in his pocket.

"Is that so bad?" Corey stepped behind Griff. Without planning to, he moved closer than he ordinarily would have, like a magnetic force compelled it. "That Erica wants you again? That I..."

When Corey didn't finish the thought, Griff whirled around until they were almost nose to nose. "That you *what?*"

"I was curious, that's all," he burst out. "I don't know why, I never have been before. But I really liked watching you fuck Erica. I loved seeing how much she enjoyed it. You knew just how to make her go wild and that was so hot. It made me think about *you*, not just her."

"Corey, shut the *fuck* up."

The harsh rebuke propelled Corey backward. His heart seized painfully. "You're not...shit. I thought you were..." His throat closed around the word, the mortification of getting it so wrong. "I thought you were bisexual."

Griff stared at him levelly while Corey's heart hammered out of control. At length he said, "I don't like labels."

Corey's breath caught. "But you like blokes?"

"Depends on the bloke." Griff's gaze flicked over Corey's face. "I can swing that way for the right person."

Dully, Corey concluded, "And I'm not right."

"Jesus, Cor." Griff lifted his hand, using it to frame Corey's jaw. "You're gonna kill me."

The contact made Corey's heart race. When Griff used his thumb to trace the outline of Corey's lower lip, Corey's mouth dried out. The look Griff was giving him was the same one Corey knew he wore when he found himself this close to a woman he was dying to kiss.

Did he want Griff to kiss him? The notion sparked confused anxiety in his chest. It also rushed his blood. There was a distinct swelling in the general area of his Levis that couldn't be ignored. Griff's nearness, the touch of his hand, aroused Corey.

"Griff." The name sounded like a plea. "I don't know what to do with these feelings."

He reached out and curled shaking fingers around Griff's shoulder, noticing the flex of solid muscle beneath his palm. Griff's hot breath puffed into the scant space separating them as he met Corey's eyes.

He wasn't going to make a move. Griff waited, the muscles in his face tense, while Corey wrestled with the possibilities. The air around them thickened, became hot and electric. It suffocated Corey, until he felt the only way he could breathe was with Griff's help.

He inclined his head and met Griff's lips with his own.

Chapter Seven

Five long years.

Griff had spent five agonizing years stuffing his emotions down, securely caging his sexual predilections and fucking anyone who'd have him, all so Corey wouldn't guess that *this* was what he'd wanted most. Corey's mouth, soft and yielding against his. His body, hard and strong, yet trembling with the force of the craving coursing through his blood.

After the first tentative melding of mouths, Griff deepened the kiss with a groan, unable to help himself. Corey responded with a moan that turned Griff's dick into a steel spike. With a mammoth effort, he kept his hands above Corey's shoulders, confining his explorations to the silky threads of his hair, the fine line of stubble on his jaw.

Corey didn't show the same restraint. He grabbed Griff's back, digging his fingers in like he needed to hang on to something. Once they got moving, his hands were everywhere, his touch frantic. Griff burned beneath the frenetic pace of Corey's fingers. His abs bunched when Corey touched him there. When he moved lower Griff pushed him back, severing the connection of their mouths.

"No, Cor. Stop."

"What?"

Corey blinked like a man with concussion. His befuddled expression reminded Griff that Corey was completely new at this, as virginal as they got. As he'd said, he was curious, that's all. Curious and confused and feeling attacked by feelings he didn't understand.

Not the time for Griff to take advantage.

With resignation, Griff pushed him away. "That shouldn't have happened. Sorry."

"I did it." Corey frowned. "I wanted it."

He needn't remind Griff of that, the evidence had been pretty stoutly pressed against his groin while they'd kissed. They'd *kissed*. As if his sleep hadn't been disturbed enough of late. Despite the lies he'd tried to tell Corey, Griff hadn't been able to stop thinking about Erica and wondering if Corey had made the move Griff had told him to. Now he discovered they'd used *him* as a phone-sex aide. He was going to turn into a freaking insomniac. An insomniac with a permanent hard-on for a man who didn't know what he wanted and a woman playing hard to get.

"You were curious, right?" Griff reminded Corey. "Curiosity satisfied."

Corey shook his head. "It felt good."

"Of course it felt good." Griff smiled, trying to alleviate the tension. "I know how to kiss."

Corey smiled back in a way that made Griff's heart turn over. "Maybe you should do it again."

"No." Griff moved farther away from him. "I can't be your experiment, Corey."

"It's not like that."

The uncertainty on Corey's face told a different story. "You don't know what you want. A few seconds ago you were mooning over Erica."

"Over the idea of all three of us, remember?"

"So what are you suggesting? We get together once or twice, have a grand time, then when you're done with kink you and Erica go on your merry way and be a normal couple?"

"No. I don't know." Corey blew out a frustrated breath. "Maybe it could work longer term."

"We're all going to play house? Do you know how tricky the dynamics of something like that are?"

"No." Corey swallowed. "Do you?"

"Yeah, I do." Griff's admission was hoarse. "A relationship between two people is hard, Corey. Between three it's almost impossible."

"You lived with a couple," Corey filled in, remembering. "When I first started at Ashton Heights. You were boarding a room from them while you renovated your place."

Griff confirmed what the look in Corey's eyes told him he'd already worked out. "I was more than a boarder—but not much, as it turned out." He feared his smile didn't appear as nonchalant as he'd intended. "Anna and Jack were already together when I met them, so I should have known how it was going to play out. They were always the main couple and I was an occasional guest star. Only I didn't realize my role was as insignificant as that until I'd already outstayed my welcome. I won't make that mistake again."

Corey shook his head. "We would never do that to you."

The cynical curve of Griff's lips hurt his face. Didn't Corey realize he already was doing it, simply by referring to him and Erica as "we"?

"I would never kick you out of my life," Corey continued, his words impassioned. "You're my friend. We'd still be friends, wouldn't we? No matter what?"

Not necessarily. Griff had considered Jack a close mate as well as a lover, but when he'd lost him as one he found he couldn't have him in his life as either.

If he did this, he could lose Corey completely. The very thought made his blood turn to ice.

"I can't risk it, Corey." Griff fished his keys out of his pocket and clicked the electronic unlocking mechanism. The beeping noise sounded loud in the deserted car park. "If you conduct your little experiment with me and decide it's not a permanent lifestyle choice for you, I'm fucked. If I get to know Erica better, if I let her in and then she wants you all to herself, I'm fucked. I might want both of you, but if I act on it chances are I'm the one who'll end up screwed."

Griff left Corey standing in the car park, staring after him as he peeled out into the street. He wondered if he'd just made the biggest mistake of his life, passed up the best thing that could have happened to him. But he'd wanted Corey for so long, risking eventual rejection was not something he relished.

As for Erica...the woman turned him inside out with little more than a glance. But what happened with Anna and Jack had nearly killed Griff. He knew he couldn't go through something like that again. Getting over one person was hard. Getting over two was murder.

Griff was glad he was about to start a series of night shifts. Lying alone in his bed, imagining Corey and Erica including him in their fantasy phone calls would surely have been the death of him.

I'd love to kiss you between your legs. The idea makes me so horny I can barely breathe. Open yourself wide, Erica. Tell me how you're touching yourself while we're both wishing it was my tongue licking inside you.

Flushed, breathless and wet, Erica awoke as the first rays of sun made the sheer white curtains draping her window glow, bathing her bedroom in shades of pink and mauve. Corey's words, murmured intimately through the phone lines last night, swirled through her mind. The remembered sound of his voice retained the power to ignite her blood, even though she'd brought herself to orgasm while Corey talked her through it.

With a groan of frustration, Erica rolled onto her side and switched on her clock radio as a distraction. The classic Chris Isaak hit that slid into the room didn't do much to divert her attention from the memory of Corey's voice in her ear last night...and the four nights before that.

Five nights in a row Corey had called to ask her out, to talk about his day, to seduce her with his words. Erica knew she shouldn't let things go on this way, but as had been the case that first night, Corey Wachawski had proven impossible to ignore.

This day of all days she shouldn't be thinking about sex. It was D-day, the day she would learn the results of the biopsy she'd had on Thursday. Unconsciously, her hand went to the spot on her left breast where the needle had punctured her skin. Her skin tingled, the reality of her situation doing nothing to dampen the remnant effects of last night's fantasy, nor the intensely erotic dreams that followed Corey's husked revelations.

I want him too, Erica. I want Griff, but he as good as told me to forget it. Talk to me about him. Tell me how he made you feel.

The words "Ashton Heights" and "house fire" punctuated the drone of morning news snippets, drawing Erica's attention away from the memories. Erica stilled, her heart thudding, as she listened to the details.

Firefighters were called to the blaze at around 2:30 this morning, but the house was well alight by the time crews arrived. Despite the efforts of emergency workers, the occupants—a young couple and their two children—could not be saved. A spokesperson for Queensland Fire and Rescue said working smoke detectors might have averted the tragedy.

In other news, the prime minister is set to...

Erica's first thought was for Corey's well-being. But he was on the phone with her late last night, so he wouldn't have been on shift. What about Griff? Erica's eyes stung as she thought of that young family, all of them perished in one terrible event. Had Griff been one of the firefighters forced to stand by and watch as flames obliterated four lives?

Shoving the melancholy and concern to the side, Erica climbed out of bed. She slipped on her plain white cotton robe and, after visiting the bathroom, wandered out to her front porch to see if the paper had been delivered.

No paper graced her lawn, but what she saw instead made her heart slam to a stop. A sleek red Ute was parked across the street. Erica recognized the car and the man sitting behind the wheel, staring at her house.

Erica stood frozen on the porch. After a moment, Griff opened the car door and got out. Even from this distance, she sensed tension in his strides as he crossed the road. He mounted her steps with heavy footfalls. Erica noticed his eyes were bloodshot and there was a shadow of stubble visible on his jaw.

He appeared irate, reckless and decidedly dangerous. Erica's fear instinct kicked in even though she didn't think for a minute Griff would hurt her. Her erogenous zones tingled. Seeing Griff again made her feel so much more than trepidation.

"I want you to break it off with Corey." His abrupt demand hit her like a slap. "If you're not going to fuck him, stop fucking him around."

"I'm not." He responded with nothing more than a sardonically quirked eyebrow which made guilt wash through her. She shifted her weight from one foot to the other. "He calls me."

"So hang up."

"Have you ever tried to hang up on Corey?"

A muscle ticked in his jaw. Erica easily read the truth in his eyes—no way could he turn Corey away so easily if he were in her situation. "You're going to hurt him," Griff said roughly.

"I never want to hurt Corey."

"Then don't." Griff took a step forward and glared down at her. "Next time he calls you're going to put him out of his misery. Either break it off or fuck the man—I don't give a shit which one you do."

"I can see that."

His eyes flashed at her terse response, a brief gleam of satisfaction. He'd hoped to needle her. Griff had not come here at six o'clock in the morning because he was in a good mood.

No, he'd come here because of last night. He must have witnessed last night's tragedy. She could feel it in the frustration and pain radiating from him. Why he felt the urge to come here, Erica had no idea. But she sensed his need for something unnamed in every ragged breath, in the flashing vulnerability barely concealed by his bloodshot eyes.

Quietly, she asked, "Is that all you came here for?"

"No. I have to check your smoke alarms."

Erica blinked. "I beg your pardon?"

"You heard me. It'll only take five minutes then I'll leave you in peace."

Erica doubted any form of peace would be in her near future. Before she could respond to Griff's odd demand, he had stalked past her into the house.

Erica hurried after him. She found him in the living room, where he had taken it upon himself to pull apart the little circular device embedded in the ceiling. His stance caused his faded red T-shirt to ride up, exposing those ripped abdominal muscles.

Her inner walls contracted and her breasts peaked. Every fantasy she'd ever had involving her tongue and those abs, his mouth and her mouth, her pussy and his cock returned to haunt her. The fact that she was aroused at the mere sight of him despite his high-handed attitude really increased her irritation. "Is this a new service the fire department is offering now? Dawn wake-up calls? I can check my own smoke detectors later."

"Later when? After this box of kindling you call a house has burnt to the ground with you inside it?" Griff swore graphically as he read something on the side of the device he'd dismantled. "These are out of date. They'd melt from the heat before they made a peep."

"Excuse me if I've been a little too busy lately to do all the requisite household maintenance. What with my aunt dying and all the legalities that came with that. Not to mention..."

When she almost blurted out the facts of her own medical situation, Erica crossed her arms over her chest. As though she needed to hide the cancer from him.

"Not to mention what?"

His golden eyes sharpened. Forcing herself to appear nonchalant, Erica uncrossed her arms and placed her hands on her hips. "I have a job. A life." The latter, not so much but Erica was hardly going to admit it. "If you're really concerned about this, I will attend to the smoke alarms as soon as I can."

"I am concerned. Do it today."

Erica frowned in exasperation. She had other things on her mind today, but she wasn't going to tell him that, so she lied to appease him. "All right."

A relieved breath eased out of him. "Great. Good. It's so bloody stupid, Red. People die all the time because they neglected something so simple as a battery or an expiry date. Good people. Whole fucking families sometimes. Young people with their lives ahead of them. People like you, damn it."

Griff stopped dragging his hand through his hair long enough to pin her with his gaze. "You live here all by yourself in a place that looks like it's itching to be firewood. There's no one here to look out for you. *You* could die, Erica."

It was such an ominous, prophetic statement, so mirroring the thought that had been on replay in her mind since that morning she'd found the lump and realized the Shannon genes had caught up with her. Erica couldn't breathe. It was as though he had curled a hand around her throat and squeezed.

Her expression must have shown her horror. He took a step toward her, his hand outstretched. "Hey, I didn't mean to—"

"Don't touch me." Erica thought if he tried to hold her she would surely break down and cry on him, reveal all her secrets. When Griff didn't immediately back away, she reiterated with more force. "I don't want you to touch me."

Griff's face turned hard once again. "Right. Well you might want to rethink the way you're dressed. That itty-bitty robe doesn't exactly scream stay away."

Erica glanced downward. The lapels of the thin cotton garment had fallen open, the gape in the fabric giving away the fact she wasn't wearing anything underneath. She gathered it together at the front, embarrassed. "I wasn't exactly expecting anyone to come over. I just got out of bed."

"You always sleep in the nude?"

His query was as rough as bark. "Not that it's any of your business, but no. Last night was...hot."

"Not really." Griff's eyes turned from glittering gems to smoking coals in an instant as realization hit. "You get naked when you're on the phone with Corey."

Erica swallowed her mortification. "Now that *really* isn't any of your business."

"You don't think?" He walked forward, lethal intent in his eyes. Instinctively, Erica backed up. She hit the wall with a soft thud. Griff pressed one hand flat on the doorjamb beside her head and leaned over her, six feet of powerful, masculine intimidation. "You don't think I have the right to know the role I played in your little tête-à-tête last night?"

So Corey had told him the nature of their conversations. Erica could have been angry, but it wasn't rage that made her blood pulse hot through her veins, that flushed her skin all over. The fact that Griff knew aroused her. The fact that he was staring down at her with a similar ferocity of lust making his eyes smolder brought the excitement to fever pitch. He was so close she could smell him—a mingling of smoke and the soap he'd used to try to erase it. So close she could touch that hard chest.

Griff slid a hand insolently into the valley between her thighs and skimmed it upward. He encountered her uncovered sex and cupped it. Erica gasped, but did nothing to stop him. "Tell me what you told Corey last night. What did I do to you in your wicked little mind? Did I do this?"

89

With seeking fingers he separated her folds and slid one digit effortlessly inside her sodden channel. Erica moaned. Her head dropped back against the wall, a sign of surrender. After the nights of sharing sexual secrets with Corey, secrets that for both of them starred the man who was now skillfully manipulating her folds, Griff's touch rendered her instantly weak. She couldn't fight the erotic promises he made with his hands or his words.

"Did I suck this sensitive little clit?" he asked, and circled his thumb lightly over it. "Did Corey and I both fuck you in your dreams? Tell me your secrets, Red. Where did I put my cock last night?"

She opened her eyes and stared at him. "You put it in Corey's mouth."

Chapter Eight

Griff froze, not game to move a single muscle, lest the one in his groin region went off like a hair-trigger pistol. Erica held his gaze without flinching, her dark irises swallowing her pupils. Her eyelids drooped over them and her cheeks blushed pink.

Nothing in her expression told him she was in any way turned off by what she'd just said. By what she and Corey had apparently fantasized about together.

Oh God.

The evidence of her arousal coated his fingers, but still he had to know. Griff had to hear Erica say it. "Does it turn you on? The idea of Corey and me. Of watching us."

Her breath was coming in rapid pants, mingling with his in the scant space between them. She never took her eyes off his. "Yes."

Jesus Christ. Instant increase in the size of his already monumental boner. He could barely get his words past the lust-induced lump in his throat. "Red, if you don't want me to fuck you right now, get out of here. Put some damn clothes on. Otherwise..." He let his gaze trail over her. The circular shadows of her areolae were visible through the too-thin cotton. He was so hard it was criminal. "Otherwise take this poor fucking excuse for cover off, before I rip it off."

She reached for the sash barely holding the flimsy material together and tugged slowly on the end. He might have thought she was being intentionally tantalizing, if he didn't recognize the tortured cast of her expression. Her limbs were simply weighed down by the magnitude of her lust, the way his were. He was impatient to be buried inside her, but everything about him felt heavy and sluggish—his arms, his dark, slowly spinning thoughts, his stiff, pulsing cock. His clothes irritated his burning flesh, but he didn't want to pull his hand out of Erica to tear them off.

The robe parted. The dusky-pink nipples he remembered so well were flushed and tight, pointing right at him. She was slumped against the wall as though she had given herself over to him. He looked his fill of her while she stood there and breathed great lungfuls of air that caused her sweet globes to shimmy and thrust.

He inserted a second finger into her lush wetness, parting them to stretch her. Erica mewled. Her hips rocked. Griff pressed the heel of his hand flush against her mound, supporting her weight with that one hand, controlling her with only that touch.

It barely took a minute. She rode his hand into the fray, her gaze never turning from his until the instant it claimed her. An orgasm achieved in an instant that rippled over his embedded hand like a languorous dance, caressing and sucking at his fingers so eagerly his dick felt tortured by the need to feel that same connection with her body.

When she passed through the core of it, she fell out the other side in a mass of spent limbs and lost breath. Her head fell forward, her forehead lolling against his shoulder as she shuddered with the aftereffects.

Griff knew he should hold her close and stroke her back to life with care and patience. She deserved at least that. But he found himself unable. His own needs ravaged his every proficiency and left him with only primal wants. He released her so she fell against the wall. He whipped off his shirt and immediately went for the fastening of his jeans.

Erica made a sound that could have been relief or joy, but most definitely signaled acceptance. She reached for his hand. "Come to bed."

Griff shook his head. The bedroom was at least twenty meters away. "No time. Get down on the floor."

Her eyes widened, shock and desire glimmering in the chocolate discs. Beyond flowery invitations, Griff pushed his jeans down his legs, allowing his taut cock to at last spring free of the stifling clothing. "I'm as serious as a fucking heart attack, Red. It's the rug or the wall—you pick."

Making her decision quickly, Erica slid down the wall and crawled to the center of the brown and white rug. The flimsy robe rode up to expose the luscious curve of her ass. Griff closed his eyes on the feral urge that almost overcame him, to take her like that, doggy-style on the floor like he really was an animal. But the urge to mark her with some bestial stamp wasn't as strong as his need to have her surrounding him, have her arms and legs draw him in while he sank into her. He needed her softness right now as much as he needed to come.

She rolled onto her back and lay there like a sacrificial virgin, and Griff all but fell onto her. He took her breasts into his hands and sunk his teeth into her neck. Then he spread her open and plunged brusquely inside.

Erica emitted a shocked sound. Griff wondered if he'd hurt her, but whatever tenderness existed in him proved elusive. He couldn't stop himself from angling his hips forward, a repetitive motion that was already getting away from him. "Okay?"

Erica sank her fingernails into his shoulders and angled her hips up to meet his. She sighed his name—not Griff. Into his ear she whispered, "Dale," and Griff was lost inside her in every way a man could lose himself.

He was almost as embarrassingly quick as she had been. He swore and pounded into her, faster and faster, until in a burst of blinding light and rushing heat he felt his climax approaching. Somehow he found the presence of mind to pull out of her, spilling his seed onto her bare stomach, on the rug. He came in jets, hoarsely crying her name like a man who wanted to be saved.

"Yes... Oh yes please."

She wriggled on the floor, frantically palming her breasts. He hadn't even waited until she'd come again before losing it.

93

Self-flagellation made Griff's actions rough and impatient. He grasped Erica's knees and yanked them apart, exposing her plump, wet sex. Then he plunged into her with his tongue, before moving up to suck hard on her clit. He only had to do it once more, and she came, filling his mouth with her tangy juice, still whimpering his name like a mantra.

Dale, Dale, Dale.

Griff moved up her body and buried his face in the curve of her neck. He detected the faint, well-remembered scent of lavender on her skin, and it made everything he'd just done rush to confront him. The lack of respect he'd shown Erica in being so rough. The dog act he'd done to Corey. While Corey had been doing the right thing, trying to romance and seduce Erica, Griff had stormed into her house screaming about fire alarms and taking her on the floor like a man driven mad by lust.

No matter what Corey said, the man still thought of Erica as his. And Griff had just fucked her into oblivion.

Long moments passed, filled only by their mingled breaths, the ticking of an old grandfather clock in the hall and Griff's shame. The last kept his face hidden in her neck, a cowardly attempt to delay the moment when he'd have to face her and explain himself.

In the end, Erica saved him the trouble. "It's not your fault those people died. I know you would have saved them if you could have."

Griff was further mortified to feel his eyes sting. *God grant me the strength not to cry in front of her.* He couldn't muster a response, so greatly was he humbled by her capacity for perception, the gift of her acceptance. She must have heard the news and known why he was here.

She must also realize he'd used her to make himself feel better. It was a cruel irony that he ended up feeling much worse.

His words rasped with regret. "Erica, I'm so bloody sorry."

She didn't seem to hear his apology. "You're right about Corey. I've been giving him hope when I have none to offer. I'll end it."

"*No.*" Griff extracted himself from her tempting softness. He rolled to his side and stared down at her. "I shouldn't have said that. You'll kill him."

Her faint smile was disbelieving. "No, it's the best thing. There can never be anything between me and Corey."

Griff hoped to God she wasn't writing Corey off because of what had just happened. He had enough guilt to carry. Even now having her so close, smelling so sweet and looking achingly fragile in her nudity, made his groin stir once more.

Turning away from the enticement she represented, Griff stood and pulled his jeans up. "I know what I said, but I was wrong. Don't break it off with Corey. Give him a chance. As for this..." Griff swallowed past the lump in his throat, the evidence of his disgrace. "Don't let it affect your decision. I was wrong to come here."

She stood as well, smoothing down her hair and self-consciously tightening the sash on her robe. A moment of sluggish silence passed before Erica asked quietly, "Why did you?"

Griff wasn't sure where to start. He hated the decimation he sometimes encountered in the course of his work. When there were kids involved, it exacerbated the horror, made frustration and anger burn a path up his esophagus. There were counselors the service provided. There were also his colleagues, his friends, people who understood only too well how he felt and could help him make sense of it.

But he hadn't gone to any of those people. Instead he'd come here. Griff wasn't sure if Erica would understand that there were times when talking to mates or shrinks wouldn't make a damn bit of difference, when all the quiet time and reflection, all the alcohol in the world wouldn't help. At those moments what a man needed above all else was the welcoming, forgiving softness of a caring woman to sooth the fire in his soul.

"I felt like shit." As an explanation it was pitifully economical. "I told myself I was coming here to tell you off about leading Corey on because I was in a foul-enough mood to do it, but it wasn't that. That fire last night made me think about you, and how easy it would be for this place to go up. Occupational hazard," he conceded wryly. "I couldn't stop thinking about you. I haven't been able to since that night. It was so much worse after Corey told me..."

When he trailed off she filled in. "What he and I talked about?"

The mere mention of it in those dulcet tones, her voice honeyed by her recent orgasm, made Griff's knees weak and his cock hard. "Yeah."

Although he knew further contact was inadvisable, Griff reached a hand out to her. Inexorably, his touch wandered, sneaking along the side of her neck until she tilted her head, acquiescing to the slow stroking motion of his hand. Griff skimmed his fingers along her collarbone, nudging at that damn lightweight robe. He was going to take her again if he didn't get control of himself.

Erica seemed equally lost in the web of temptation that bound them. As though she couldn't help herself, she took a small step forward, resting her forehead on Griff's shoulder. If she'd stripped off her robe and climbed onto him, Griff couldn't have wanted her more. And he felt bad for wanting her, because the vulnerability inherent in her gesture signified a need to be held, not fucked.

He wanted to do both, but alighting on the former he wound his arms around her and settled her body close to his chest. She sighed and burrowed deeper, her frame shuddering. After a moment Griff felt warm wetness trailing over his bare skin. He said nothing about the silent tears she shed. He simply held her until they ran dry.

He moved his hand gently over her hair, brushed his lips across her temple. Against him she quaked, her body melting to meet his. A small sound of surprise escaped her, as though she hadn't had an honest-to-God hug in so long she'd forgotten how it felt. The thought softened Griff's heart, and he found his lips trailing downward, tracing over her cheek until Erica tilted, meeting him halfway.

The press of her mouth was so luxurious that Griff groaned, helpless to stem the rising tide of desire. He'd tried to offer comfort, nothing more. But Lord help him, her kiss was so giving it encouraged a man in need to take, and Griff found himself delving into her velvet-wet mouth and tasting the particular mix of sweetness and secret anguish he discovered there.

Erica kissed him back with a helplessness he recognized, her lush tits molding to his chest, burning his skin. He cupped her face in one hand, angling her mouth to allow a deeper exploration. With the other hand, he grasped her hip and drew her to him.

She couldn't miss the hot swell of his erection. When it pressed into her stomach she gasped, wrenching her mouth away so she could look at him. In her dark brown eyes, Griff saw sharp astonishment and smoldering lust. But the way her cheeks reddened was all about shame and remorse. It reactivated Griff's sense of culpability, which had conveniently fled the instant he'd succumbed to the enticement of just one more kiss from Erica Shannon.

Muttering a curse, Griff set her away from him. The loss of her body heat was as chilling as an icy wind. Griff hastily retrieved his T-shirt from where it still lay crumpled on the floor and dragged it on.

What a fucking mess. He wanted Erica Shannon like he couldn't remember wanting another woman. Was it this intoxicating in those first months with Anna? Right now, Griff could hardly remember what Anna Hendricks, the woman he'd thought one of the loves of his life, looked like. He couldn't recall her scent or the sound of her voice. His memories had been obliterated by the waft of lavender shower gel and needy little moans he was unable to strip from his mind. His lust for Erica had grown into an irrepressible creature, unruly and resistant to any attempts he made to tame it.

Erica gathered her robe tighter around her, avoiding his gaze. "You'd better go."

"Yeah." It was all he managed to say before he stalked out the door. He had to find a way to talk to Corey, had to confess all and hope the other man had been serious about wanting to share Erica.

Because despite all his misgivings, a three-way affair loomed before Griff as the only solution to this growing problem. If he could keep his heart out of it, he wouldn't be risking the same pain he'd endured when it had ended with Anna and Jack. He was older now, and he had to believe past experience had made him smarter. If he could stay friends with both of them, if the two of them ended up together, he could wish them well and walk away without regret.

That was all he had to do; keep his heart out of it.

Erica moved through the morning in a daze. Her appointment was at two in the afternoon, when the doctor assured her the lab results would be available. She went to work because it beat the alternative—waiting all day on tenterhooks, forced to mull over what she'd done with Griff that morning.

Guilt was her unwelcome companion throughout the day. The emotion aggravated her. Why did she feel guilty about being with Griff when Corey had repeatedly reiterated his desire to share her with the man? Neither had she made Corey any promises or led him to believe there was a future for the two of them. She could have sex with anyone she pleased.

But that was precisely the problem. She wouldn't describe what she'd done with Griff as mere sex. Making love didn't seem the correct term either, but there was certainly a wealth of emotion, of connection in what had passed between them, as much as there had been in her long, sultry conversations with Corey. The fact that she'd allowed herself to cry in front of him terrified her. She hadn't felt safe enough to cry in front of any man in years, not since she was a little girl. Her father hadn't handled her tears well, and Erica had learned not to let her anguish show. Ironically, it was that very feeling of safety she'd experienced in Griff's arms that seemed so dangerous.

Despite her efforts to remain uninvolved, Erica felt a strong bond had developed between her and Griff *and* Corey, and she had no idea how she was going to break it.

She was no closer to an answer at two o'clock when she walked on wobbly legs into her doctor's office and gave her name at reception.

"Dr. Singh is running a little behind schedule," the receptionist explained apologetically. "If you'll take a seat, someone will call you when she's free."

Great. Erica smiled through her tension, telling herself it wasn't the woman's fault the doctor was behind. The last thing she needed was more time to brood, but the outdated magazines in the waiting area didn't have a hope of catching her interest.

From the way Griff had stormed out of her house that morning, she didn't think he intended to return. But she had to make it clear to Corey, once and for all, that a relationship between them was impossible. Thus far he'd chosen not to believe her protestations, but Erica was willing to concede her behavior hadn't exactly backed up her words. Telling a man she wasn't interested and then following up with phone sex was hardly an unambiguous message. She had to call him and lay her cards on the table, exactly as Griff had told her to. She had to cut him off completely.

There was little point in waiting until after her appointment. No matter the outcome of her lab tests, it didn't change her ultimate prognosis or the fact that she had to face her future alone. Pressing the numbers she'd unintentionally memorized into her mobile phone, Erica stepped outside and waited for Corey to pick up.

Erica closed her eyes on the shudder of desire that rippled through her at the now intimately familiar sound of his voice. "Corey, it's me, Erica."

"Hey, baby." The wealth of pleasure in his tone made remorse at what she was about to do grip her. "You called."

"Yes, I..." Erica swallowed the lump of dread in her throat and tried again. "I had to talk to you."

"I like the sound of that."

"About us, Corey. The phone calls—they have to stop."

"Uh-huh. You rang to tell me this?"

Erica wasn't in the mood for his gentle teasing. "I won't do it again, and you can't call me anymore either."

"Erica, we've been through this."

"No, we haven't, not really. I realize I haven't been clear enough with you. I've sent you mixed signals and that isn't fair."

"There's nothing unclear about the way we affect each other," Corey countered calmly. "You want me as much as I want you. Why can't you admit it?"

"Because what I want doesn't matter. My life is more complicated than you realize, and it's not something I'm able to talk to you about right now. You have to trust me on this—getting in deeper with you is out of the question. You have to stop phoning my house. If you do it again..." Erica pushed against the bubble of pain that had formed behind her sternum, "...I won't pick up. I won't call back."

"Right." A tense note had found its way into Corey's voice. "So what's to stop me dropping by? How long do you think you can hold out if I set up camp on your doorstep? Because I'm telling you, Erica, I'm willing go that far."

"For God's sake, Corey," she huffed. She knew what it was going to take to stop him, and Erica barely hesitated before she employed the biggest weapon in her arsenal. "I slept with someone else."

The ringing silence on the other end of the line told Erica all she needed to know about how accurate her aim had been. She felt like the worst person in the world. She'd intentionally hurt the nicest man she'd ever met because she didn't want to admit the truth and have him reject her for that instead, the way Doug had. She couldn't have handled it.

She shouldn't have been surprised by Corey's question, but she was. It took her breath away. "Was it Griff?"

"Yes," she admitted in a threadbare voice.

"So I was right." His words were more sad than angry. "You like him better, you always have. You didn't want to share, you wanted him to yourself."

Erica remained silent, unable to adequately explain the effect they'd both had on her, how impossible it was to apportion her feelings in percentages like slices of a pie chart. After a moment Corey went on. "When did this happen? *How* the hell did it happen?"

"This morning. He came over."

"*He* went to see you?"

Realizing too late the trouble she'd inadvertently caused between the two men, Erica implored, "Please don't blame him, Corey. It was me. I wanted it. I needed him."

"You needed him, but not me. I get it. I've made an idiot of myself. I thought you wanted the both of us, but those fantasies were all about Griff, weren't they?"

It wasn't true, but denying it would only muddy the message she was trying to get across. "Corey, I'm sorry. He told me I ought to be straight with you and I want to do that. That's why he came over this morning, because he was concerned about you. The rest just...happened."

"Right."

Erica was ashamed of herself for using such a lame excuse. Sex didn't simply happen, like an act of fate. It was an act of

101

will. She'd willingly let Griff into her body. She'd willingly hurt Corey, let him think she'd used him to get to his friend. Was there any end to her sins?

"I have to go," Corey eventually announced. "I'm at work and can't chat on the phone all day."

"Corey, I'm..."

He hung up on her before she got the chance to apologize again. Feeling nauseous, Erica braced her weight on the brick wall behind her with one hand while she bent at the waist, waiting for the bile in her throat to eject itself. Fortunately she'd barely eaten all day, or she might have made a mess right on the pavement.

"Miss Shannon?" Erica lifted her head to see the receptionist regarding her with a concerned expression. "Are you all right?"

Erica nodded, the gesture making her dizzy. But she remained steady as she straightened. "Is Dr. Singh ready?"

"Yes, you can come through now."

"I'm sorry to keep you waiting," Dr. Mariana Singh began as she ushered Erica into her office and closed the door behind her. "I know you must be anxious."

"I have to know. What am I dealing with?"

"I received your results from the lab." The doctor took a seat opposite Erica and indicated the file on her desk. "You'll be relieved to know the biopsy identified no abnormal cells."

Erica's breath suspended. She didn't think she could have been more shocked if the news was bad. "What?"

"They could find no indication of cancer. The lump you discovered was a benign cyst."

Benign cyst. Those two words might as well have been *lottery winner.* Erica was as shocked and disbelieving as she would be had someone rung to say she'd won a million dollars. "Benign? Are you sure?"

"I had the lab double-check the results. In fact I phoned them again before I called you in here. Yes, the cyst was benign. You don't have cancer, Erica."

Dr. Singh had guided her Aunt Claire through the process of her own discovery, one which had an ending not nearly as elating as this one. Her familiar, faintly accented voice washed over Erica, soothing her distress like the tide smoothes out a rough stone. "My God, I can't believe it."

"You are a healthy young woman." Dr. Singh smiled kindly. "Believe it."

Healthy young woman. It seemed such an alien concept. She'd spent the past year mired in her aunt's medical issues and her own genetic misfortune. It seemed she'd been focused on cancer for so long it had shifted her attention from anything good or healthy that might exist in her life.

A burgeoning euphoria quickened Erica's breath, but it was tempered by another harsh reality. She caught the doctor's gaze. "This is just the beginning. It wasn't breast cancer this time, but what about next time?"

Dr. Sing inclined her head. "There are no guarantees in life, and your risk is very real. We both know that. But with continued regular checkups, a good diet—"

"My chances of getting some form of cancer at some point are around eighty-seven percent," Erica interrupted. The stress of the past week had taken a massive toll on her. She couldn't go through it again. "I can't simply wait around and hope for the best, not anymore. There are other ways to deal with this, and I think I need to start seriously looking at them."

"Of course, you do have several options at your disposal," the doctor agreed. "Your genetic abnormality need not be a death sentence. Let's discuss what we can do in terms of preventative measures."

Dr. Singh provided Erica with a wealth of information, most of which Erica had already familiarized herself with online over the past year. She knew what her options were, and for the first time they started to seem like exactly that—options. Not invasive surgeries, not disfiguring procedures, but realistic alternatives to the life of fear and dread she'd been living. There were methods of thwarting this disease. Many others did it, and right now in Dr. Singh's office, Erica decided she could do it too.

She wouldn't let cancer win. She would take control of her fate.

The impact jarred Corey's body as he slammed into his opponent. Steve Waller landed on his back on the dew-damp grass, the air rushing out of his lungs in a gasp.

It took a moment for Steve to catch his breath. When he did he sounded pissed. "Fucking hell, Corey. You got your period tonight or what?"

Corey offered him a tight smile. "Trying to stay in shape for next year's game, that's all."

Every man at the evening's footy practice knew there was more to Corey's zealous performance than an attempt to perfect his tackling technique. The annual Guns and Hoses rugby league stoush, where the fieries challenged local law enforcement to a grudge match, had already been played, and won. Tonight's post-season practice was more an excuse for some rowdy exercise and male bonding than anything.

Not that Corey was in much of a bonding mood tonight.

As he got back into position, fully prepared to take on the next man who tried to pass him with the football, Erica's words rang in his head.

...getting in deeper with you is out of the question. You have to stop phoning my house. If you do it again, I won't pick up. I won't call back.

She'd punctured his lung with those words, but what followed was worse. More than twenty-four hours later Corey was still prone to bouts of breathlessness that had nothing to do with physical exertion.

Steve Waller came running at him with the ball, and Corey made a beeline for him. The other man shook his head and quickly offloaded. Corey pulled up just before he slammed into Steve again.

Too bad. Corey really wanted to body slam someone.

Admittedly, Steve wasn't his preferred target.

I had sex with someone else.

"Here he is now. You're late."

Steve's greeting made Corey whip his head around. Sure enough there was Griff, dumping his duffel by the sideline and giving the team an unapologetic shrug. "Stuff to do, Waller. It's called a life."

"Funny. For that, you can take my spot for a while. Wachawski's broken my spine."

Corey took little notice of the mock-filthy look Steve sent him as he pretended to limp off the field. He had eyes only for the man's replacement. He tracked every step Griff took as he moved into the vacated position. Griff didn't look him in the eye once.

Coward.

Corey continued to stare at Griff, until he finally looked up. What he saw in his golden eyes knocked the wind out of him.

Not regret, but defiance. *The bastard.* All that talk about standing aside so he could have Erica, about how the three of them could never work. He hadn't meant any of it. He'd been waiting for his moment to waltz in behind Corey's back and steal her.

His blood pumped with impatience as the game got going again. Corey took a pass and ran straight for his mark, not bothering to sidestep or feint, even when Curly called for the ball. He ran straight for Griff, who came equally hard toward him.

At the last minute, Griff ducked, grabbing Corey around the waist instead of meeting him chest to chest. The surprise caught Corey off-guard and he was propelled backward. He fell onto the earth like a sack of cement, Griff landing with an *oomph* on top of him.

Grinding his teeth, Corey pushed at Griff's body weight until the other man stood. Griff offered his hand to Corey, but Corey ignored it, standing on his own with a glower. He bent to play the ball through his legs. When he straightened, he was still glaring.

Griff faced the look levelly and came to a simple conclusion. "She told you then."

The cavalier words made Corey so mad his blood burned like acid. "Told me what?" he spat. "That you fucked her or that you told her to dump me?"

He thought he saw Griff wince but he couldn't be sure. His vision was a little blurred from that body-shaking tackle. Griff turned his attention back to the game, and Corey barely resisted the urge to push the other man into the dirt.

The game proceeded. Penalties were awarded, scrums conducted. Griff's team scored two tries, Corey's three. All the while Corey grabbed every opportunity to slam his opponent into the ground. Most of the time it could be chalked up to legitimate score-line defense.

Sometimes not.

"I thought you wanted to share her with me," Griff drawled after one such incident had them both sprawled flat out on the field.

Rage gave Corey the energy to stand again. "Not like this," he hissed.

"So only on your terms. Anyone else have a say in how this plays out?" Griff pondered, standing too. "Obviously not me. What about Erica?"

"Fuck you."

Mitch, who acted as referee on account of a recent knee injury, blew his whistle. "You guys need to sit out for a while?"

"No," Corey denied immediately.

He wasn't done hurting Griff yet.

Never one to admit he might be bested in a matchup, Griff let Corey see his lips twitch. A few minutes later when Griff was passed the ball and started making a run for it, Corey flew straight for him in top gear.

Griff showed no fear as he hurtled forward. He had opportunities to offload, guys in position and yelling for the ball. But he held on to it and kept running.

Bring it on, Corey thought, a second before they collided.

Griff had more speed but Corey had the size advantage. Griff hit the ground with a loud thump and Corey followed him down.

For a second he panicked, thinking he'd actually caused Griff damage. He sat up and surveyed Griff's body. "You okay?"

"Do I fucking look okay?" Griff wheezed.

The shrill of Mitch's whistle was ear piercing. "Wachawski! Griffin! What the fuck is wrong with you?" Mitch lit into them in a diatribe fit for the occasion and ended it with a screamed instruction. "Both of you, off! You're sin-binned for ten!"

"There's only eight minutes to go," Corey pointed out.

"I know," yelled Mitch. "Both of you out of my sight now."

"Fair enough." Griff staggered to his feet. "I'm too old for this shit anyway."

Remorse mingling with his simmering anger, Corey followed Griff off the field. They each headed to their bags in silence, drank water and wiped their faces on the hems of their ratty T-shirts. Although they didn't face each other once, Corey was aware of every action, every sound Griff made as he threw his stuff back in his duffel and closed it. Corey zipped up his own bag and stood.

Griff stood in his path, his gaze steady in a way that made Corey's blood skip. "Do we need to finish this discussion elsewhere?"

"My oath we do."

"My place." It wasn't a suggestion, but a command. "Now."

Chapter Nine

Corey never lost sight of Griff's taillights as he traveled the same roads in his wake. Griff's house was on the outskirts of Ashton Heights. Griff had bought it years ago before the suburb had boomed and spent the intervening time renovating the timber cottage into a three-bed, two-bath showpiece with floorboards polished to a high shine and a plethora of chrome fittings throughout.

Corey had been to the house on numerous occasions, but never like this. Anticipation made his heartbeat thump erratically. His tongue was so dry it stuck to the roof of his mouth. Whole body throbbing, Corey screeched into Griff's driveway after him. He didn't think to lock his car as he stalked down the front walk. Griff pushed the door open with his foot and tossed his bag carelessly down the hallway. Corey followed, his steps eating up the polished floorboards.

Griff didn't turn to face him until he stood in the middle of the open-plan living room he'd decorated with modern black couches and red-patterned rugs. When he did, his expression was bland. "Come on, out with it."

Corey hardly knew where to start. "What the hell was it about the other night? All that shit about how you didn't want her and I should go for it?"

"I meant it. I lost my head for a moment, that's all."

"You lost it. That's it?"

"Okay, so I lied too when I said I didn't want to make a play for her. I only stepped aside so you could do your thing."

"Thanks for the fucking favor," Corey spat.

"Hey, you used me in your little phone-sex games. Knowing what you do about me, didn't you think that would drive me out of my mind?"

"What Erica and I talked about has nothing to do with this."

"Bullshit. You made it my business when you told me about it. You made me as horny as hell, and a man can only deny himself so much."

Corey's dick flexed as Griff's admission penetrated. *You made me as horny as hell.* His anger morphed into something else, something equally as hot that gave him an instant erection. Concentrating on why he was pissed off became difficult. "How do you mean?"

"Knowing you two fantasized about me like that is hot," Griff said, his tone lowering. "Three-way sex, it's the ultimate payoff for me."

Because he liked to be with a man as well as a woman. Corey's blood pulsed, just thinking about it. *The ultimate payoff.* "Would it be that way for me, too?"

"Are you asking if I could make you love it, Cor?"

He was supposed to be furious, wasn't he? How come all his bodily energy was now channeled into creating an erection the size of Queensland?

"I could, you know." The turn of Griff's lips was arrogant in a way that was more sexy than annoying. "I could make you scream my name 'til your throat's raw, the way she did."

Corey swallowed. "I thought you didn't want to take the risk of getting screwed."

"I won't risk a relationship, Cor. I'm not going there again. But sex is a different story." Griff took three languid steps toward him. "Since I can't seem to help myself around either of you, I might as well reap the benefits."

Corey's dick twitched, receiving another blood infusion. His lips were so dry he had to wet them. Griff's gaze tracked the movement of his tongue with a look that could only be described as predatory.

"I'm not going to push, Cor." Everything radiating from him told Corey that was one of the hardest things Griff had ever said. "I know you're not ready to go that far."

Heart pounding without restraint, Corey asked, "What makes you think I'm not ready?"

Griff eyed him steadily for a long moment. In the vacuous silence of the open-plan house, the only sound was their combined breathing, raspy breaths drawn in with difficulty. Then Griff grasped the hem of his T-shirt and drew it over his head. The garment hit the floor, followed a minute later by his shorts and jocks.

He stood there, nude, administering some kind of test. Gripped by the determination to pass it, Corey let his gaze trail downward. At the sight of Griff's red-flushed erection, he caught his breath, refusing to shy from what lay before him. A naked, aroused man. A line he'd never thought to cross until recently. Untold, unknown pleasures—if he had the guts to explore them.

Fingers trembling, Corey fisted his shirt at his back and hauled it over his head. He didn't pause to think before removing his own shorts and underwear, letting them fall to the floor beside Griff's.

Just as he hadn't shied from ogling all Griff had to offer, he didn't flinch when Griff now looked his fill. The thoroughness of the other man's scrutiny made Corey hot with a tumultuous mix of pride and pure carnal excitement.

Without a word, Griff turned and walked to the bathroom. He left the door open as he got the shower running. Corey couldn't stop staring at the taut globes of Griff's ass. The shower stall was clear glass, and Corey's view was unobstructed as Griff stepped under the spray and started soaping himself.

His breath shallow, Corey followed. Taking up Griff's implied invitation, he opened the shower door and stepped inside. The last time he'd shared a shower with Griff, Erica had been between them. In some ways she still was. Yet Corey's anger about how things had gone down with Erica drifted to the back of his mind when Griff wordlessly handed him the soap.

Unable to speak, Corey turned the soap to lather in his hands. Then he put those hands on Griff.

Griff's eyes fell closed as Corey rubbed the soap into his skin. His flesh was smooth and hard, so different to a woman's. Fear evaporated in the face of fascination. Griff's muscles were as inflexible as boulders, the tension in them thrumming against Corey's fingers.

Touching him felt better than good, and Corey's groin burned in response. He'd seen Griff shirtless before, but the tactile sensation of his flexing muscles made him seem more impressive, hot and real beneath Corey's fingers. Tracing the line of Griff's armband tattoo, he said huskily, "I've thought about getting one."

"Nah." Griff's own voice was threadbare. "Don't mess with perfection."

The compliment warmed Corey's chest. He'd always been susceptible to the slightest hint of praise from Dale Griffin. The thought sobered him. Was that why he was doing this? Was he seeking Griff's approval?

"Problems?"

Griff's gaze had sharpened on Corey's face. He was ready to put a stop to this any time Corey showed signs of hesitation. Corey sensed it in the way Griff held back, the fact he still hadn't reached out to touch. But Corey didn't want to stop. He had to see this through—he needed to. He didn't want approval. He needed to see where this was going.

He needed Griff.

He shook his head. "No problem."

Then, heart hammering, he reached down and curled his soapy fingers around Griff's dick.

"Ah, yeah." Griff swayed a little and his fingers dug into Corey's shoulder. Encouraged, Corey stroked up and down his length, marveling at how it felt to touch another man this way, to feel that rod of smooth steel pulse within his grip. Familiar, yet a little awkward. "Jesus, that's good."

"Really?"

"Did you think you wouldn't know how to do it?" Griff smiled. "You've touched your own enough times, I bet."

Corey looked at him. "Is everything a joke to you?"

Griff sobered, studying the tension in Corey's face. Without responding, he snaked his hand downward, seeking Corey's erection. Using some of the soap from his own body, Griff cupped Corey, stroked him.

The touch of his friend's hand made Corey grow longer, harder. He filled Griff's grip as his hips rocked helplessly.

"Don't stop."

At first Corey thought he'd spoken his thoughts aloud. Then he realized he'd stilled the motion of his hand on Griff's dick, was simply holding him tight while Griff drove him insane with the best hand job he'd ever had. "Shit. Sorry."

"Shh." Griff silenced Corey with a kiss that was little more than a wet glide of their lips until Corey opened against him, inviting him inside. Griff swept in and teased Corey's tongue, never losing the rhythm and pressure he applied to Corey's shaft.

Corey couldn't say the same for himself. He was pretty damn sure he was doing a terrible job of pleasing Griff, but he was so overwhelmed by the sensations coursing through him that he didn't have the mental capacity to make improvements.

Drawing back a little, Griff observed roughly, "You're going to come pretty quick, Cor."

Embarrassed to have it pointed out, Corey shuddered. "I want to see you..."

"I know. You will, after."

"I loved watching you come inside Erica."

"She was the prettiest, tightest little ass I've ever fucked. Made me unload so hard I saw stars."

Corey's achy balls contracted, drew up into his body. "She made me come too. On the phone when she told me what she wanted to do to you."

Griff gave Corey's shaft a squeeze. "And when you told her how you wanted this."

"Yeah. Oh, yeah. *Griff.*"

Griff continued to stroke him, increasing speed when he sensed Corey needed it. A heartbeat later a gasp seeped out of Corey as he shot wet heat from his body.

Griff captured Corey's lips, murmuring against them, "God, you're gorgeous."

Corey was beyond words, beyond actions. Lathering more soap, Griff eased Corey's hand out of the way and started working himself. Still reeling from his own climax, Corey could do little but watch in rapt fascination as Griff's breath came in staccato pants and his palm worked overtime on his hard cock. He let go within a minute, his semen arcing out of the tip and onto Corey's stomach.

Hooking an arm around Corey's neck, Griff brought him close until their cheeks touched.

Corey dropped his head onto Griff's shoulder, weakened. He couldn't prevent the way his frame shuddered with the aftereffects, even when Griff angled him into the spray and washed them both off, like he thought Corey needed taking care of.

Shit. He had to pull himself together. He couldn't fall apart in front of Griff.

"How do you feel?"

"Fine. Good. Great." *Fuck. Settle on a word why don't you.*

Griff didn't tease him about his lack of adjectives. "You still shitty with me about Erica?"

"I...I forgot to be."

"Don't blame her. I started it."

"All right, I'll blame you." But Corey couldn't work up the ire to really do it. How could he hate the man who'd made him feel this blissed out? He sighed. "You're the most frustrating prick I know."

"Yeah, but I'm also hellishly sexy. Right?"

Corey let out a sound somewhere between a laugh and a groan. "Erica will never want me again."

"I don't think that's true, Cor."

"How could she want me after she's had you?"

Griff swore and tightened his hold on Corey, placing his lips against his temple. The rough brush of his stubble made Corey's pulse skitter. *So much different than a woman.* The post-orgasm dynamics had Corey's mind reeling. He had no idea how he was supposed to act now. Women tended to look for reassurance after, which Corey was more than happy to provide. Griff was so damn sure of himself already that offering to hold him for a while would be ridiculous.

Acknowledging with no shortage of mortification that he was the one seeking reassurance this time, Corey took a step away from Griff, proving he could support himself. Griff turned off the shower and they both got out, using towels to dry off.

Corey could sense Griff's eyes tracking the motion of his hands, and the heat that had left him with the furious burst of his climax returned. Then Griff started using his towel to dry Corey's hair. A softness pervaded Corey's chest, making his heart stutter. What the hell was Griff doing to him?

Griff finished and hung the towel around Corey's neck, still holding onto the ends so Corey was forced to face him. "We won't do anything else tonight."

"Why not?"

"You're not ready."

Geez, now Griff decided to activate his protective streak. "Again with that. It's me, Griff. I'm not a girl."

Griff's lips quirked. "I did notice."

"Stop being so freakin' gentle with me."

Griff's voice was serious, quiet. "Don't think I can help it. Hell, Corey. I'm more gentle with you than I have been with women lately."

Corey stared him down. "Did you hurt Erica?"

Griff stared back. "Nothing she didn't want."

Corey could well imagine the scene, remembering the way Erica had screamed Griff's name when he'd taken her in the shower. He remembered too the many things he and Erica had discussed, the varied ways she'd said she wanted Griff to bring her to orgasm.

Fantasies he'd encouraged her to share. Corey had no right to act like a possessive creep, not when he'd encouraged Erica's attraction to Griff.

Griff left the bathroom, walking across the hall to his bedroom. Corey caught up in time to see Griff dragging a pair of jeans over his bare butt. The knowledge that he went without underwear made Corey's mouth dry out. *Who says I'm not ready?*

"No fair," Corey said. "The only clothes I have are all sweaty."

"I'd lend you some jeans but you're bigger than me."

"Oh you noticed that too?"

Griff sent him a droll look. "Don't start with me, Wachawski. It's what you do with it that counts."

A little shiver ripped through Corey. "So what do you do with it? I mean when you're with a guy it must be different."

"You asking who gets to be the boss?"

"I suppose."

Griff smiled slowly. "I usually like to be in charge."

That shiver coursed over Corey's skin again. "No kidding."

Riffling through his drawers Griff found a pair of baggy sweatpants and tossed them over. "I told you, Corey, not tonight. You need time to let the big head wrap around what the little head wants." He glanced downward with a knowing smile. "Not that you're so little."

Heat flushed Corey's skin, made him tighten below the waist. He dragged the sweatpants on to hide the response. Griff was flirting with him, and it made Corey's brain scramble. Maybe his big head did need more time than the rest of him to work this whole thing out.

He sat on the bed while Griff went looking for a shirt. "How did it happen?" At Griff's questioning look, Corey clarified. "Your first time with a man."

"It was stupid. I was at a party with this girl I was going with. Actually I thought it was getting serious, but she didn't seem to be of the same opinion." Pulling a button-up flannel from his wardrobe, Griff handed it over. "She was flirting with this other guy to make a point. When I took issue, Becca came up with a way we could battle to win her affections. We all ended up in one of the bedrooms together. I was drunk. I don't really know how it happened, but somewhere in the middle of it he started kissing me and that got out of control pretty fast. Becca went ballistic."

Corey still held the shirt balled up in his fists. "She broke up with you over it."

"And called me a few choice names in the process. Pervy faggot was my personal favorite."

"Shit, Griff. That sucks."

Griff shrugged. "Not everyone's as freakishly understanding as you are, mate."

"Did you ever think you were...you know?"

Griff came to stand before Corey. He looked down at him, stroking back his hair in that tender way that took Corey by surprise. "You're not gay, Cor."

"How do you know for sure?"

"Because women give you a hard-on, dork."

Corey held Griff's gaze. "You give me a hard-on too."

Silence fell, as bulky as a blanket. Corey could see the pulse thudding at the base of Griff's throat. When he spoke his voice was as thick as molasses. "I'm gonna order a pizza. No pepperoni, right?"

When Griff made to move away, Corey grabbed him around the waist and held him still. "You had to take care of yourself before. Maybe you ought to show me how to get that right."

Corey leaned forward and pressed his lips to the flat muscles of Griff's abdomen. Twisting his fingers in Corey's hair, Griff used the grip to tip his head back. He swooped down and claimed his mouth for a brief, hot kiss. "Am I going to have to tie your hands to keep them from wandering?"

Corey's cock flexed even as his blood cooled. Talk about his body giving him mixed messages. "I don't know if I'd like that."

"Exactly my point. You don't know what you want yet. Like you said, it's different with a guy. Give it time."

Griff moved away again and Corey let out a breath that shuddered.

Griff went to order the pizza, and the two of them sat with a couple of beers and the supreme-without-pepperoni in the living room. They found a game on and watched it while they ate, the sound turned down. Mostly they talked like a couple of guys sharing brews and junk food and nothing else between them.

But Griff's flashing grins and occasional flirtatious comments kept electric heat fizzing in the air. Corey was half-hard the whole time, his skin prickly and hot.

"So how is this going to work?" Corey asked at one point, his impetuousness getting the best of him. "I mean with Erica."

"I still want her." Griff smiled ruefully. "There I am, being upfront about it."

"That hasn't changed for me, either. But..."

"She wants you like crazy, Cor. Don't doubt that. The two of you are like horny little peas in a pod."

"She told me to stop calling her."

"Only because some prick went over there and forced her to make a decision before she was ready."

"Yeah, I heard that guy's a massive tool."

"I heard he *has* a massive tool, and he really knows how to use it."

Corey wadded up a napkin and threw it at Griff's head. "You're a jerk."

"Who makes you hot, right?"

The glance Griff sent Corey's crotch would have clued Griff in to the truth, so Corey didn't do Griff's ego the favor of confirming it. "This is messed up."

"Not really. It's simple. Erica said you should stop calling her. She didn't say anything about visits, did she? And she never actually told me to piss off."

"What a shocker." Corey's gaze narrowed. "What did you have in mind?"

"I can fix this for you, Cor. The three of us can have some fun and then, when the time is right, you and Erica can make a go of it."

The suggestion gave Corey a cold feeling in his chest. "You think you can start something like that and just...stop?"

"Sure." Corey saw the way Griff's Adam's apple worked and wondered if he was back to telling lies again. "I'll get bored eventually."

The thought of Griff getting bored with him made Corey's gut burn. Griff was more practiced at hiding his emotions than Corey could ever be, and the notion made Corey wonder if he was well out of his depth. But it was too late to go backward. The lure of that *ultimate payoff* Griff had mentioned was too strong. If he didn't follow this through, Corey would always wonder what he'd missed.

Corey asked, "Are you going to help me get her back? It's the least you can do."

"Fair enough."

"Are you going to put me out of my misery at some point too?"

With a smirk, Griff once again glanced down at the place where Corey formed a bulge in his sweatpants. "Oh yeah. Believe it."

But not tonight, Corey mentally added, wondering if Griff's determination to take the slow road with him was going to prove beneficial or as frustrating as hell.

Wondering if he wasn't headed for a big fall either way.

Chapter Ten

Five days after Erica had received her get-out-of-cancer-free card, the phone rang.

The phone never could ring these days without making her think of Corey, and Erica's heart clutched. The one thing tempering her relief at being given a reprieve from a terminal disease was the sadness that still rested like a decaying thing in the pit of her stomach whenever she thought of Griff or Corey. Of those wild moments in Griff's arms, of the cold, hurtful truths she'd used to push Corey away the last time they'd spoken.

No, it would not be Corey on the other end of the line this time. The thought weighed Erica's heart down as she lifted the receiver.

The voice she heard stopped it altogether.

"What are you wearing?"

Erica gaped for several moments, flabbergasted by Griff's question. "What?"

"What? You're happy to do the kinky phone thing with Wachawski, but I don't rate?" Erica blew out a stunned breath. Griff went on as though she hadn't made a sound.

"Lucky for me I'm not the sensitive type. So, watchadoing on this fine Saturday morning?"

"I'm very busy." Erica glanced down at the rag and bottle of cleaning spray on the kitchen bench. "There's no need to come over and check my smoke alarms or anything."

"Shame," Griff said smoothly. "I so enjoyed it last time."

Heat flushed through Erica. She was stunned into silence by Griff's nerve.

"Besides," Griff continued. "It's too late to stop us."

"What do you mean?"

"Look out your window, gorgeous."

Erica broke into a sprint to get to the living room window. Down there in her front yard they stood, both wearing khaki shorts and stretchy T-shirts. Corey's was black and Griff's faded red, the same shirt he'd been wearing the morning he'd come over and they'd...

"Surprise," Griff said into the phone. Corey lifted a hand and gave her a wave.

Astounded, Erica waved back. "What are you doing here?"

"Yard needs mowing," Griff stated. "We're going to mow it."

They were going to *mow her lawn*? "You don't have to do that."

"Hard work and sunshine are good for the soul."

Erica saw Griff's wink, his cheeky lopsided smile, even from a distance. He was fifty meters away and still he could make her belly flutter. It was darned exasperating. "I don't need you to do my yard work. I'll hire someone."

"Why would you do that when you've got us?"

There was a click in her ear as Griff hung up his mobile phone, leaving Erica to ponder what he meant by saying she *had* them. She watched as they turned, walked to Griff's Ute and started pulling gear out of the back.

Shell-shocked, Erica wandered back to the kitchen and retrieved the cloth and bottle of cleaning spray she'd left on the bench. She held on to them without moving for several moments, until the phone rang again.

Erica picked up the receiver, her heart pounding.

"Look, Griff can be an ass sometimes." In the background Griff issued a disgruntled objection to Corey's opening line. "You won't hold that against me though, will you?"

Erica shut her eyes against the pleasure of Corey's whisky-smooth timbre pouring over her. Oh, he had such a voice on him. Just right for slow sexy conversations that weakened a woman's resolve. "Corey, I don't understand. Didn't you hear anything I said the other day?"

"I heard you say your life was complicated, that's why we're here. We want to make it easier for you. You don't have to do everything alone, Erica."

Erica warmed, his words as effective as a comforting hug. His generosity made guilt eddy inside her. "Don't you hate me, Corey?"

"Baby, I could never hate you."

"I slept with Griff, remember? I refused to go out with you and then I slept with your best friend."

"It's not as simple as that. All those nights on the phone... I knew what you wanted, that it wasn't just me. I encouraged it. I get it, Erica." Corey's voice softened in a way that made Erica's heart skip a beat. "Griff sort of gets under your skin in a way you can't ignore."

Walking back to the window, Erica looked out at the front yard. She couldn't see either of their faces, could find no clue as to whether Corey's statement implied what she thought it did.

Had something happened between Griff and Corey?

"We're going to get started," Corey announced. "Anytime you want to come down and say hi, that'd be just fine with me."

He hung up the phone.

A short time later the lawnmower started. Erica remained ensconced in the safety of the house, carrying out her usual raft of Saturday-morning chores and glancing out the window about a thousand times in the process.

She had to go down there at some point, at the very least offer them something to drink. But she delayed, afraid of how she might react once she was in close proximity with those two hunky, sweaty men.

After months and months of burying her emotions, either for Aunt Claire's sake or to avoid facing the reality of her situation, she now felt raw and sensitive. All the feelings she'd numbed had come alive with a vengeance, making the very surface of her skin seem to pulse with awareness. In the past two days, she'd simultaneously felt a hairsbreadth away from laughter or tears. If she came within a meter of Corey and Griff, she was liable to either break down or launch herself at them and beg them to make love to her.

But the moment of truth couldn't be put off forever. Manners dictated she offer them refreshment for helping her out, even if she hadn't asked for it. Erica opened the fridge and found a bottle of juice. At the sink she mixed it in a jug with some ice, then she retrieved some bread from the freezer and started making sandwiches.

The men were working in the backyard now. Erica watched as Corey paused in his duties to wipe the sweat off his face with the hem of his T-shirt. The action exposed the flat expanse of his abdomen and the impressive bulge of his pectorals. Erica's mouth dried out as everything below her waist grew moist.

Griff approached, butting shoulders with Corey. He said something close to Corey's ear, and Corey laughed, color stealing into his cheeks. Every cell in Erica's body went still as Griff placed his hand on Corey's stomach, spreading his fingers over the ridged muscles there. There was something beyond platonic in the gesture, close mateship with sexual currents running through it.

Then Griff moved his hand up so it slid beneath the raised hem of Corey's T-shirt.

Erica stood, transfixed, as their foreheads came to rest against one another's. Griff's hand moved around underneath the black fabric of Corey's shirt, caressing and teasing. Corey slanted his face sideways. Erica's heartbeat extended, became a slow painful thing that vibrated in her chest as Corey's and Griff's lips whispered against each other's.

Erica had never seen anything as breathtaking, as erotic as those two hard-bodied men being so achingly gentle with each other. Arousal curled like a cresting wave inside her, causing her entire body to tremble. Realizing they were going to catch her watching if she didn't turn away, Erica dragged her attention back to the refreshments. She tried to lift the jug onto the tray she'd set up, but her hands shook so badly she dropped it. The juice spilled all over the counter, the ice making a succession of loud thumps as it tumbled to the floor.

She glanced out the window to see Corey and Griff both staring straight at her. Instinctively, she ducked out of sight. She slunk to the floor, feeling like the biggest fool who ever lived. Why on earth was she hiding? It had nothing to do with her what Griff and Corey did to each other. But her mind raced with curiosity. Had her instincts been right? Were they lovers now?

"Erica?"

Erica hastened to meet Corey at the back door just as he was pulling open the screen. She placed the flat of her hand on his chest, intent on pushing him back. The feel of his rock-hard pecs beneath her palm, the same pecs Griff had trailed his hand over but a moment ago, made desire run wild inside her.

The abject concern on his face ripped at the shield around her heart. "Are you okay?"

"I'm fine. I dropped a jug, that's all."

"I'm sorry." The apology tore out of him, a sound like ripping paper. "I'm so sorry. I know you saw. Griff and I... We've become more than friends. But we shouldn't have flaunted it like that."

Erica bit her lip, an agony of sorrow twisting her organs. He thought she was repulsed by what she'd seen, when the truth was the absolute opposite. "You can do whatever you want."

"I know we talked about it before, but that was talk. This is different. I hope you can learn to accept it, because I don't think I can stop what's happening with Griff."

"Of course not," Erica said, surprised. "I would never want you to."

Footfalls on the stairs heralded Griff's arrival on the porch. Erica glanced past Corey's shoulder to see him standing there, the shade of the awning casting his face in shadows. She sensed rather than saw the defiance in his expression. Erica knew then that this side of him, his sexual flexibility, had not always been embraced by others.

Erica smiled at both of them, making sure they could see the unadulterated acceptance in her eyes. "I think it's beautiful. How could I think otherwise? You're both so wonderful. I'm glad you found your way to each other."

Corey said, his expression intense, "I'm glad we found *you*."

Then he kissed her.

The first touch of his lips was like a drug being reintroduced into her system. Despite everything she'd been through with Corey, his lips had not touched hers since that first night. Erica opened eagerly, sensible thought fleeing. All that mattered was the engrossing magic of Corey's kiss, the warm support of his arms wrapping around her, the scent of musky male sweat mingled with freshly cut grass.

Cool timber hit her back as Corey urged her into the shade, pressed her up against the house. His lips never left hers, as though he was as unwilling as she to relinquish the contact. He didn't release her when she gasped at the way his hand gently cradled her womanly flesh. He relented only when that gasp of pleasure turned into one of shock the moment a second pair of lips brushed across her cheek.

Corey moved aside, transferring his kiss to her neck as Griff took his turn at her mouth. Erica was already pliant and aroused from Corey's kiss, so made no objection when Griff immediately sought entry. She moaned at the back of her throat, overwhelmed by the skillful, demanding thrust of his tongue.

Corey's thumb swept back and forth across her nipple, which had grown distended beneath her cotton shirt and soft-cup bra. Erica shuddered in the grip of pleasure when Griff slid his hand to cover her other breast and began gently kneading it.

Breathing became impossible, and she had to wrench her mouth from beneath Griff's. She dragged warm spring air into her lungs, but it only seemed to increase her dizziness. She forced her eyes open. The rest of the world looked so normal, old houses mixed with new, their tin and tile roofs shining red, grey and black in the midmorning sun.

Her neighbors possibly in their own yards, perhaps glancing over to see her being fondled by two men.

The idea wasn't entirely unappealing, and Erica let out an appalled gasp at her own wickedness. Exhibitionism now? What else were Griff and Corey capable of drawing out of her?

Corey pulled back and looked into her face. His blue eyes shone with understanding and an intense desire he fought to control. "Let's go inside."

Yes.

"No."

Griff was the one who'd spoken, using the answer she should have been prepared to give. Corey glanced at his friend with a frown. "No?"

"No." Griff's hot mouth brushed over her temple. His hand continued to massage her flesh as though he had no intention of stopping anytime soon. "We're all sweaty and I'm not taking this further in the shower again. I want more room to maneuver."

A shiver raced over Erica's skin.

Griff tilted her chin up so their eyes met. His hazel ones were filled with hot passion, but his lips curved sardonically. "Tonight, seven o'clock. Be ready."

"For what?"

Stupid question. They were seducing her. They wanted her, still, although they were now involved with each other. How could that be?

But Griff didn't give the bald sexual response Erica expected. He flashed her a grin. "The best steakhouse in the city. You own anything black and tight?"

Erica blinked. "Do I look like the kind of woman who wears black and tight?"

"No, but you ought to. Not to worry, one of those prudish skirt-and-blouse sets of yours'll do for tonight."

Prudish?

Erica was about to offer Griff a piece of her mind, even as she conceded he might be right about her usual wardrobe. But Corey completely muddled her thoughts and her annoyance when he ran his hand over her stomach, making her muscles bunch. "Can't we make her come just once right now?"

He moved his hand downward until he cupped her mound through her cotton shorts. Erica couldn't stifle a moan.

"Much as I love the way Red screams when she comes...no." Griff's smile bordered on satanic. He knew how close to the edge she already was. He traced the outline of her lips. "We'll make it up to you tonight."

With a sigh of disappointment, Corey took his hand away. Erica cut him a look. "You take your orders from him now?"

Corey smiled at her annoyance. "He knows what he's doing."

If only Erica knew what he was doing—what they were both doing. The events of the morning had made her head spin. Corey and Griff simply showing up like this, doing her yard chores, flaunting the nature of their relationship and now pulling her into it for reasons she didn't understand.

Why did they still want her? What could they possibly need her for?

The questions had not assembled coherently in her mind by the time they'd packed up in preparation to leave. She was too stunned, too aroused to utter her confusion. She would simply have to go out with them tonight to find out what it all meant.

At least that was her excuse for not refusing the date.

"Remember, Red, six o'clock." Griff told her as he prepared to get in behind the wheel of his car.

"I thought you said seven." That demand had burned into her memory.

Griff smiled. "I decided not to wait that long. Want to make it five?"

Erica was sorely tempted to suggest four. She bit her tongue to keep from sounding quite that desperate. "Six is fine."

They left a moment later, Corey waving through the windshield as the Ute backed out of her driveway. Erica was left standing there wondering what was going on, questioning her own blind obedience in the face of Griff's demands, and mentally cataloguing everything in her wardrobe.

She definitely did not own anything black and tight.

Am I the only woman in the world who doesn't own any black lingerie?

At a quarter to six Erica stood before the full-length mirror in her bedroom, cursing her conservative tastes. Brown was the best she could do. *Brown.* Could she be any more boring?

In actuality the matching bra and panty set was closer to the color of cinnamon. It wasn't even a dark chocolate brown that brought to mind edible desserts. It was like satin, and Erica had always gleaned a tactile enjoyment from the way the underwear cupped and caressed her skin. But there was nary a wisp of lace on the full-cup bra and the pants were *pants*; built for coverage, not seduction.

She simply didn't know how to drive a man to distraction with her choice of underthings. In fact she had no clue how she'd sustained Griff's and Corey's interest at all—especially now they had each other.

A rush of lust throbbed through her veins. Erica had no idea where her fascination with the intimate side of Griff and Corey's relationship had sprung from, but she couldn't stop picturing the two men together, doing things to each other. Hard bodies straining, soft lips exploring, undressing each other. It was fascinating—and shockingly arousing.

Erica's fingers trembled as she pulled her best dress off its hanger and slipped it over her shoulders. It was a wraparound style with three-quarter sleeves that she usually wore with a black camisole beneath on account of its plunging neckline. Tonight she went without it.

Unused to revealing quite so much cleavage, Erica had the immediate urge to change. But the only black dress she owned was high necked and dour—*prudish*—the dress she'd worn to her aunt's funeral. This one was a dark emerald green that flattered her red hair and pale complexion. She'd bought it years ago for the first time Doug had taken her to dinner and a show. She'd hoped for passion that night, but it had never eventuated. If she'd worn it without the concealing camisole then would Doug's reaction have been stronger?

Probably not. Erica had come to realize that for Doug she had been little more than convenient company when he found himself in the mood for some. His passion had been reserved for his dusty history texts and for the convoluted politics of academic life. Any attempts Erica had made at spicing things up had been met with lukewarm bewilderment. But when the issues of her genetic test and Aunt Claire's diagnosis had begun to consume her, the resultant lack of attention she'd afforded Doug had irked him.

He'd dropped her like a hot potato. Would Griff and Corey do the same thing if they knew the truth?

Erica pushed thought of the future from her mind, concentrating instead on the moment. Her recent cancer scare had illuminated the fact she hadn't been enjoying life because of her fixation on somber possibilities. Soon enough she would have to deal with her situation and the probability that whatever novelty factor she represented for her two firemen would wear off.

Soon enough—but not yet. Not tonight.

A solid knock on the door made Erica bolt into action. Surveying her reflection in the mirror one last time, she prayed the dark eye makeup she'd applied didn't make her look like what her students would call a *try-hard*. Then she slipped on her black heels, grabbed her purse and rushed for the door.

Corey stood on the veranda, dressed in black pants and a cobalt-blue button-down shirt that drew attention to the color of his eyes. The material stretched tight across his chest and arms, and Erica wondered if he had trouble finding shirts to accommodate his size. The thought brought to mind his considerable girth in other departments, and a hot blush infused her throat.

Surveying her appearance, Corey let out a low whistle. "Holy smokes, Erica. You look incredible."

The heat in Erica's throat moved to her face. She fought against the compulsion to refute the compliment. "Thank you. So do you."

"Are you ready?"

As ready as I'll ever be. Erica nodded and switched on her porch light. As she went to lock the door, Corey stopped her. "You might want to leave the light off. I don't think you'll be coming back here tonight."

The presumptuous statement was so unlike Corey that Erica glanced at him askance. There was a glimmer of abashment in the curve of his lips, but the sparkle in his eyes was all irascible self-assurance, so reminiscent of Griff's usual demeanor that Erica shook her head in bemusement. "I think Griff is rubbing off on you."

"Maybe."

"Where is Griff?"

"We're going to meet him there."

Corey escorted her to an older-model Ford and settled her into the passenger seat as though she were a princess being handed into a carriage. Once he was behind the wheel and they were on their way, he apologized. "Sorry about the car. I cleaned it up the best I could."

"I don't care that you drive an old car, Corey."

"I know. I still wish I had something nicer to take you out in. Especially when you look so amazing."

Lifting one of her hands from her lap, Corey held it in his and rested them both on his thigh. The warmth of his muscular leg permeated their linked hands, making Erica's heartbeat turn from an erratic fluttering to a pounding, steady rhythm.

How could he arouse her and calm her at the same time? That simple contact generated an acute sense of longing inside Erica, a longing that grew and swelled and peaked time and again as they headed toward their mystery destination. Yet at the same time Corey's touch was reassuring. They barely spoke but there was no awkwardness in the long stretches of silence. It was as though they'd been sitting beside each other holding hands for years.

Or as though they would for decades to come.

Quickly, Erica quashed that wistful thought. Tonight was about enjoying the *now*, not trying to analyze what it all meant or agonizing over the fact it couldn't last.

The best steakhouse in the city looked very much like a suburban house. Erica looked out the window, her surprise evident to Corey in the confines of the car.

"This isn't a restaurant."

Corey explained. "Best steakhouse in town, Griff said. He's not one for modesty, you might have noticed that."

"This is Griff's house?"

"Uh-huh."

Corey went around to open the passenger door for her. Taking her by the hand—he couldn't seem to bring himself to let it go—Corey led Erica to the front porch. He paused before opening the door, turning her toward him. "Erica, before we go in..."

She raised her eyebrows expectantly, her brown eyes wide and soft. "Yes?"

With a groan Corey dipped his head and sampled the cherry-flavored lip gloss he'd been aching to taste since she first opened the door. Erica whimpered something unintelligible and pressed up against him, those gorgeous breasts cushioning his chest.

Corey held her elbows and battled the compulsion to pull her more tightly to him. He'd promised himself he'd make this night special, and that meant not rushing her into bed the second they walked through the door.

Suddenly the front door opened, and there was Griff, leaning on the doorjamb, watching them. "Shit, Wachawski, I can't trust you for a minute, can I?"

Making a sound somewhere between a groan and a laugh, Corey pulled back and turned toward Griff. "Nope."

Griff's lips twitched, letting Corey know any irritation in his voice was only for show. His gaze roamed Corey's face before trailing downward, blazing a trail over his body. Then his attention shifted to Erica, and his eyes lit like flares in the dim light of the hallway. Corey knew Griff was having the same reaction to Erica as he'd had himself when he'd first laid eyes on her. "God help me," Griff muttered.

He took Erica's hand, the one Corey didn't already have clasped in his, and led her inside. Corey brought up the rear, admiring the way the soft green dress caressed Erica's thighs as she walked. Affording Griff's ass its due attention too. He wore a black shirt he'd left untucked so the tails hung over his dark jeans. It didn't entirely obstruct Corey's view of his ass, fortunately. The man looked criminally good in well-fitted denim.

Corey had to force himself to breathe. This was intense. It was one thing to admit to himself he wanted them both, Griff *and* Erica, quite another to be here with them, knowing full well what was to come. Anticipation made Corey as edgy as hell, and as gleeful as a kid locked in a toy store overnight.

"Welcome to my humble cave," Griff said as he guided Erica into the open-plan living area.

The stereo played The Rolling Stones's *Forty Licks* softly in the background as Erica twirled on her heels, surveying the vast space. "Humble? This is incredible. From the outside it looks small."

"I knocked down some walls in here, made it all one room. It's not as big as it looks."

Corey shot Griff a look. Was he being *modest*? "He did this all himself. Increased the resale value by a bomb."

"But I'm not selling. This is home."

"I wouldn't sell either," Erica agreed, giving Griff a soft smile. "Your home is beautiful."

Griff took a lazy step toward Erica, leaning in a little—encroaching on her personal space but stopping short of invading it. "More beautiful with you in it," he said, his voice low. When Erica blushed prettily, Griff lifted a hand and stroked it lightly up and down her arm. "Do you want a drink, beautiful?"

Her voice was raspy, as though she needed to wet her throat now more than she ever had. "Yes, please."

"Make yourself at home."

"I'll give you a hand," Corey said, following Griff to the kitchen. Once there, he leaned over the open fridge door and lowered his voice. "What are you doing?"

Griff pulled out a bottle of chardonnay and lifted it. "Getting your girl a drink."

"She's not just my girl."

Griff's gaze strayed past Corey's shoulder, resting for a moment on the woman now wandering around his living room, inspecting CD collections and wall art. "We've been through this, Cor. I'm not the one who's head over heels for the busty redhead."

"You were cracking onto her."

"Of course I was." Griff pulled three glasses down from an overhead cupboard and placed them on the granite-topped bench. "She looks smoking hot."

133

"No, I mean you're trying to impress her."

"Same thing, Wachawski."

No, it wasn't, not to Griff. Corey had seen him with women before. He flirted, teased and all around made his intentions clear. But he never went too far out of his way to get laid—he never had to.

"Look, you asked me to be gentle with her, not to scare her off." Griff shrugged. "This is me being gentle."

Corey watched as Griff poured the straw-hued liquid into three chunky wine glasses. He thought of all the women who had made a fleeting appearance in Griff's life, thought of how he'd been by his side to see most of them waltz right back out. He knew this was different but Corey decided not to pursue it for now. Griff with all his bravado could be as easy to scare off as Erica.

And for the first time Corey acknowledged that he didn't want either of them going anywhere. It was going to take every power of persuasion he had to keep Griff and Erica from bolting out of his life.

So instead of pushing the issue of Griff's true feelings for Erica, Corey asked, "How come you never put moves like that on me?"

"What? Throw you up against the lockers at work?"

"Not at work. I know you don't want anyone there finding out about us." That had been abundantly clear from the way Griff had returned to ignoring Corey while they were at the fire station, much like he had after that first night with Erica. Corey tried not to let it sting, but he missed the easy comradeship they used to share.

"It has to be kept separate, you know that, right?" Griff asked. "I have to keep my mind on the job, that's all. I'm not ashamed of anything, least of all you."

"You sure about that?"

"Yes. Forget about work. Forget about who knows or doesn't know. It's what we do in private that counts."

134

The reminder of how everything changed when they were alone caused Corey's body temperature to soar. When they'd left Erica's this afternoon, Griff had dropped Corey off at his apartment. Without waiting for an invitation, Griff had followed him inside and slammed the door with his foot. He'd shoved Corey up against the wall and kissed him like he wanted to take his soul in the act. Then Griff had dropped to his knees and taken Corey to heaven.

Corey's cock twitched at the remembered feel of Griff's tongue bathing it in heat. As if being so close to Erica and her signature lavender scent hadn't gotten him hard enough, now he was as immovable as Griff's granite bench tops.

"I like what we do in private," Corey conceded when he found his voice. Maybe that was all that mattered. It wasn't like they were at work twenty-four hours a day. "But when are you going to let me return the favor?"

Griff's gaze dropped to Corey's mouth, his irises sparking with heat. By the time their eyes connected again, Corey was blushing. "When I know you really want to, Cor. When you want it so bad you can't go one more day without tasting my cock, without knowing what it's like to have it fill you right to the back of your throat."

Corey's insides went all spongy and his face flamed. The sensations only intensified when Griff rounded the counter and hooked an arm around his neck, drawing him into a quick, close embrace. He smelled faintly of herbs, beer and aftershave, a spicier scent than the one Corey used. His smooth, warm lips brushed against Corey's ear as he murmured, "Jesus Christ, you're cute when you get bashful."

Griff was gone the instant the words were out of his mouth, headed back to Erica. The effect of his touch, of his words, lingered like an aftershock, shaking up Corey's world. He hung back in the kitchen, grappling with a tumult of emotions that had sideswiped him.

He looked across the room, watching as Griff stood behind Erica, brushing ever so subtly up against her as they discussed one of the paintings that hung on his wall. Corey saw her reaction to his nearness, the way she rubbed her arms as if he'd raised goose bumps, the way her body swayed backward as though yearning to melt into him. Corey understood exactly how she felt. She was fighting a losing battle against falling for Griff.

For Corey it was already too late.

Chapter Eleven

Griff had no idea why he was so goddamned nervous, but his palms were sweating like he was sixteen again and losing his virginity to an eighteen-year-old goddess by the name of Shauna Thompson. He'd been so keen to impress Shauna that he'd tried to unclasp her bra with one hand like a schoolmate had advised him to. She'd ended up doing the job herself with an impatient roll of her eyes Griff still couldn't recall without wincing.

You're trying to impress her. He'd shrugged off Corey's observation about his intentions toward Erica, but the truth nagged now as the three of them sat around his distressed timber outdoor table, replete after the meal he'd spent the afternoon carefully assembling. He'd dropped a tidy sum on the best porterhouse steaks he could find, a gourmet potato salad and a couple of bottles of fancy wine, thinking of Erica as he made the preparations. She'd been on his mind, too, when he'd strung the fairy lights along the railings rimming the back deck to create atmosphere, and when he'd bought scented candles as a table centerpiece.

Scented frigging candles.

Griff used to put on airs for Anna too. Without being fully conscious of it, he'd cleaned up his language and refrained from wearing his worst T-shirts in her presence. Anna had been an ambitious player in corporate banking, the daughter of a well-to-do surgeon. Jack had been an architect. Not an impressive-enough job to suit Anna's snobbish father, but a guy with a degree at least. As a professional, Jack Chambers had passed muster. As a lowly public servant, Griff had not.

In the beginning that hadn't mattered. Despite their varied backgrounds, he and Jack and Anna had clicked, in and out of bed. That was rare enough that Griff overlooked the small gripe that he was forced to act like nothing more than a boarder in their house. But a few years in the pretense had gotten too uncomfortable to keep up, like a prickly wool coat worn in the heat of midsummer. Griff had pressed for a more open relationship.

Unwilling to buck her family's and society's conventions, Anna had cut him out in a heartbeat. Jack had supported her because the two of them had always been the primary couple.

Sitting across the table from Erica and Corey now, Griff watched them interact like long-lost friends aching to be lovers and couldn't shake the sense of history repeating itself.

It'll be different this time. Walking away will be your choice.

"No, that was not Kate Winslet, it was Kate *Hudson.*" Erica fired another shot in the little game of who's-that-starlet that she and Corey had entered into when he'd asked her to name her top five favorite films. "And *How to Lose a Guy in 10 Days* is a much-underrated classic of the romantic-comedy genre."

"I'm surprised, Erica. I thought you'd be into serious, important movies, not screwy chick flicks."

"I read a lot of serious books for my job. When I watch movies I'd rather relax. Anyway, I'm appalled that you're into scary slasher films."

"*Scream* is really more funny than scary."

Erica made a face. "There's nothing amusing about all that blood. What about you, Griff?" She turned to him, gazing at him over the rim of her wine glass as she took a sip. "Don't tell me you like that sort of thing too."

If pushed to nominate a favorite movie Griff would probably cite *The Shawshank Redemption.* But he wasn't in the mood to be so informative. He flashed a grin he didn't feel all the way to his insides. "I like *Debbie Does Dallas*—a classic of the genre if there ever was one."

As expected, Erica rolled her eyes. "Sex and violence. I don't think I'll ever understand what makes men tick."

"Maybe the fun is in trying to work us out anyway," Griff suggested.

Her lips curved then, her whole face—hell, everything in a ten-foot radius—brightening as a result. "Perhaps you're right."

That smile, beatific and sincere and a little goofy from one-too-many glasses of chardonnay, wrapped warm fingers around Griff's heart and squeezed. *Fuck no. Your heart's supposed to stay out of this, remember?*

"So tell me." Corey reached across the table and gently tugged on a strand of Erica's hair, bringing her attention back to him. "We didn't get to number one. What's your all-time favorite movie?"

"Oh, that's easy." Erica's smile widened as she reclined against the back of her chair, a dreamy expression on her face. "If it's a rainy Sunday afternoon, my favorite thing to do is curl up on the sofa with a packet of Tim Tams and watch *An Affair to Remember*."

"Haven't heard of it."

"Corey!" Erica admonished. "How can that be? Cary Grant and Deborah Kerr in the most romantic movie of all time."

"Come on," Griff chimed in. "You call martyrhood romantic?"

Erica returned her attention to him. "You've seen it?"

"My mother loves old movies." It occurred to Griff that Erica would get on well with his mother. He quashed the random thought before it could take root. "I think I saw it twenty times growing up in that house."

"Then you know. They're both involved with other people but the attraction is so strong that they *have* to be together."

"But then when she has the accident and doesn't show up at the Empire State building, she never gets in touch with him to tell him why. That's pretty stupid."

"How could she tell him she couldn't walk?" Erica argued. "She knew she'd be a burden to him and she couldn't bear that."

"Jesus, Erica. If he really loved her, looking after her wouldn't have been a burden, and if she'd loved him she would have realized that. You know what I think? I think she never contacted him because she was scared—scared that he'd reject her because she wasn't perfect."

"His name was Nickie." Erica studied him with those soft brown eyes, as though trying to work out if he meant what he said or if he was having a lend of her. "And maybe she was right to be afraid. Nickie was used to ideal women, he fell in love with Terri when she was perfect in his eyes. How could she be confident he'd choose to be with the lesser version of her out of anything other than pity when he had so many other, easier options?"

Griff got the strangest feeling they weren't talking about the movie anymore. Familiar clouds had gathered in Erica's eyes, and it was only when he recognized them that Griff realized why she looked so different tonight, so much more breathtaking than she ever had. It wasn't only the incredible dress or the sultry makeup. The sadness he'd always sensed in her had lifted. Her smile tonight had been heartfelt, her manner lighter, even playful.

Now, that aura of sorrow had returned, and Griff cursed whatever it was about this discussion that had brought it back. If she'd still been sitting forward, Griff knew he would have reached across the table to take her hand, so powerful was his desire to reassure her there was no need to be wary or frightened around them. The last thing he or Corey wanted to do was hurt her.

Forcing himself to remain seated instead of going to her, Griff finally replied. "Love isn't about doing what's easy, Erica.

Love is hard, and sometimes it hurts like hell. But it's real and it's human. It makes us what we are."

He hadn't meant to sound so bloody deep and meaningful. He was trying to keep this thing purely sexual—at least as far as Erica was concerned. In Corey's case, the love boat had left port years ago. But Griff figured he could still protect himself from Erica and the probability that she would eventually take Corey away from him. *If* he refrained from bandying the L word around like it held some special significance.

It didn't—couldn't. He was going to have wild sex with Erica and Corey tonight simply because if he didn't his brain might well explode. In every other way he had to keep himself separate or risk losing his mind.

It was time to stop pussyfooting around Erica for Corey's sake, because Corey still thought this could be some grand affair and he didn't want to blow it by scaring Erica off again. Griff wasn't so sure Erica was that easy to frighten, not the way she seemed tonight—calm, self-assured and confident.

No more Mr. Nice Guy.

"You know what? I never told you how damned delicious you look tonight, Red." When the door had opened and he'd been bombarded by the twin enticements of Corey filling out his sexy blue shirt and Erica wearing a knockout green dress that skimmed her impressive curves, he'd nearly tripped over his own tongue. He was going to have to take better control of this situation—starting now. "Actually, I think the word I'm looking for is fuckable. You, Erica Shannon, look good enough to fuck, and once Corey and I get started with you, I don't think either of us is going to stop until sunrise."

The sudden shift in Griff's demeanor shocked Erica, but she stifled the gasp that threatened to pierce the quiet. The fragrance of blooming gardenia floated around them on a warm October breeze, mingling with the vanilla scent of the candles. The soft lighting and the comfortable conversation had lulled her into a sensual trance, keeping her desires simmering when they could easily have boiled over.

Griff had gone to a lot of trouble to create a romantic atmosphere, and that had touched the traditional, feminine side of her that wanted to be romanced. Why would he do that if he was only going to revert to brash, blunt type?

"I want you to go sit on Corey's lap." Griff's voice was husky, his tone low. "Tell me if he's as hard for you as I think he is."

Erica flushed hot, unspeakably aroused despite the instinct that told her she ought to be affronted. Beside her, Erica sensed the tension in Corey's body. "Go easy, Griff."

Griff flicked Corey a look before returning his focus to Erica. "What do you say, Red? You want me to go easy on you?"

This Griff was the man she knew, the one who'd initiated their first threesome, who'd taken what he'd needed from her on the hard floor of her living room without explanation. This man, she realized, was easier to handle than the one who'd stocked his fridge with the wine she liked and decorated their outdoor nook in candlelight, all so she'd feel more comfortable. Meeting Griff's challenging gaze, Erica found that the answer came more readily than she would have expected. "No."

Griff smiled and there was something almost like pride in his expression. "There's my girl. Now, go on and do what I told you."

Heart galloping, Erica pushed back her chair. Corey watched her approach, his blue eyes smoky. His chest moved up and down in the taut confines of his shirt and through the black material of his trousers she saw the bulge of his erection.

Erica could hardly wait to feel that hardness against her, but when she went to sit down Griff stopped her. "Wait. Give me your panties."

This time her gasp was audible in the thick atmosphere. "Pardon me?"

"You heard me. I want your panties, Red. Give them to me."

Wet heat pooled in the pit of her belly, sliding downward, spilling onto the underwear in question. He'd know how drenched she was if he had access to her panties. *That's probably the point, Erica.*

Slipping her hands beneath her dress, Erica pulled the underwear down and off. When she handed them over she *really* regretted that she didn't own anything black and brief. Griff examined them, an amused smile tugging at his insolent mouth. "These are cute, but we're going to have to buy you something prettier one of these days."

Then he brought the underwear to his nose and inhaled the perfume of her excitement.

Erica's knees buckled. Corey reached for her, grasping her by the hips and settling her onto his lap before she fell. "Hey, baby. Are you okay?"

In answer Erica sought his mouth with her own. He responded with hunger, sweeping her up into passion even as his sturdy arms grounded her. The rock-solid length of him nudged her hip. When he lifted a hand and settled it over her breast, Erica wanted that fabric gone. She longed for the burn of his hands on her skin.

"Turn her around so she's facing me, Cor."

With a stuttered breath, Corey did as Griff said. Erica wiggled in his lap, getting comfortable on his groin. Corey grabbed her hips to still her. "God, baby."

"You like the way that feels?" Griff asked her. "Corey's hard cock pressed between your sweet ass cheeks?"

Erica nodded. She shifted on Corey's lap once more, forcing a groan from him. His breath was hot on her neck as he placed his lips to it and swirled his tongue over her skin. "I like the way *that* feels," Corey said. "You turn me on so much."

She dropped her head back on his wide shoulder, angling her face so her lips were a hairsbreadth away from his. "So does Griff. Doesn't he?"

"*Yes.*"

From across the table there was the sound of creaking timber as Griff shifted in his chair. His words carried a harder edge than they had a moment ago. "That dress looks easy to take off. Just like unwrapping a gift. Corey, unwrap our sweet little present now, our own wet and willing fuck toy."

On her hips, Corey's fingers flexed. Erica sensed his struggle not to tear at her clothes. "We're outside."

"No one can see through the hedges." His tone held amusement. "There would have been complaints long before now."

So he'd had other women out here—probably in every room of his house. Erica knew she wasn't the first or the last, and that was okay. She'd decided to live in the moment, hadn't she? A person in that frame of mind didn't think about the future, didn't care about the past. To Griff, she was one of many, nothing special. His own wet and willing fuck toy.

It was a truth she could hold on to. No matter how dangerous Corey was to her heart, Griff would be there to remind her that all she had with either of them was sex. She was an amusement, a novelty to be indulged in when they wanted the variety of a woman between them.

Taking Griff at his word about how concealed they were from the neighbors, Corey tugged at the bow that held her dress in place. The material fell open. Although the night air was sultry, gooseflesh rushed over Erica's skin. No matter their level of seclusion, there was something undeniably naughty about having her flesh bared to the open air.

Easing her forward, Corey slipped the dress off her shoulders and unhooked her bra. The layers of covering fell away, leaving her sitting on Corey's lap, naked. Her thighs rested atop Corey's, so when he spread his legs hers moved too. The night air didn't seem so balmy when it caressed her heated folds. Corey was free to touch her everywhere and Griff... Erica looked across the table to find him watching with hot intensity as Corey cupped her breasts, lifting them as though showing them to his friend.

Corey brushed his thumbs over Erica's nipples and they pebbled under Griff's watchful gaze. "Such beautiful, perfect tits." He murmured the praise as though entranced.

Erica's arousal mounted to painful heights, and she ground her ass into Corey's crotch. The fabric of his pants was an irritant, a reminder that both men were fully dressed while she had been laid completely bare for their enjoyment. Being placed in such a vulnerable pose should have made her uneasy. Instead it excited her, made her feel free.

In this position, she felt like a woman with nothing left to fear.

Corey's hands trailed downward. His fingers burrowed into the thatch of hair at the apex of her thighs, finding it damp and sticky. "Jesus, Griff. She's so wet."

Griff took something out of his back pocket and tossed it across the table with a flick of his fingers. The foil-wrapped condom landed in front of them. "I want to see you fuck her."

Finding her slick entrance, Corey buried two fingers deep inside. Erica rocked into the touch, emitting a helpless moan at the deliciousness of it. "Do you want that, baby? You don't mind if Griff watches while I put my dick in this tight space?"

Looking across the table, Erica saw how Griff's gaze was fixed on the movements of her body as she ground against Corey's crotch. "I want him to watch."

Griff's eyes burned as they met hers, their irises glowing gold in the amber light cast by the candles and the myriad lights strung around them, dotting the darkness like tiny fallen stars. "Dirty girl," he said. "Corey's going to have to fuck you extra hard for that comment, so hard it hurts."

That kind of pain Erica would gladly accept. "All right."

Behind her, Corey's breathing grew harsh. "Stand up for a sec."

Erica did as he said, bracing her weight on the table in front of her. Corey groaned, grasping the backs of her thighs and easing them farther apart. With his thumb he breached her core, probing her depths in teasing little bursts, in and out. Erica's arms trembled. She lowered to her elbows, relieving some of the burden of supporting herself. Her breasts pressed against the tablecloth, the cotton teasing the tender points as she moved back and forth in time with Corey's playful thrusts.

Across the table, Griff watched her, his eyes hooded and his manner lazy, as though he could enjoy seeing her suffer like this for hours. The tension inside tightened unbearably. "Corey, please."

"I think she's letting you know she's ready for your cock now. Is that right, Red?"

"Yes. Oh, yes, I'm ready."

Corey reached for the foil package and tore it open. A moment later there was the sound of his zipper rasping apart and the rustle of fabric. Then his warm fingers gripped one of her hips and he began drawing her backward. Erica could picture him holding his cock steady with his other hand, taking aim with it as he brought her down onto the broad head.

The initial stretch of her flesh around his girth made a grateful whimper seep from her lips. She lowered herself over him, the sounds she made rising in pitch as she forced her flesh around his, inch my inch.

"God, Erica," Corey groaned. Then he angled his hips upward as she moved the last distance.

Erica cried out when he was fully seated inside her. He and Griff had taken her from behind before, but sitting on him this way created a more acute penetration. It was as though he filled her all the way to her womb and beyond, to some central part of her she'd never known existed.

For a moment she was unsure how to move. Then Erica found purchase on his feet—he still wore his shoes, his trousers bunched around his ankles. She pressed the balls of her feet onto his shoes and used the leverage to begin a slow up-and-down cadence.

"That's right, baby. Oh yeah, do that. Fuck me, Erica."

Erica continued the rhythm, gradually increasing the pace. She grasped the arms of the chair on which they sat, using the grip to steady her as she ground her ass into Corey's hips, seeking every inch of his length. Corey wound his arms around her, keeping her back pressed to his chest, apparently seeking the same closeness.

Griff's chair scraped against the deck as he pushed it back. Opening her eyes, Erica saw him walk toward them, his strides unhurried. She marveled at his controlled facade. He was excited, the evidence was there in his eyes and in the significant bulge of his jeans, but he approached as though he was still deciding what to do with them.

He came to stand before Erica, brushing a wayward hank of hair back from her face. "I swear, you are the two sexiest damn people I've ever seen. Watching you together is almost enough to make me come."

A vision came to Erica, of Griff taking his cock out, stroking it, not taking his eyes off the slow, sweet way Corey fucked her until his semen erupted from his body. "I want you to."

"Oh, I will." He traced the shape of her lips with his finger. "But around here, ladies always come first."

Holding her gaze with the wicked intent in his, Griff lowered to his knees. His mouth was warm and wet as it enclosed the tip of her breast. Erica threw her head back, resting it on Corey's shoulder as she arched into the exquisite sensation of Griff's lazy sucking. Corey cupped her, tenderly massaging her flesh, offering it up for Griff to sample. Griff did more than sample her, he tasted, teased and devoured, working her nipple until it was distended and hard as flint. Then he transferred his attention to the other one.

Corey took her now-abandoned peak between his thumb and forefinger and gently squeezed. The twin assaults had her soaring upward before she could stop herself. Her body quivered and strained, reaching for orgasm with clasping, desperate hands.

Griff slid one hand downward to find her burning, pulsing clit with his finger. Ever so lightly he flicked his fingertip over the swollen knot of flesh, never taking his mouth from her. Behind her, Corey rocked his hips, moving with relentless purpose in and out of her pussy.

Her climax exploded inside her, ripping an animalistic sound from her throat. Her inner walls clutched at Corey, her orgasm stretching out for long glorious moments. She was moving in spasms over Corey's cock when Griff stood and tore open his fly. Corey shifted his hand to cover her mound, rubbing her clit to keep her orgasm alive. Erica was still coming when Griff took advantage of her gasping mouth, plunging his cock into it.

Erica's exclamation of delight was muffled by the hot hard rod of Griff's erection as it moved over her tongue, filling every recess of her mouth. Still teetering on the edge of her orgasm, Erica responded with enthusiasm, sucking him with eager movements of her lips and tongue. Corey kept up the pressure on her clit, stroking it while Griff thrust his fingers into her hair, holding her in place for his invasion.

Astoundingly, Erica came again, gyrating her hips and taking Griff in so deep she almost gagged. She fought against the urge, willing to suffer any physical discomfort to avoid disappointing Griff. Moving past the psychological barrier, Erica concentrated on breathing through her nose and relaxing her throat muscles so she could accept the greater depth he sought.

"Holy mother of Christ," Griff swore as he eased in to the hilt. "You have a fucking fantastic mouth."

Behind her, Corey groaned. "I don't know how much more of this I can take."

Over Erica's head, Griff pinned him with a stare. "Jealous?"

"Fuck yes, I wish she was sucking my cock."

"Wanna switch?"

Corey ground into Erica, licking a trail over her neck. "No. I like being here more, watching her take you in and out of her mouth."

Griff's cock pulsed against Erica's tongue. She moaned and increased the pressure she exerted, clamping her lips around him, tightening the fit as he thrust inside her. His movements grew more harried, his hand twisting in her hair. "That's it, Erica, milk me. I'm going to spill my load any second now."

"Oh shit." Corey jerked harder, rougher into her, until her ass bounced on his thighs. Griff held her as steady as he could while he used her mouth. The sensation of being stuffed so full overwhelmed her, causing her clit to pulse where Corey still rubbed it with his fingers. With a final, brutal push Corey released himself with a primal roar. The knowledge of his climax brought on another one for herself. Erica's eyes stung as tears of shock and pure physical ecstasy threatened. She'd had no idea her body was capable of sustaining such prolonged pleasure.

A moment later Griff swore and dragged his cock out of her mouth. He held the base while pearlescent liquid spurted from the tip, bathing Erica's chest in streaks of wet heat.

When he was at last spent, Griff rested his weight on the table behind him, grabbing a napkin and handing it to Corey. Corey remained buried within her while he cleaned her off with tender swipes. He held her against him, pressing his face into the curve of her neck. "Did I hurt you?"

Erica shook her head. A second later her half-empty glass of wine appeared in front of her. She took it from Griff's fingers, gulping some of the contents down because she was thirsty. When she saw the concerned look on Griff's face, she wondered if he'd offered the drink because he assumed she'd be impatient to wash the taste of him from her mouth.

The thought made her eyes sting again. "Thank you—both of you—so much."

The string of words Griff spat was particularly virulent and inventively vulgar. "Christ, Erica. We're the lucky ones."

Erica shook her head in amazement, wetness pooling in her eyes. "I never realized I was capable of so much."

Corey said, his voice threaded through with anger as he repeated something she'd told him during that first, revealing phone call, "The last guy made her think she wasn't good at giving head."

"You've got to be fucking kidding." Griff's expression hardened, matching the ire in Corey's voice. "Not good at it? Sweetheart, you just deep-throated me like a pro."

Laughter burst out of her, causing the tears to spill over. Immediately, Griff muttered regretful words and lifted her from Corey's lap. He wrapped her so tight in his arms her lungs compressed. "Shit, I'm sorry. That was a bad comparison."

"No, it's fine. I think I'm actually flattered." The incredible sex must have done something to scramble her brain. The woman she'd always thought she was would never have taken being compared to a prostitute in her stride. "You're very sweet in your own, totally unique way, Dale Griffin."

He grunted. "No I'm not. I'm an insensitive asshole."

Corey stood, pressing his chest to Erica's bare back. His arms moved to enfold them both. "You're our insensitive asshole."

Against her breast, Erica felt Griff's heart give a few hard thumps. In that moment she understood how completely Griff loved Corey, and the affection she felt for both of them blossomed, expanded into something more miraculous, more dangerous.

Yet the notion that she could easily fall in love with them, that in fact she was already halfway there, wasn't the issue. When it came time for her to move on, to go back to her solitary existence, she would always be comforted by the knowledge that Griff and Corey had each other. That she had played a part in bringing them together. She would have her memories and that would have to be enough.

"Let's head inside," Griff suggested. "Take this woman to bed and show her how much we appreciate her doing us sexual favors."

Corey smiled against Erica's shoulder. "Best idea you've ever had, mate."

As Griff lifted her legs around his waist and carried her, Corey following close at his side, Erica silently agreed with Corey's assessment.

The night and the following day passed in a blur of want and sensation, gasping sighs and mind-numbing ecstasy. As Erica hadn't brought a change of clothes with her, Griff lent her a faded navy fire-service T-shirt that came to mid-thigh and was so soft from years of wear that it brushed her skin as sensuously as the finest lingerie. She remained completely naked beneath it—Griff wouldn't return her underwear. More expedient, he'd said.

Erica lost track of how many orgasms she'd had by the time she found herself stretched out on the couch sometime on Sunday afternoon with her head in Corey's lap and her feet on Griff's shoulders, moaning as Griff lapped at her bared pussy. Griff's T-shirt was bunched at her throat, giving Corey easy access to her naked breasts.

His touch was so tender, almost reverent as he circled her areola with one finger. Between her legs, Griff kept up the slow steady pace. Corey looked into Erica's eyes. "Does that feel nice, baby?"

Nice didn't begin to cover it, but Erica was beyond offering appropriate superlatives. She merely nodded and bit her lip when Griff teased a particularly sensitive spot.

Corey cupped a breast in his hand, strumming the swollen tip with his thumb. He watched avidly as she squirmed beneath the twin assaults of his hand and Griff's mouth. "Griff knows what to do with that tongue."

The suggestion that Corey might speak from personal experience had juice spilling from her depths for Griff to feast on. All night and all day they'd concentrated their energies on her, rather than each other. Were they holding back for her benefit? Didn't they believe that she not only approved of their relationship but wanted to witness the intimacy they'd begun to develop?

"Corey..."

"I know, baby." Softly, he pinched her nipple. "He'll end it soon."

"Like hell." Griff lifted his head, only to blow a teasing stream of air across her sensitized nerve endings. "I'm having way too much fun down here."

Erica could only squirm, the declarations she'd wanted to utter lost in her throat. Perhaps they'd think her a pervert for wanting to watch them pleasure each other, or maybe their relationship hadn't progressed as far as she'd thought.

Now wasn't the time, she decided. What woman in her right mind would interrupt what was happening already?

Corey took both her hands in one of his and eased them over her head, pressing them into the soft leather couch. "Open your legs wider, Erica."

Beyond independent thought, Erica arched and let her legs fall open farther. She planted one foot on the floor while Corey helped her hook the other over the back of the couch. "Oh yeah. That's so pretty, Red."

Griff returned his mouth to her pussy, but this time he had access to everything, every part of her—and he took full advantage. He added a finger to his technique, shafting her with it and fluttering it deep inside her, hitting the spot guaranteed to send her into the stratosphere. He flattened his tongue and bathed her clit in wet heat.

Corey kept her wrists trapped above her head, his other hand kneading her breasts, teasing the aching tips, while Griff kept up what he was doing. Erica felt her climax approaching, already recognizable in its intensity. She rode it out with a taut cry that could have been Griff's name, or Corey's.

It didn't matter. She was helpless at the hands of either one of them, completely powerless against both. The last twenty-four hours had been like an occupation, the Germans invading France—if the Germans had brought decadence and utter joy with them. Erica had no desire to defend herself against Corey and Griff. It was so much more glorious to lose herself.

Corey swooped down and kissed her hard on the lips. "You are so sexy when you come. And I love it when you call out Griff's name."

Against her inner thigh, Griff's groan vibrated. He rose to his knees, his shirtless form tense, his muscles flexed. He curled insistent fingers around Corey's neck and pulled him into a savage kiss.

Corey moaned, relief in the sound. Erica could only watch, rapt, as Griff worked Corey's mouth open and swept inside. Possessing him as he had just possessed her. She knew her own flavor must have been shared between them, and the knowledge made everything in her pulse with life.

All too swiftly, Griff dragged himself away. As he lifted Erica's pliant leg from the floor and placed it on the couch, she detected the slightest tremble in his fingers. "It's getting late. Corey better take you home, Red."

His brusque order made her flinch, but she managed to keep her expression from showing it. Griff had retreated, just like that, and she for one wouldn't challenge his behavior. It was exactly what she needed to do to keep her heart protected. This was sex, Griff had indicated as much when he'd labeled her their fuck toy. Erica refused to be some weepy female who lamented that they couldn't give her more. Especially as she could offer nothing deeper herself.

No dwelling on the past, no obsessing on the future. Live in the moment.

Griff went in to take a shower and Erica gathered her things. A short time later she left the house with Corey. Twilight lit the sky a velvety mauve by the time he dropped her at her house. Erica felt a little wicked, like a woman who'd spent all weekend partying only to stumble home on Sunday wearing her evening clothes.

So this is living.

Corey kissed her, a thorough, lazy caress of his mouth on hers. He promised he'd call—or that Griff would, depending on who was working what shift. He saw her inside, holding on to her hand to say one last thing, his smile lighting his eyes. "I had the best weekend I've ever had."

Erica smiled back. "Me too."

"Anytime you need either one of us—or both of us," he added with a grin, "you call, okay? A light bulb changed or a spider stomped. We'll help."

"I can change my own light bulbs, Corey."

"I notice you didn't jump to say you'd kill the spiders."

Erica arched a brow. "Who do you think has been dealing with them all this time?"

Corey's expression softened. "You're not alone anymore, Erica. Promise you'll call if you need to."

Reluctantly, Erica nodded, knowing she wouldn't phone either one of them. If they wanted her, they knew where to find her. She wouldn't force herself on them or beg for affection. Doug, her father, they'd both taught her that way led to humiliation and disappointment. She refused to appear that needy and weak in front of Corey or Griff and taint the memories of this time, which she planned to keep with her, always.

As she watched Corey drive away, Erica wondered exactly how long the attention of her two virile firemen would last. Eventually, they would move toward each other, and Erica had every intention of encouraging that. Because her role was temporary and that was okay. Perhaps Corey needed her to transition to loving Griff, a woman between them until he felt one hundred percent comfortable with the shift in his sexuality.

Until Griff learned to show his feelings for Corey more openly.

Until Erica had to book her operation, turn her body into something they would no longer want.

Temporary. A series of finite moments destined to end, but which she would live with all she had in her.

Chapter Twelve

The pitter-patter of light rain sounded like the crackling of a slow-burning fire as it peppered the tin roof of Erica's house. It was cold for midspring, the grey light of an overcast sky emphasizing the unseasonable morning chill. It was the kind of morning a man yearned to stay curled up in bed—especially if there was a softly sleeping woman warming it with him.

Corey lifted the sheet until it more fully covered Erica's shoulders. She shifted against him but didn't wake. Not that Corey could blame her for sleeping so soundly. Between them, he and Griff had kept her up late and active almost every night for the past week and a half.

The drifting aroma of percolating coffee reminded him that Griff was out in the kitchen fixing breakfast. Last night, they'd once again shared Erica's body, her passion. Other nights it had been only he and Erica, or when he worked night shift, Corey knew Griff spent his time here or at his own house, having kidnapped Erica in order to have his wicked way.

Corey didn't mind that, the possessiveness he'd felt a few weeks ago crumbling in the face of his desire to see Griff and Erica happy. He knew Griff satisfied a deeply primitive need that existed within Erica, a longing to be mastered, inundated by carnal urges that took her to a place where conscious thought didn't intervene. Corey now understood it, taking contentment in the knowledge that he was the one who made Erica feel safe—safe enough, he hoped, that she would one day open up to him completely.

He had to believe it would happen, that the clouds he sometimes saw gathering in her eyes would dissipate if only she accepted that he cared about her more than he'd ever cared about another woman. That he would do anything to see her happy.

His Erica. Still his, even though she was Griff's now as well.

Erica moved against him with a groggy mumble, stirring Corey out of his thoughts. "What's the time?"

Corey glanced at the bedside alarm clock. "A little after seven."

She grunted unhappily. "School day. Have to get up soon."

He shifted so the jut of his morning hard-on bumped her hip. "Not right now I hope."

"Hmmm...you're insatiable."

"That doesn't sound like a complaint."

"It's not, but eventually I'm going to wear out."

Concern sparked inside him. He gave her shoulder a squeeze. "You're not sore, are you?" It was something he'd worried about a time or two, that his needs and Griff's would prove too much for her.

Erica showed him a slow smile as she ran her hand up and down his chest. "Not that sore."

Corey loved it when Erica was like this—dazed and relaxed after wild sex followed by a deep sleep. She gave off a special glow that dimmed far too much when she was wholly awake and fretting over whatever problems she imagined looming in their future.

Rising to her knees, Erica bracketed his hips with her thighs. Her movements were lazy as she rocked forward, rubbing her slick nether lips against his cock. "Where's Griff?"

"In the kitchen fixing breakfast."

"Really? I should probably go help."

"I thought you were about to help *me* out."

"Because I owe you for the amazing way you two interrupted my sleep last night?"

Griff had started it, rousing Erica into a semiconscious state by working his tongue over her pussy. Her drowsy squirming had woken Corey, and he'd happily joined in the fun, taking turns with Griff between Erica's thighs until she muttered their names in broken whispers, over and over again. "Griff will get really pissed off if he hears you talking like that. You never have to pay either of us back for giving you an orgasm."

"Or three, but who's counting." She smiled. "But if that's the way you see it..."

She made to hop off his lap. Lightning quick, Corey dug his fingers in the flesh of her ass to keep her in place. "Take pity on me, baby."

Erica laughed. "You don't need my pity. I've never been so easily aroused in all my life."

Corey used his grip on her ass to move her up and down his hard length. "I believe it. You could come just from rubbing that sweet spot against my dick."

"Uh-huh."

Corey angled his hips to add pressure. Erica closed her eyes on a moan and leaned into him. "I could come from doing this too, and from watching your gorgeous breasts sway as you rock into me. I loved that you let us come all over them last night."

He'd worried that she might think it disrespectful, the way he and Griff had jerked off on her tits after they'd gone down on her. But Erica smiled. "I liked it. Watching the two of you get all worked up is exciting." Her eyelids fluttered up and she pinned him with her dark eyes. "I loved watching you kiss."

And Corey had adored the way Griff had taken his mouth in a rough, desperate possession that had tangled their tongues and shared Erica's feminine essence between them. It wasn't the first time Griff had kissed him like that, and each time it thrilled Corey. Yet Griff hadn't allowed their physical relationship to progress beyond kisses and hand jobs, the occasional blow job when Corey sensed Griff couldn't resist temptation. The heat and skill of Griff's tongue amazed Corey, and he liked it when Griff went down on him as much as when Erica did.

But Griff still insisted he didn't need the favor returned. That night at his house he'd said he'd only allow that when he knew Corey wanted to do it. *So bad he couldn't go another day without it.*

If Griff's intention had been to tease him to the limits of his endurance, it was mission accomplished. Corey had never wanted to do anything so much in his life, and he was starting to wonder when Griff was going to intuit that. If someone had told Corey a month ago that a man could make him feel this aching sense of yearning, he would have thought they were crazy.

But Corey yearned—he yearned to hold Griff's pleasure in his hand. And his mouth.

Noticing the way his cock jerked against her, Erica reached down and stroked him. "You should kiss him more often. You should do whatever you feel like doing."

"Okay then." He lifted a hand and cupped her breast. "How's that?"

Erica arched into his hand. Then she whispered words she usually only said for Griff, because he forced them out of her. "Fuck me, Corey. Now."

Hearing her offer up those words for him had blood flushing his dick. Corey never made Erica beg for it the way Griff liked to do because he couldn't bring himself to make her suffer—even though seeing her lose her mind at his friend's hand was a massive turn-on. Now, he wanted to see her go into a frenzy. Had to know Griff wasn't the only one capable of stripping away her polite mannerisms to reveal the wild wanton beneath.

He growled, "Say that again."

Erica's eyes widened at the tone of his voice. Against his cock he felt the lips of her pussy quiver. "Fuck me, Corey."

Corey grabbed her ass and ground against her. "Louder."

She raised her voice. "Corey, please. I want you to fuck me."

"Hell, yeah."

Reaching for the bedside draw, Corey opened it with a yank. The whole thing clattered to the floor beside the bed, underwear and foil packets spilling out. Swearing, Corey grabbed one of the condoms, ripped it open and sheathed himself. Then he positioned Erica above him, until her damp entrance sucked at the head of his shaft.

He rose up as he lowered her, impaling her in one smooth plunge.

Erica cried out. "Yes! Oh my God."

"Touch your breasts, Erica. Play with them for me."

The slightest brush of her thumbs over the already pearled peaks caused them to distend into flinty points. Her nipples were so sensitive, all Corey ever had to do was tickle them with his tongue to have her writhing against him.

"You're my girl, Erica. Say it's true."

"I am." She panted the words. "I'm your girl."

"And Griff's. You belong to both of us."

She braced a hand on his chest, seeking the leverage to push her body harder onto his. The new depth made her gasp and Corey clench his teeth. "Corey…"

Reaching behind her, Corey found the tight hole between her ass cheeks and probed it. "Has Griff been sticking his dick in this tight spot all week—the nights he was with you and I wasn't?"

Biting her lip, Erica nodded. "He puts it there…and everywhere else."

An image of Erica taking Griff's cock deep into her mouth assailed Corey, made his balls draw up tight. Christ, he loved watching Griff fuck Erica's sweet mouth. "I haven't fucked you here." Corey eased his finger into her body, until the ring of muscle clenched around him. "I've never done it to anyone but I want you to be my first."

"Oh, God. Corey, I'm already..."

"Yeah baby, I can feel your pussy rippling over my cock." He brought her down over him in a series of frantic thrusts. "You're going to come so fast and hard, thinking about the way Griff and I both want you. But you're with me now, Erica. Scream my name when you come."

"Yes! Oh Corey, don't stop."

"I won't, baby. Never."

Corey felt every contraction of her muscles right to the steel-rod core of his shaft. The delicious friction coaxed his own orgasm closer to the surface and as Erica bounced on top of him, her breasts swinging against his chest and her beautiful ass in his hands, Corey let her body take him over the edge. He spurted into the latex, so forcefully he feared he might break the damn thing.

As Erica wilted against him, landing on his chest like a warm, wet noodle, Corey was filled with a sense of rightness, of completion. All his concerns over Griff's reluctance to get too involved and Erica's trust issues melted away. Everything would be all right. Better than that—everything would be perfect. Because they were equals, the three of them.

This was *right*. So right he didn't care if he did break the frigging condom. He'd be stoked to father Erica's baby, or even to have Griff do it.

Way ahead of yourself, Wachawski.

Corey knew it, but the knowledge didn't stop him smiling. When something felt this great, it didn't simply fall apart over a few minor issues.

"Oh my goodness." Erica breathless exclamation sounded so dainty after the bawdy demands she'd made only moments ago. "Do you suppose Griff heard that?"

"What, you think I'm deaf? I reckon the neighbors heard that."

Corey turned to see Griff standing in the doorway, his shoulder leaning against the jamb. Corey chuckled while Erica hid her heated face in the curve of his neck.

"If you're done working up an appetite in here, Red, I made some of those oats you like. Come get it." Griff's lips twitched. "If you can tear yourself away."

Behind Erica's back, Corey flipped Griff the bird. Griff returned the gesture as he swung around to leave.

"Griff, wait."

Griff stopped and turned back, facing the rueful look on Erica's face. Still half-groggy from sleep and the athletic fuck-session he'd heard clear down the hallway, she didn't remember to grab the sheet or a robe to cover herself like she usually did. Her blushed-pink nudity was a call his dick heard loud as a siren. Not that it hadn't already stood to attention at the sound of Erica begging Corey to fuck her.

"I'm sorry," Erica said. "You were out there making my favorite breakfast and I was in here...goofing off." That was one way to put it. "I didn't mean to exclude you."

Griff was horrified by the notion that he might have come across petulant at being left out of the morning activities. He was the one who kept pushing Corey to think of Erica as his and his alone. But hearing Erica and Corey going at it like such a hot-for-each-other *couple* had hit too close to some touchy place that remained buried inside. Anna and Jack had woken like that, all over each other in a way that Griff had often heard from his downstairs bedroom. He'd never gotten up the nuts to go join them because he hadn't been explicitly invited to what seemed more like "them" time.

When was he going to man up and get over that old crap?

Griff reached for a flippant response. "Not a problem, Red. I enjoyed the auditory entertainment."

Erica let her gaze drift downward meaningfully. "I see."

He barely resisted the compulsion to adjust his jeans. "Keep looking at me like that and I'll think you're up for another round."

Her expression was an irresistible combination of goofy post-orgasmic dreaminess and still-gagging-for-it invitation. She lifted a finger and curled it toward her. "Come over here."

That throaty command caused his heart—the heart that wasn't supposed to be *involved* in any way, shape or form—to break into a samba. His erection strained against his fly, making Griff doubt his ability to walk the distance without limping.

Chuckling, Corey climbed off the bed and headed for the bathroom, presumably to take care of the condom. Griff noticed the way Corey's pecs rippled when he stretched his arms over his head. "Not my fault you're an early riser."

"So are you, I've noticed."

Corey merely grinned, a cocky lilt to his lips that made Griff want to bite them. But he could hardly blame the other man for his self-satisfied expression. If Griff had made Erica climax with that primal scream, he'd feel pretty big-headed as well.

Speaking of big heads. Griff sauntered into the bedroom when a large part of him—a *very* large part—wanted to run. Erica knelt on the mattress, rising to meet him with an open-mouthed kiss that almost made his knees buckle. She smelled of warm sheets and hot sex, the faintest hint of lavender and a heavy dose of Corey. The mixture was thoroughly intoxicating, like every wet dream he'd ever had rolled into one.

Deciding not to point out they'd probably both be late for work if they went on this way, Griff skimmed his hands down to cup Erica's bottom. Hell. He'd write her a note if he had to. "Have you got more in the tank for me, Erica Shannon?"

"I seem to have a never-ending supply these days, Dale Griffin."

Griff nibbled at her lower lip, murmuring against it. "I liked the way you screamed for Corey. Did it get you off, thinking I could probably hear you?"

Her hips rocked into his, a telling gesture. "A little."

Perhaps he wasn't above petty rivalry, because the idea that he'd entered her mind while she'd been riding Corey like a cowgirl does a bronco made Griff smile. "A *lot.*"

"Okay, a *lot.*"

"You are one naughty girl, aren't you?" Her licentiousness was all the more appealing because nobody else knew about it— nobody but him and Corey. "I can give Wachawski a run for his money, seeing as you're still a little revved up."

Erica pulled out of the kiss-chat-nibble thing they were doing with their mouths and shook her head as though to clear it. "It's your turn."

Griff could have objected once more to her penchant for keeping score about this stuff, but who was he kidding? When she sat on the bed and reached for his jeans to open them, all he could think about was how good it would feel if he simply let her blow him. "I have to appreciate your sense of fair play, sweetheart."

"I'm not doing you any favors." A few more movements of her hands and his jeans were resting low on his hips. Erica stared at the substantial boner he'd worked up on account of her—her and Corey. "I really enjoy having you in my mouth."

"I really enjoy being there."

Enjoy was such an inadequate word to describe the drugging ripple and spark of sensations that overtook him when she parted her lips and wrapped them around his pulsing head. Griff groaned as she moved down and over him, circling her tongue on his shaft for lubrication until he slid more easily into her sultry recesses. "Oh yeah, like that. Christ, that's so soft and wet."

Closing his eyes, Griff let his neck go rubbery until his head drifted back. He couldn't believe Erica had ever lacked confidence in this area. She had a way of drawing a man into a trance with the tender press of her lips and the lazy swirls of her tongue. Griff fast lost himself in it. Then something in the atmosphere shifted, like a hot breeze travelling past him. The whine of bedsprings made Griff open his eyes.

Corey had returned from the bathroom and now sat on the edge of the mattress beside Erica. His avid gaze fixed on the slow bob of her head with a look Griff could only think of as hungry. Corey shifted the curtain of Erica's hair out of the way so he could get a better view of what she was doing.

In Erica's mouth, Griff's cock flexed. The leak of precome was quickly swallowed with an excited little moan that made Griff fear the real thing was already on its way. He braced his hand on her cheek, the one that Corey wasn't touching, and gently urged her off. "Give me a sec."

Erica released him but continued delivering soft licks to his head and the tender spot just under the crown. "Hmm...you taste nice."

Beside her, Corey groaned. There was such longing in the sound that Griff had to grab the base of his shaft and apply pressure to stop an embarrassing premature incident.

Corey's baby blues burned like lasers as he assessed Griff's reaction. Erica stared at him too, her fathomless dark eyes all-knowing, all-seeing in a way that was scary but somehow also soothing. As Griff watched, she stuck out her tongue and gave his cock a little butterfly flick. The steady eye contact was as sexy as the tickle on his taut skin. She repeated the maneuver a few more times, before shifting aside to place a soft kiss on his hip.

Corey stared at him, a question in his eyes. *Ah, Christ.* Griff knew what Erica was up to, what she was encouraging Corey to do, and it made him suck in a breath.

Erica cupped her hand around Griff's girth and began a slow up-and-down stroke. Griff moved his own hand out of the way, threading it through her hair and letting her cadence hypnotize him. He stared at her, but his peripheral awareness of Corey didn't dim. He sensed his friend's curiosity, his craving, but the trepidation was there as well, as real as his hot, uneven breaths fanning across the tip of Griff's cock.

Griff wasn't going to ask. He couldn't bring himself to discourage Corey either, not this time.

Erica's free hand wandered, exploring the contours of Griff's chest. The tip of her pinkie finger grazed his nipple at the same moment as another butterfly flick rushed his blood.

Jesus fucking Christ. Griff watched, tortured by anticipation, as Corey leaned forward and did it again, this time ending the flick with a swirling lick the way Erica had been doing.

Afterward he sat back, his eyes wide as though he'd surprised himself. Then he made a sound at the back of his throat and dipped his head again.

Corey's lips were cool on Griff's fire-hot shaft. Where Erica's movements were soft and teasing, Corey's were tentative and awkward. Widening his mouth, Corey pushed down on Griff's cock, trying to take too much in at once.

When he gagged and pulled back, Griff felt like he'd been slapped. "You don't have to."

"Shh." The admonishment came from Erica, who put her hand on Griff's ass, keeping him in place when she sensed he might retreat. "It's okay."

She drew the tip of his dick into her mouth, pressing her lips together and sucking in a way that made Griff groan and forget all about Corey's rebuff. A moment later she released him, keeping up the motion of her hand.

Once again Corey lowered his head. This time he was careful to only take the tip of Griff's cock between his lips. He kept the fit snug, sucking on the mushroom head like a lollipop, exactly as Erica had done.

Damned if Erica Shannon, his prudish, reserved English teacher, wasn't giving Corey a blow-job lesson. Griff had never been so happy to be a guinea pig in his life.

"That's it, Corey, just a little at a time." With her free hand Erica stroked Corey's hair, encouraging him as she kept her other hand wrapped tight around Griff's shaft, pumping him as

Corey licked and sucked at the tip. "Rotate your tongue around the top, he likes that."

When Corey did it, Griff swore and shoved his hands into his hair. All the better to keep from grabbing the back of Corey's neck and thrusting his cock all the way into his friend's virgin mouth. "Jesus, Red. You've gotta hurry it up or I'm gonna die."

Erica merely smiled.

"Keep doing that, Corey, but move a little bit more in every time you swallow." Corey groaned, his lips vibrating on Griff's staff. He did as Erica said, inching more of Griff's meat past the back of his tongue. "That's it. Now hold him here, stroke up and down the way I've been doing."

Corey grabbed Griff's dick and the added pressure, the fine-sandpaper sensation of calluses on his fingertips dragged a groan from Griff's throat. He started moving his hand up and down in time with the motion of his head.

Heaven. Utter heaven.

Griff gave himself over to the rhythm, though it wasn't always consistent or smooth and the occasional scrape of Corey's teeth made him wince. He'd dreamed of plunging his hard cock into Corey Wachawski's sexy mouth more times than he should have, he was hardly going to correct the guy. Especially not when Erica was so good at it anyway.

Yet a coolness on his right side told Griff she'd moved away. *Where?* He opened his eyes to see her reclining on the bed watching them. Between her legs, her hand moved in a harried motion.

Oh fuck, Erica you beautiful thing.

It hit Griff then, the emancipating, glorious truth. Erica was nothing like Anna Hendricks. Anna, who'd tolerated Jack's interest in Griff only so long before ensuring through subtle machinations that all eyes were once again on her. Anna had never been aroused by the sight of Griff and Jack together, although she'd never outright told them to hurry up so she could have her time. Anna had never once had to get herself off watching her boyfriend give Griff a blow job.

And Corey... How could he ever have compared Corey to Jack Chambers? For Jack this act had always been about control, not giving pleasure. The innate generosity shamed Griff. He should have been more open with himself. He should have been the one doing all the giving instead of Erica and Corey, who were more uncertain of themselves than any two people he'd ever been with.

Trouble was, Griff wasn't sure that kind of emotional courage was in him anymore.

Gently, Griff wound his fingers through Corey's hair, noting how glossy it was—as glossy as Erica's. He lifted him off. The anguish in Corey's blue irises pierced Griff through. "Did I stuff it up?"

Griff shook his head. "No way. You're doing great. I'm so fucking hard for the feel of your mouth, but I'm not gonna blow my load in there."

"Griff..." Corey rolled his eyes.

"Trust me, it takes some getting used to." Griff pulled Corey close, pressing his cheek to the flat expanse of his stomach. "Look at Erica. You're turning her on too."

Erica lay on her side now, her eyes soft as she watched their exchange. Her fingers still worked in languid circles on her clit.

"Oh, baby," Corey breathed, reaching out to touch her cheek.

"You hard there, Cor?"

"Shit yeah."

Griff stepped back. "Show me."

Corey's Adam's apple bobbed as he swallowed. He leaned back on one elbow and grabbed his cock with his free hand, giving the stiff column a few good tugs. Despite having come like gangbusters not so long ago, he was as big and red as a damn fire hydrant.

Oh to be twenty-five again. "Keep doing that. Erica, come over here and help him out."

Getting up on all fours, Erica stalked the bed until she reached Corey. Corey's eyes and head rolled back when Erica about swallowed him whole, moving her mouth with the motion of Corey's hand.

Griff climbed on the bed, settling on his knees beside Corey. He presented him with his throbbing hard-on. "Lick it like you did before."

Corey stuck out his tongue and ran it up Griff's length. God, he was so close he could almost come from that one swipe of the other man's tongue. "That's it, Cor. You know what to do with that mouth of yours. You like sucking cock while you're getting your own blown?"

His only answer was a moan that he wrapped around Griff's dick as Erica increased the pace of her sucking. Griff turned to see her bent over Corey's supine form, working him like she was greedy for his taste. Between her legs, her hand moved faster and faster, and her hips thrust back and forth into her own touch.

Beneath him, Corey hollowed his cheeks and Griff knew he was going to lose it. He pulled out of Corey's mouth and started pumping hard, massaging his balls, feeling the eruption reaching its peak. Erica made a muffled squeal, her hips gyrating hard. Her orgasm ripped Griff's from him. He came in powerful jets, streaking his come all over Corey's chest.

"Oh, God...Griff." Corey reached down and grasped Erica's head, holding her to him as his hips jerked. "Baby, yeah. I'm coming now."

Erica drank every last drop until Corey was flat out panting on the mattress, staring at the ceiling like a man who'd had a not-unpleasant knock on the head. Griff knew exactly how he felt. He dropped down beside him, while Erica found her way to the narrow space between them.

No one said a word for long moments while the rain continued to fall on the tin roof, trickling into the gutters and down the drainpipes. Gutters probably needed clearing. Griff made a mental note to take care of that when it fined up.

First lawn mowing, making breakfasts and now gutter duty. You're acting very domesticated, Dale. Domesticated and ashamed of himself for not being more emotionally accessible. *This way lies danger.*

"Darn it!"

Erica sat bolt upright, staring at the bedside alarm. "I'm going to be so late. Darn it, darn it, darn it!"

As she scrambled off the bed, Griff drawled, "Why don't you go ahead and say fuck it, Red. The profanity ship's sailed already."

"That word is only appropriate in certain circumstances." Erica slapped him on the leg as she ran for the bathroom.

Griff laughed. Beside him, Corey didn't say a word. Quietly he used the sheet to wipe off Griff's stickiness. "You all right?" Griff asked.

"Yeah. You?"

"Yeah." *Way to make the dialogue sparkle.* Sitting up, Griff reached for his jeans and dragged them on. "You were great, by the way. Phenomenal first-time effort."

"Do I get a gold star with that glowing review?"

Griff winced. "I didn't mean that the way it sounded."

"I know, I'm sorry." Corey sat up and reached for his own pants, which were hanging over the timber post at the foot of the bed. "I'm not sure what to say. Is this how it always is after?"

"What do you mean?"

Corey averted his gaze. He stood and pulled on his jeans. "Do guys never hug?"

Griff's heart fissured, expanding so far it felt like it could crack his rib cage. He stared at Corey's broad, strong back and was amazed anew at the guy's willingness to show vulnerability when so many men wouldn't dare. When *he* didn't dare.

In two strides Griff was behind Corey, wrapping his arms around his waist and drawing him back into a fierce embrace. "Shit, Cor. Anytime you want a hug, you only have to ask."

He laughed ruefully. "Now I know why chicks always complain when you can't read their minds. Can't you tell what I want, dickbrain?"

Griff slid one hand down to cup Corey through his jeans. "I'm better at reading this dick than anyone's brain. Sorry I'm such a shit. Next time you blow me I'll make a note to cuddle after."

"Shut up. Next time you can blow me."

Placing an open-mouthed kiss on Corey's neck, Griff murmured, "That can be arranged."

"What about the time after that?"

"Meaning?"

Corey turned so he could meet Griff's gaze over his shoulder. "Are you going to make me beg for what I want the way you do Erica?"

A mental picture of Corey bent over, screaming at Griff to fuck his tight ass fired Griff's nerve endings. He gave the package he still had his hand on a tender massage. "Only if you like it that way."

Griff heard him swallow before answering. Beneath Griff's hand, Corey's heart thudded. "I think I would."

Damned if Griff's thirty-six-year-old dick didn't stir to life like it was twenty-five again. "Tease. Now I gotta go to work with a hard-on."

Corey laughed and Griff released him with a curse. A moment later Erica came tearing back into the room throwing on clothes in fast motion. Griff went to the kitchen and put her oats into a Tupperware container, handing it to her as she grabbed her purse and keys.

"Thank you." She leapt up and kissed him hard on the mouth. Then she did the same to Corey. "Remember to lock up when you leave. Sometimes you have to use the key though because the lock is temperamental. Here." She fished her spare off the key ring and placed it on the kitchen counter.

Erica stared at it a moment, paling at the implications she must have only then acknowledged. She'd given them a key to her house. Whether she dismissed her concerns or simply didn't have time to deal with them, she said nothing further as she offered them a watery smile before racing out the door.

When she'd gone, Corey glanced at the key. "Did you see that?"

"I'm not blind."

"She gave me a key."

"Us, mate," Griff corrected. "She gave *us* a key."

He tried not to grin or let his heart beat out the thrill that burrowed inside him. Could this really work, the three of them? *They're nothing like Anna and Jack, remember?*

Tamping down the surge of hope, Griff reminded himself that was no guarantee a relationship between the three of them would work. The inherent complexities of a triad provided difficult-enough waters to navigate, but the fact he and Corey worked together added another dimension. Watching him take risks on the job had never been easy, but now it was downright heartrending. Griff's emotions ran so deep he had to cordon them off altogether if he was to continue functioning as a firefighter. He couldn't sustain that level of self-restraint long term. Something would have to give—the job or the relationship.

Fighting fires was what Griff did. He'd been doing it for fifteen years and he couldn't see himself switching careers. He knew Corey felt the same. No two ways about it, if he had to give something up in order to save his sanity, it would be the relationship.

Besides, he'd already promised Corey he'd walk away.

Just not yet, Griff told himself as he watched Corey pick up the key and kiss it like it was a winning lottery ticket. *Just let me have a little longer.*

Chapter Thirteen

She should never have given them that key.

The changes had seemed harmless enough in the beginning. Instead of calling first to ask if he could visit, Erica arrived home from school one Tuesday to find Corey's dilapidated Ford in her driveway and him already inside, making himself at home by using her shower. The surprise made her heart jump with a mixture of ire and excitement. Determined to lay down some ground rules about what he could and could not use her spare key for, the intended diatribe died on Erica's lips when Corey emerged from the bathroom in a cloud of steam, wrapped in only a towel and a whole lot of sex appeal.

"Hey, baby." The lingering dampness on his body wet her blouse as he walked into the kitchen and wrapped his arms around her, lifting her feet off the ground. "God it's good to see you."

All thought of haranguing him disintegrated at the weary words. "Bad day?"

"One thing after another since I started this morning. There was a three-car prang on the inner-city bypass, and this afternoon an old couple lost the house they've lived in for fifty years because of a faulty tumble dryer."

Erica stroked the tired lines on his forehead. "How awful."

"I know. They were a nice couple too." Corey brushed the hair back from her face and offered a ghost of a smile. "Do you always look this good when you get home from work? If so, I'll have to make sure I'm here to meet you more often."

That reminded her why she was supposed to be peeved at him. "What do you think you're doing, letting yourself into my house, by the way?"

"Saving time. I was going to come around anyway, and this place is closer to the station than my apartment."

Erica arched a brow. "Oh you were going to come over anyway, were you?"

His slow smile brimmed with self-assurance. The soft kiss he placed on her lips teased her annoyance away. The feel of those lips, the hard crush of his body molding hers to it, took Erica's breath. Against his lips, she asked, "Don't they have showers at the fire station?"

"I wanted an excuse to be naked in your house."

Erica reached for the towel wrapped around his waist, barely concealing the jut of his erection. "Since when do you need an excuse?"

He pleasured her right there in the kitchen, hoisting her onto the counter and feasting on the cream that dripped from her pussy. Then he took her to bed and stretched her body with his, twice, before they even thought of dinner. They ordered Chinese food and stayed up late watching movies—Erica made him sit through *How to Lose a Guy in 10 Days*, for which he declared she owed him a favor. They tussled that one out in bed and Corey didn't leave until morning lit the sky.

At no time during those hours did Erica ask him to give the key back.

Two nights later she arrived home to find a note stuck to her fridge.

Red,

You never did get those smoke alarms replaced, did you? Bad, bad girl. Have gone to get stuff to cook dinner, your pantry is in a sad state. No end to your sins, is there? I'll be back in a bit to feed you and discuss appropriate punishment. Warm up for me, G.

While Erica tried to control her wild speculations about what Griff meant by *appropriate punishment*, she walked from room to room. Her old alarms had been replaced by some state-of-the-art-looking system that would probably go off if one of her neighbors lit a cigarette. Erica battled to keep the spark of her annoyance alive, but it suffocated beneath the heavy weight of her arousal. Griff was coming back and he wanted her *warm* for his *punishment*.

By the time he walked in the door, Erica had showered and changed into a more casual skirt and top that Griff seemed to appreciate. She'd already surpassed warm, and her body teetered on the edge of spontaneously combusting all through dinner. But Griff talked about his day, asked her about hers, discussed world politics and conspicuously said nothing about his note or his intentions until Erica burst out impatiently, "What did you mean by punishment?"

Griff merely arched his brows as though he had no idea what she was talking about.

"In your note." Erica scowled. "You said you'd be back to discuss appropriate punishment because I'm apparently a poor housekeeper."

"Oh, that." He grinned. "Your punishment was me deciding to have you for desert instead of an entree. Why, what did you think I meant?"

Erica flushed so hot she regretted not turning on a fan. "Nothing."

Griff smiled knowingly. "You're blushing, Red."

"It's like summer weather tonight. I'm hot."

"You bet you are. A hot, dirty schoolmarm who wants me to spank her pretty behind."

"Oh, you horrible man!" Erica pushed back her chair and tossed her napkin onto her empty plate. "I'd never even thought of it until you put it into my head."

"But it's in your head now. Why not give it a go?"

Griff's chair scraped as he shoved it away and stood. The lethal intent in his golden gaze made Erica take several steps backward. "No. I never said I wanted to…" Her protest trailed off as Griff started moving toward her. "Griff, please. I couldn't."

"Oh, you could. And you will."

Griff kept coming, unbuttoning his shirt as he stalked her. Erica's heart pounded, her backwards steps hastened. When Griff pulled the hem of his shirt from his jeans with a forceful yank, Erica squealed and bolted down the hallway, into her bedroom. She tried to slam the door shut but she wasn't fast enough. *How hard did you really try, Erica?* Deep down she knew the semblance of protest was merely for show, part of the fantasy she hadn't even been aware of having.

Dale Griffin brought out the most perplexing behavior in her.

"I mean it, Dale." Erica tried to inject a stern tone into her voice. "I'm not the kind of person who does things like this."

"You mean the kind of person who fucks two guys at once? Who eats cock like it's the last meal she's ever going to have? Who comes extra hard when she takes it up the ass?"

"You bastard." Did he have to go out of his way to remind her how depraved she'd become? "A gentleman would never throw a woman's sexual performance in her face. *Corey* would never push me to do something that frightened me."

He showed her an acidic grin. "A *lady* would never throw my obvious deficiencies compared to Saint Corey in *my* face. Admit it, Red, you're no lady. You're a naughty little tart who gives it up at the drop of a hat, and you want to be punished for it."

"No!" Erica tried to scramble across the bed to the opposite side, but Griff caught her easily with a firm grip on her leg. He dragged her backward until she fell facedown on the mattress. Shoving her floral skirt up to her waist, he grasped the waistband of her underwear and yanked it down her legs.

When they were dispensed with, Griff spanned her bare ass with his hands, squeezing her cheeks. "Damn you have a nice ass on you—as firm and ripe as a couple of tasty melons. I've always been an ass man."

"Probably why you like boys too," Erica spat.

Griff slapped her behind, causing a sharp sting that made her gasp. He growled close to her ear. "I never liked boys, but I love men. So do you. That's why you're always gagging to have some guy shove his dick in you here."

Griff inserted two fingers into her pussy and found it already drenched with arousal. Erica moaned at the intense pleasure and pure indignity of it. He was right. She did want this.

Removing his fingers, Griff delivered another blow to her backside. This time she couldn't hide her gasp of delight or the thrust of her hips that silently begged for more. Griff gave it to her in a series of harsh spanks that made her flesh catch fire.

When she was panting and her ass felt red raw, he swooped down and bathed the places he'd marked with his tongue. He kissed all over her backside, quickly making his way to her dripping entrance. He lapped up the evidence of her arousal, fluttering his tongue on her lips before driving it inside her channel.

Erica thrust her hips, seeking a deeper intrusion. "Oh, Griff. Sometimes I hate when you're right."

He chuckled, causing pleasant vibrations within her. He started trailing kisses over her bottom again, gradually moving up until he followed the path of her spine. "Damn, sweetheart. If every guy could see what you're really like underneath that serene exterior, there'd be a queue at your door, scores of men just dying to fuck you."

Erica shook her head, the image both arousing and repelling her. "No. Only you and Corey—no one else."

Ever. She didn't speak the word, but it imprinted itself on her subconscious, ready to come back to haunt her later—when she lost them.

Erica let the rough possessiveness in Griff's voice push the reminder of her lonely future to the far recesses of her mind. "Damn straight. We're the only guys for you. We own this ass."

He delivered one last, resounding slap that had Erica crying out. "Griff, please!"

"Tell me where you want it, you sweet, horny bitch. In your wet cunt or your tight little asshole."

How could she possibly choose? "I want both."

Swearing harshly under his breath, Griff yanked open the bedside drawer. A moment later Erica heard the tear of a foil package and the familiar low hum of one of her vibrators.

Oh God. She had no idea which of her toys he had or where he would put it, where he would stick his thick member. Anticipation thrummed inside her. She rotated her hips, showing her eagerness for whatever Griff had in store.

The coolness of lube was a balm to her heated flesh. He smeared it over her ass and down to cover her pussy—not that she needed it there. The push of the quivering sex toy against her puckered back entrance made her bite her lip. Griff pushed it in a little farther, and Erica gasped.

It wasn't the bullet or the nice safe butt plug. He'd selected the bigger dick-shaped toy with the giant purple head. "Griff..."

"Bet you've never used this one up here before. Big, isn't it? Not as big as Corey though." He eased the instrument deeper into her body, the vibrations facilitating its entry. Griff delved into her pussy with his fingers, moving them in and out as he worked the battery-operated penis in her ass. "We'd better get you ready to feel Corey's massive stick in this tiny hole."

Erica could imagine it all too well, had thought about it constantly since Corey had mentioned his desire to take her anally.

Griff invaded her hole with the toy, inch by inch, all the while keeping up the teasing movement of his fingers in her pussy. He hit a spot that made her shudder and clutch at his fingers with her internal walls. It was then he replaced his fingers with the broad head of his erection.

Her muscles spasmed when he entered her in a smooth stroke, withdrawing the dildo as he came in. "Oh yeah. You feel so damn good. I'm never going to get enough of this. You know what I want you to say, sweetheart. Let's hear it."

Had it only been a month ago the words seemed impossible to speak? "Fuck me, Griff. I'm yours to fuck."

"That's right, you are." He thrust hard inside her, bumping her cervix. Then he drew back and stuck the vibrator into her ass.

He continued that way, the cadence of the alternate entries steadily increasing in pace until Erica was wild with the need to climax. The twin invasions filled her completely, made her yearn for the same thing but with Corey the one filling her backside. The very thought of it made the spasms begin.

"Yeah, oh yeah. Come for me my beautiful, dirty little redhead."

It seemed as though she shattered everywhere—in her pussy and her ass, in her old view of herself. Her orgasm rocked her to the depths of her soul, breaching what she'd thought were impenetrable walls shielding her heart. When Griff came with a litany of muttered curses, it was as though he seeped into her while her defenses were down.

In that moment, Erica wasn't sure if she was ever going to be able to force him back out.

A minute later when Griff started laughing, Erica rethought that assessment. She glowered at him. "You're *laughing* at me?"

"No way, Red. I'm laughing at myself."

"Oh, sure."

"I mean it." When Erica made to roll off the bed, Griff covered her body with his, pinning her down. "You may not believe this, but I've never spanked a woman before."

"You're right. I don't believe it." He'd made it feel so darned *good.*

"Seriously." Griff chuckled. "Didn't I sound like a first-class dick? Sorry I called you a bitch."

"That's all right. I think I liked it." Erica groaned. "Dear Lord, what's wrong with me?"

"Nothing." Griff's expression turned momentarily serious, almost pained. "I can't think of a damned thing wrong with you."

Erica's heart raced. Oh no, not Griff. Corey looked at her with that tender expression sometimes, the one that scared her into thinking they weren't on the same page in the this-is-purely-a-temporary-sexual-affair department. But not Griff. He cussed and criticized and bossed her around, generally treating her like a sex object. Griff kept her grounded, kept this whole situation impersonal.

"Don't, Dale. Please don't."

Her agonized whisper seemed to make him snap out of whatever trance he'd been in. Griff pulled back, his expression turning blank. "Whatever you want, Red."

"I want..." ...so many things she couldn't have. Erica focused on something that might actually be attainable. "I want to be there the first time you make love to Corey. I want to see it."

Griff stood and chucked her on the chin. "How can I say no? I know how much you love to watch, kinky minx."

"I do." It meant more to her than a vicarious thrill, but Erica didn't want to explore that with Griff. *Let him think it's nothing but a voyeuristic desire.* She watched as Griff went about getting dressed. "Do you have to go?"

"Early shift tomorrow. I'll hit the hay at home."

Erica nodded, schooling her features to appear as bland as Griff's. This was what she wanted—sex and nothing more. She might not be able to resist Corey's tendency to invite himself to stay all night and cuddle, but at least she didn't have to worry about that in Griff's case. Over the ensuing weeks he didn't stay overnight once. When she visited him at his house she tried to grant him the same courtesy.

At school the hours crawled by, characterized by the mounting heat of approaching summer and the subsequent irritability of her teenage charges, who wanted nothing more than for the term, and the year, to be over. Erica understood how they felt. For the first time in her life, work loomed as an aggravating distraction from the unpredictable variety and excitement of her private life. Every night she raced home, never knowing who she'd find waiting for her there—Corey, Griff or both of them. If the house was empty, her momentary disappointment would soon be allayed by a phone call or a knock on her door.

Corey would often take her out to a movie or for Thai food. He'd tell her about his family, whom he obviously adored. A sister on the Southside raising three kids, another currently in Canada on a working holiday. His parents had been married for thirty-one years after meeting through friends and falling instantly in love. Corey had flashed her a smile when he'd said that, and taken her hand across the restaurant table.

Sometimes Erica worried that Corey considered himself her boyfriend. Pam even thought he was, since Corey had picked Erica up from school a couple of times and fussed over her like she was a delicate, precious thing. He carried her folders of student assignments as he walked her through the car park, causing twitters of speculation amongst the other teachers and exclamations like "Nice pull, Ms. Shannon!" from the cheekier teenage girls. Corey didn't recoil, hamming it up by kissing her full on the mouth to the background noise of cheers and whistles.

When Corey treated her like that, Erica experienced a painful sense of guilt that she hadn't told him everything about herself. If he was really her boyfriend, she would owe it to him to reveal everything—the cancer scare, her genetic prognosis, and most of all the mastectomy she had decided to have as soon as a date for the procedure could be confirmed. But the thought terrified Erica. Every time they made love—and she'd begun using that term in her mind before she could stop herself—Erica felt his growing affection soothing her soul. Even a flicker of the distaste she'd seen in Doug's eyes flashing through Corey's would be devastating.

Besides, Griff's presence in her life was a constant reminder that she wasn't a girlfriend. She was an affair, a fuck toy. When Griff decided to visit her, he rarely called first. He didn't take her out to restaurants or the cinema. Griff's *modus operandi* involved waltzing into her house with food that would sit on the kitchen counter growing cold as he stripped her out of her clothes. It involved taking her bent over her couch or up against the wall in the hallway on the way to her bedroom. It involved whispered dirty words and harsh commands that Erica followed because his masterful manner made her so wet she couldn't deny him anything. He bought her gifts, not of flowers and chocolate, but of lingerie and sex toys. He'd insist she wear and use them for his benefit, and for Corey's the next time all three of them were together.

At first Erica felt awkward doing it, but the looks on Corey's and Griff's faces made that all float away. She grew bolder as the weeks passed, wearing the naughty underwear beneath her unofficial school uniform of knee-length skirt and buttoned-up blouse. She even bought something for herself, a tight black dress she doubted she'd ever be game to wear in public. The mere fact it hung in her wardrobe made her feel like a new woman—a sexy, bold woman.

Griff did that to her—turned her into a person she hardly recognized by nudging her sexual boundaries, forcing her to discover parts of herself she never knew existed. And Corey with his steadfast strength and gentle ways gave her the sense of security she needed to go out on those limbs. The two firemen were a dynamite combination, making her feel cocooned and reckless at the same time.

As time wore on Erica had more and more trouble picturing a future without them in it.

Griff woke with a jerk, his body bathed in sweat. The nightmare held him tight, like black quicksand trying to pull him back into the horror. The scent of smoldering timber was sharp in his nostrils, and for long moments he struggled to convince himself the nightmare wasn't real.

The disturbing dreams had grown more frequent in recent weeks. This time the burning building wasn't an unfamiliar storage shed or apartment block. This time it had been Erica's house. The thought of Erica being trapped inside the crumbling walls had exacerbated the panic. Griff had stood by, frozen and helpless, his limbs like solid blocks of cement, as Corey had rushed in and the flames had swallowed him. The fire had taken them both.

The imagined sound of their screams had jolted Griff awake, the terror so fresh his throat felt clogged with it. He rolled to his side and wrapped his arm around Corey's torso, pressing into him, chest to back. His nearness was reassuring and it diminished the clarity of the dream. Corey was here, safe and sound. On the other side of Corey, Erica slept, her breathing even and clean, unhampered by suffocating smoke. Griff breathed a sigh of pure relief.

It was so much easier when they got together at Erica's place. That way, Griff could slip out anytime he wanted. He didn't have to lie beside them and feel the inherent intimacy of sharing a bed scratch at his resolve. He didn't have to acknowledge how close they were to ensnaring his heart completely.

But tonight Erica and Corey had stayed over at his house, the three of them falling asleep in mutual exhaustion after they'd gorged on each other. Times like this it was getting more and more difficult to subtly suggest he preferred to sleep alone.

Countering his dark thoughts, the full-body contact with Corey caused a stirring in Griff's groin. When he'd wrapped an arm around the man his knuckles had brushed the warm body curled into Corey's front. Now, the curve of Erica's bare breast was warm and smooth, an enticement too tempting to ignore. Griff cupped her, gently caressing. A soft moan fell out of her and she arched, responsive as hell even in sleep.

Instantly, Griff turned hard, his erection jutting into the crevice of Corey's ass. The twin assaults on his libido, combined with the lingering distress of the dream, tore his willpower to shreds. Angling his hips to better announce his physical state, Griff swirled his tongue around Corey's ear. On the other side of Corey, Erica began to squirm, rubbing herself against Corey's chest as she drifted toward wakefulness.

The simultaneous activity eventually roused Corey, who pressed his ass backward, drawing a curse from Griff. Momentarily abandoning Erica's breast, Griff slipped his hand downward until he encountered Corey's very impressive hard-on. Wrapping his hand around it, Griff rasped into Corey's ear two words he'd never before dared to utter. "Need you."

As though the admission undid him, Corey curled his arm around Griff's neck and drew him forward for a kiss that seared. Griff thrust his tongue into Corey's mouth as he thrust his hips against his backside. His cock slipped along the gap between Corey's ass cheeks, over and over, mimicking the act he wanted so badly to perform.

Fuck. Want was not a strong-enough word. He ached to stick his dick in Corey's ass, burned for it. He'd played with that tight hole before, used his fingers or one of Erica's toys to prime Corey for what Griff wanted. As preparation it would have to suffice. He was going to fuck Corey tonight. He had to fuck him *now.*

Breathing heavily, Griff broke away from Corey's kiss. He found Erica watching them, her dark eyes almost swallowing her face. In the meager moonlight filtering through the blinds Griff thought he saw her smile before she tilted her face and offered her lips to Corey.

Corey sank into her, lost in the lush invitation of her lips as always. Griff took the opportunity to reach behind him for the bedside drawer. He rolled on the condom then poured a generous amount of lube on his fingers. Turning back to the couple in his bed, he watched them kiss for a moment, their bodies a series of pale curves and angles silvered by the moon as they shifted against each other. He appreciated the sight for what it was—a thing of beauty beyond compare.

Then he smeared the cool substance all around Corey's back entrance.

The slide of Griff's lubricated fingers in and out of Corey's ass made Corey's stomach curl in on itself. His heart pounded harder against his ribs as anticipation gripped him. He was going to do it. Griff was finally going to stop teasing and fuck him.

Against Erica's stomach, Corey's cock twitched. Her kiss drugged him, distracted him so he easily accepted the first nudge of Griff's cock. His body opened willingly, and Corey thrust his hips backward, silently asking for more.

Griff drove in farther and Corey couldn't control the instinctive way his body tightened. Griff paused, his breath hot on Corey's neck. Tearing his mouth away from Erica's, Corey said, "I want it, Griff."

"I know." With a barely suppressed groan, Griff advanced farther. "Take me, Cor."

The husked demand gave Corey the presence of mind to exhale slowly and focus on relaxing. He wanted to do this for Griff. He needed to do this for himself. With Griff's barely restrained urgency at his back and Erica's writhing softness at his front, Corey was on a knife-edge of need. Erica ramped things up when she scratched her nails down his chest, over his abs, then took his thick hard-on in her hand. Corey groaned when she started pumping him, leaving Griff's hands free to clutch at Corey's hips, holding him captive for the dogged invasion of his cock.

Between the two of them Corey could barely move. He couldn't escape the rush of sensations—not that he wanted to. His breathing grew labored. His ass burned where Griff breached it, but the deft stroking of Erica's hand, the luxurious gift of her kiss, turned him to jelly. His heart expanded and his body opened, allowing Griff to sink in deep, past the opposition of unused muscles, until he filled Corey completely for the first time.

From the tone of Griff's harsh curse and the trembling of his arms, Corey could tell he was using all his strength to hold back from thrusting hard and fast. Corey wanted to tell him to go for it, but he couldn't quite bring himself to. There was no denying it hurt to have Griff buried so deep, even though it made him feel so damn good at the same time. Especially when Erica kept stroking him, palming his balls, occasionally releasing him to flick her fingernails over his stiff nipples. The urge to come was a hot orb of fire inside him, banked and waiting for a whisper of oxygen so it could explode.

Griff retreated a little, re-entering with careful determination. Corey groaned into Erica's mouth, feeling something begin to pulse inside him as Griff repeated the move, over and over. His nuts drew up, tight and hot. Erica used her thumb to swipe the precome from the tip of his dick. She coated his shaft with it, making her hand slide over him more easily. Corey sensed it building inside him, a release like none he'd ever known.

Corey protested when Griff pulled out of him abruptly. "Don't stop," he groaned, not even caring that he sounded weakened and desperate. He *was* desperate. He had to know what was on the other side of the blinding heat that had gathered inside him, had to know what it was like to come from the rough motion of Griff fucking his ass.

"You're going to come soon, I promise."

Griff handed something to Erica. The familiar sound of a condom wrapper being torn open made Corey's penis ache. When Erica rolled it on he almost lost it because he knew it meant he'd be inside her soon, buried deep. As deep as Griff had just been buried in him.

Christ, it was too much. He couldn't handle this much pleasure.

"I want you inside Erica when I fuck you."

Griff's command made hot anticipation flare through Corey. He rolled Erica onto her back. She opened for him instantly and he drove deep in a smooth stroke. She was tight and hot and so incredibly wet that Corey couldn't resist plunging in again, and again.

"Yes, Corey," Erica moaned. "Use me."

Corey did, using the maddening grip of her muscles to take himself to the edge. Griff stopped him before he went over, grasping his hips to still his frantic thrusting. "Wait for me, babe."

Griff had never used any kind of endearment with Corey before. The rough tenderness of it made Corey's heart skip. He was ready, more than ready, to do anything Griff asked of him. He waited, his body suspended over Erica's as Griff positioned himself. Corey grunted when Griff propelled forward, filling him once more. Too turned on to be hesitant this time, Corey pushed his ass back, inviting the incursion. Erica moved with him, lifting her hips so he didn't withdraw from her completely. Corey sank back into her and this time Griff moved with him.

Griff was buried to the hilt while Corey was enveloped in Erica's slick heat. Corey could never have prepared for the sheer blast of sensation, of emotion. He was fucking and being fucked at the same time.

The ultimate payoff. Griff's words of weeks ago reverberated in Corey's head as Griff began to rock wildly inside him. Corey grabbed Erica's thigh, holding her wide open. Every time Griff plunged into him, Corey was compelled forward, deep into Erica's willing body.

He would never get enough of this. Now that he knew *this*, there was no way Corey would ever willingly give it up.

"Erica, baby," Corey rasped. "I'm going to come."

"Yes, oh yes."

Her muscles spasmed as though attuned to Corey's announcement. Her body always responded so easily to his, like they were made to fit together. And now it felt right with Griff too. So right Corey couldn't hold on another second. With a primal roar he released himself inside Erica, his own exclamation mingling with Griff's. The knowledge that Griff pumped his seed into Corey's body even as his own rushed out of him made the climax pulse on and on. Corey had never felt so exhilarated, so replete.

So *owned.*

Griff had claimed him just now, put his indelible stamp on Corey's body, his heart. This was what it was like to give yourself completely, to let someone else possess you. Corey looked at Erica and understood more fully what it was she offered every time they made love—and loved her for it.

Corey loved her, the truth was undeniable. He loved them both.

Griff caressed Corey's ass as he pulled out carefully. "Are you okay?"

Corey managed to nod. "Better than okay."

Placing a kiss on the base of Corey's spine, Griff left without another word, presumably to dispose of the protection. Corey rolled onto his side, bringing Erica with him. He didn't want to release her just yet. He traced the outline of her face. In the bluish light something glistened, and Corey realized it was a tear rolling its way down Erica's cheek. "Hey, baby. What's up?"

Her voice trembled. "Nothing."

Of course there was more to it, but as usual Erica kept her own counsel. He tightened his arms around her. "You can tell me anything."

She shook her head. "I should go. Griff likes it better when I don't stay."

"Fuck Griff." The moment of anger coming so swiftly on the heels of sheer bliss caused pain to lance Corey's chest. When was Griff's attitude going to change? Even now, only moments after Corey had granted the man access to his body, Griff had retreated to the bathroom, avoiding any semblance of post-coital closeness.

And Erica was trying to do the same thing. This time Corey couldn't bring himself to let her. He tightened his grip on Erica and slanted his mouth over hers until she moaned a little and wriggled against him. "Stay," Corey whispered against her lips.

Corey took the way her body melted as agreement. A moment later the bed shifted as Griff slipped back in with them, and Corey realized this was what he wanted most, all three of them together. Always.

The one thing Griff refused to give him.

As Erica buried her face in the curve of Corey's neck, Corey glanced over and found Griff watching him. The pained expression on the other man's face made Corey's heart seize. He looked so lost, so forlorn. Corey repeated the same request he'd made of Erica, but this time he was asking for more than just the next few hours. "Stay."

In answer Griff leaned over and kissed Corey, a rough, deep kiss that took Corey's breath and made him hope that maybe, just maybe, Griff was starting to change his mind about walking away.

Chapter Fourteen

By December the heat of early Brisbane summer made its presence known. Only one day of school remained, and the imminent Christmas break lifted the students' spirits, making Erica's job a lot more enjoyable than it had been around exam time. Her steps tripped down the hallway only a minute after the last bell of the day sounded. Students rushed all around her, parting for her like river rapids parting around a boulder.

As she passed Pam Spencer's classroom, she gave her friend a wave. Pam held up two fingers, and Erica leaned on a row of lockers as she waited for the other woman to come out.

Pam emerged bouncing from the classroom, singing "Friday on my Mind". "Only one more day of this, Erica, then six glorious weeks of holidays. I for one can't wait."

"Me neither."

"Summer plans?"

Erica shrugged noncommittally, but she couldn't stop a smile from tickling her lips.

Pam grinned. "Spending every possible minute with *Corey* I bet. I still can't believe you managed to nab one of Ashton Heights's most lusted-after bachelors. You do know you've become somewhat of a legend around here."

Erica wondered what kind of *legend* she would become if the rest of the staff knew she'd not only nabbed Mr. July, but Mr. October from four years ago as well. Would the astonished questions and moans of envy turn nasty? Would everyone think her a brazen slut?

Did she even care if they did?

Not really. The only person whose opinion mattered to Erica was Pam. Pam, who went on terrible date after terrible date, who had nothing but misfortune with men. What would she think of Erica taking two such fine specimens out of the availability pool?

Temporarily, of course.

Erica hadn't gotten up the courage to tell Pam the truth. Her friend fully supported her decision to have the mastectomy, and had pledged to be there to help her through surgery and recovery. Erica couldn't bear the thought of going through the procedure alone, and if Pam found out what Erica had really been up to these last two months, she might be disgusted or angry or both. As Griff didn't make surprise appearances at the school the way Corey did, Erica had never had to explain his involvement in her life.

"I suppose you're busy tonight, as well," Pam prompted. "My little sister's in town and we were thinking of hitting a couple of clubs."

Corey and Griff were both working the day shift. Tonight it would be all three of them once more, and Erica's body already pulsed with the knowledge. "Booked, I'm afraid."

"Seriously, Erica. That man is going to ask you to marry him one of these days."

Erica's heart fluttered for a moment then sank as heavily as an iron anvil. "You know that's not going to happen."

Pam sighed. "You still haven't told him, have you?"

Just as she hadn't revealed everything to Pam, she hadn't detailed her medical issues to Corey or Griff. If she had a doctor's appointment, she told them she was with Pam. If she was with Griff when Pam knew Corey was working, she made up some other excuse to fob off Pam's invitations to the movies or out dancing.

What a lying sneak she'd become, all so she didn't have to give up the deliciously decadent sex she'd been indulging in for the past couple of months. Make that a lying *selfish* sneak.

"Once I tell him, it'll be over." The notion tightened her chest. She'd known it all along but somehow Corey had still burrowed into her heart, creating his own space that she doubted would ever be occupied by anyone else.

"Maybe you're underestimating him."

Pam didn't understand. Corey was completely enamored with her breasts. He couldn't get enough of looking at them, fondling them or kissing them. Erica relished every moment of his attention, appreciating her body as she never had before. It was unbelievable what the simple act of taking off a blouse could do for a man's arousal levels—and for a woman's sexual confidence. Griff, as he'd once said, was more an ass man but Corey was definitely one individual who loved boobs. How was he going to react when she told him she was going to get rid of hers?

"I will tell him—when I have to."

"And in the meantime?"

"I'm enjoying a hot fling while it lasts. Gosh, Pam, I've never had one before." Erica knew her expression must have turned dreamy. "Am I wrong to take what I can for now?"

"I don't know, Erica. Maybe."

They stepped out into the car park, where the sun beat down on the black asphalt, raising the air temperature by several degrees. But it was the conversation as much as the humid atmosphere that made Erica's blood heat.

She turned to face Pam. "I thought you were happy for me."

"I am. But what about Corey? He seems like a terrific guy and you're just using him."

Pam's accusation sucked the breath from Erica's lungs. "He's using me too."

The statement didn't ring true. She'd bet Corey Wachawski had never used another human being for his own selfish ends in his life.

Gently, Pam queried, "Have you considered the possibility he's in love with you?"

"You don't understand." Corey wasn't in love with her, he was in love with Griff. "The thing I have with Corey...it's never been heading toward some picture-perfect happy ever after. He knows that. And I won't let myself believe in something that can't happen."

"Why can't it happen? You should tell Corey the truth and it might have a chance."

"He's not the only one I've been sleeping with," Erica blurted. "There's someone else too, and Corey knows."

Pam stepped back, agape. "Someone else?"

"A friend of his. More than a friend, actually. Corey has a male lover and they...share me."

The silence was as palpable as the summer humidity. Pam stared at her for so long Erica wondered if the other woman had gone into shock. At length Pam rasped, "Whoa."

Erica pushed out a sigh. The truth was out now, for better or worse. "Do you think I'm disgusting?"

Pam merely repeated, "Whoa."

There goes my one source of sisterly solidarity. "I get it, it's weird. But you understand what I mean. Corey and I are not going down any traditional paths here, no marriage proposals, no nothing. I'm just a novelty to him and Griff."

"Okay." Pam blinked. "If you say so."

"If I don't see you tomorrow, have a good holiday, Pam," Erica said sadly.

When she made to leave, Pam touched Erica's arm. "I don't think you're disgusting. I think I might be jealous though."

Relief made Erica laugh a little too loud. "I know it takes some getting used to."

"I bet." Pam eyed her steadily, concern in her eyes. "I hope you know what you're doing, Erica."

So do I.

Erica walked in the direction of the train station but ended up veering across the street instead, not yet interested in going home. Corey and Griff wouldn't be finished work for a while, then they would have to shower and change. It would be hours before she saw them.

A little desperate, aren't you, Erica?

Pathetic or not, Erica *was* desperate to see them. It was as though her body had become addicted to the release only they could give her. Even playing with her toys—or the new ones Griff had bought her—didn't hold the appeal it once had. On her own it wasn't nearly as much fun.

When her meandering steps brought her within blocks of the Ashton Heights firehouse, Erica admitted the truth. Her wanderings hadn't been aimless at all. Getting an idea, Erica ducked into a bakery around the corner from the station and bought a tray of pastries.

The fire-station doors were open and water ran out from inside, wetting the pavement. Erica stepped gingerly over the shallow rivers in her black pumps, passing the front of a huge fire engine which gleamed damp and shiny in the slanted afternoon sun. At the driver's side of the vehicle, a man stood hosing off the massive wheels. He had blonde curly hair that brushed hard shoulders encased in a tight black T-shirt.

"Excuse me."

The man turned suddenly, swinging the hose as he did so. Instinctively, Erica squealed and leapt out of the path of the spray. The man was quick to apologize and turn off the water, but her yelp had gotten the attention of his coworker, who yelled from the back of the truck. "Curly, what are you doing down there?"

Following the sound of the voice, Erica looked up and saw a familiar pair of hazel eyes staring down at her from on top of the truck. The mere sight of Griff made her heart beat out a crazy rhythm against her rib cage. "Hi."

"Hi yourself."

"I come bearing gifts." Erica indicated the box she held. "There's enough for everyone."

Curly exclaimed, "What a champion!" and took the pastries out of her hands, opening the lid and mooning over the contents.

"Don't mind the ravenous hound there, that's Curly," Griff drawled. "Curly, this is Erica."

"It's Rob, actually. Nice to meet you, Erica."

Erica smiled. "Likewise."

Rob flashed her a grin that made two adorable dimples appear in his cheeks. With his curly blond hair and soft brown eyes, he reminded Erica of a particularly friendly Labrador.

Griff whistled at Rob as though that was exactly what he thought as well. "Down, boy. You'd better take those out back and tell Wachawski he has a visitor."

As Rob aka Curly went to do as suggested, Griff used a ladder mounted on the side of the vehicle to climb down. His booted feet landed on the cement beside Erica with a resounding thud. "What's up, Red? You get a better offer for tonight?"

Surely he didn't think that was possible. "No, I just thought the guys might like the afternoon snack."

He smiled shrewdly. "Couldn't wait to see our blue-eyed boy, could ya?"

Griff always had been able to read her so well it sometimes frightened her. Her gaze trailed over him as though of its own volition. The yellow rubber pants held up with braces was the same outfit he'd worn in the firefighter's calendar—except in that photo he wasn't wearing the black T-shirt he wore today. It was all so eerily similar—the outfit, the gleaming red fire truck and Griff's lopsided, brashly confident smile—that arousal gripped her with hot fingers, teasing every nerve ending in her body.

Her lips were so dry she had to wet them. "I didn't only come to see Corey."

Griff's eyes tracked the movement of her tongue. Because the way Griff looked at her incited something impish inside her, Erica repeated the maneuver especially for his benefit.

"Jesus, Red," Griff breathed. "The ideas you put in my mind probably aren't legal in all states."

"Erica?" Corey emerged from out back, sporting a wide smile. When he reached her, he swooped down and kissed her on the mouth. "It's great to see you."

"You too." Corey's obvious pleasure at the sight of her made Erica's throat close over.

"The guys are going crazy for that stuff you brought in. You didn't have to do that."

"Maybe you can pay her back by giving her the tour," Griff suggested. "Girls always love to check out the equipment."

Griff's blatant innuendo made Erica flush, and Corey slap him dead center on the chest. At the playful contact Griff froze. "I'll be out back supervising the crowd. Take your time showing Erica the trucks, Wachawski."

He left so abruptly it was as though a cold breeze had blown through the garage. Corey glanced after Griff, his expression for once unreadable. Then he turned back to Erica with a warm smile.

He showed her around the facilities, explaining the difference between the truck they called a Firepac 3000—which carried a 1000-liter water tank and was perfect for the urban environment—and the Aerial Ladder Platform, which was designed to rescue fire victims from multistory buildings. The gleaming red machines were huge and impressive, much like the man showing them off as though they were his very own.

Erica smiled at Corey's exuberance. "You love the trucks, don't you?"

"What's not to love? They're big and powerful." Corey leaned in a little, backing her against the cool, hard surface of one of the vehicles. "They have everything you need to put out your fire."

High on all the testosterone floating around a shed full of huge trucks and hard-bodied firemen, Erica was happy to play with the innuendo. She fluttered her lashes. "You mean like a really big hose?"

Corey settled his lower body against hers. "You know it, baby."

"So this is the equipment Griff was referring to." Erica arched a little, causing their hips to bump. "The stuff all the girls like."

"I'm not interested in *all* the girls." Tenderly, he touched her face. "Just this one right here."

The softness in his gaze made Erica's heart race. Pam was wrong, she assured herself. Corey was interested in having sex with her, that was all. He wasn't in love with her. "Can I tell you a secret? I'm wearing one of those lacy corsets Griff bought me."

Corey's brows hiked. "The blue one or the white one?"

"The white one with the little pink bows on it."

Corey groaned. "I *love* that one." He leaned farther into her, pushing her flush against the truck. "Will you show it to me?"

Erica pretended to demure. "You've seen it."

"Only once." He dipped his head and trailed his hot breath over her neck. "Come on, baby. Just a little peek."

The light brush of his lips on the sensitive skin of her throat made Erica quiver. "There are several of your workmates in the next room."

"Griff'll keep them from coming out here. He knows the second you turned up today I wanted to kiss you more than I wanted anything."

To prove it, Corey transferred the press of his lips from her neck to her cheek, then to her mouth. Instinctively, Erica arched against him, needing what he gave her as much as he wanted to take it—right here in a shadowy corner of the fire station against the Firepac 3000.

Corey cupped her breast through her blouse, groaning softly as he pulled out of the languorous kiss. "Show me."

Trusting him at his word that Griff would ensure their privacy, Erica worked her buttons free with trembling fingers and parted the fabric. The corset was made of satin that cinched in her waist and did a great job of lifting and separating everything else. She was breathing so hard the bra cups barely contained her breasts. Corey's gaze smoldered as it landed upon the pebbled tips, visible above the pretty pink bows lining the garment.

Releasing an epithet, Corey brushed a thumb over one nipple until it jutted toward him eagerly. His other hand slipped beneath her skirt, lifting it higher on her thigh as he fitted himself more closely to her body.

Erica had to wind her legs around his waist to keep her balance. The rubber of his pants chaffed her inner thighs and Corey winced. "I guess turn-out gear is not exactly a turn-*on*."

He had to be *kidding*. The rubber pants might conceal a lot of his lower body but the tight black T-shirt he wore with them defined every perfect muscle. Bunching the cotton in her fist, Erica lifted it so she could touch skin. "Why do you think they make you put it on for the calendar shoot?"

"Oh." Corey smiled in understanding. "I figured that was a gimmick."

"Corey." Erica rubbed her wet crotch against him. "I am so turned on right now."

"I can help with that." Slipping a hand between their bodies, Corey found the front of the lacy G-string that matched the corset and stroked her heat. "But you'll have to be quiet, baby."

Silencing her cry of pleasure when Corey pushed aside the miniscule panties and delved into her wetness with his middle finger was the hardest thing Erica had ever done. His pecs grazed her nipples, heightening the sensations as he used his thumb on her swollen clit.

He watched her face as she mouthed the words *yes* and *oh please*. The only sound between them was that of their shallow breaths and the soft shifting of fabric as they moved against each other. Wearing the underwear all day had already put Erica's arousal levels on full alert. It took no time at all for Corey to bring her to a furious orgasm. He kissed her as she broke apart, swallowing her whimpers into his mouth so no one would hear them.

Afterward, his chest heaved and even through the thick material of his pants Erica could feel his hardness. "I have condoms in my purse," she whispered.

His groan tickled her earlobe. "Not here."

It was only then the sound of voices filtered back into Erica's consciousness. The other men were still talking in the common room, not too far away. Heat stole into her cheeks as she quickly began refastening buttons. "God, I'm shameless."

"Hey, I don't want you thinking you have anything to be ashamed of." Corey tilted her chin up with his fingers, holding her gaze steady. "Unless you think Griff ought to punish you for what you did here today."

The heat in Erica's cheeks intensified. "He told you about that."

"A while back. I don't care that he did that to you, as long as it was what you wanted. I couldn't though, Erica. I couldn't hurt you, even if you wanted me to. I care about you too much."

Care, not love. Corey cared about complete strangers and abandoned animals. The soft look in his eyes didn't mean he loved her. "I care about you too." Guilt assailed her at Pam's remembered words. *You're just using him.* She rushed on, suddenly desperate for him to believe her. "I really do care, so much. I want you to be happy more than I want anything else in the world."

"Baby, *you* make me happy."

"What about Griff?"

"Griff drives me up the wall most of the time. Especially here." Corey glanced around the garage. "We have to ignore each other here—at least that's what he said. We can't let our other 'stuff' interfere with the efficient working of the unit."

Erica recalled the way Griff had frozen earlier when Corey had done nothing more than casually touch him. "Does it hurt that he ignores you?"

"He has to, I get that. But the guys are starting to speculate that we've had some kind of falling out. It's all different than how it was before."

They'd lost the easy friendship they'd had because their relationship had grown in other ways, forcing the camaraderie to change shape. "But when you're both with me, he doesn't ignore you, Corey."

His grin was a touch shy. "I know."

"It'll work out." Erica stroked his cheek. "But you need to tell him how you feel. That you love him."

Corey looked about to say something, perhaps to protest. But then he sighed in resignation. "I don't think he feels the same way."

"He does, I know it. I've watched the two of you make love, remember?" Erica lowered her voice from a murmur to a whisper. "I was there the first time you let him into your body. You didn't see the look on his face, but I did. Griff loves you. He's not going to let you go."

"He said he would, Erica. He told me that months ago."

Erica dropped her hand and took a step back. "What?"

"He thinks you and I have a better chance of making it as a normal couple, without him involved. He was always going to walk away—when *he* decided it was time."

Erica stood motionless, stunned by Corey's confession. Griff had always intended to walk away from her—from Corey too. It had been her intention as well, to take her leave when either of the men had had enough of her cramping their intimacy. But to hear Corey say Griff had planned to do the same hurt more than it should have.

She had no right to take offense for herself. On Corey's behalf she could let her anger flow freely. "He can't do that to you. Is it what you want?"

"It never was. I want both of you—I always have."

Erica shook her head. "Your future is with Griff. I can't be a part of it, Corey. I've never lied to you about that."

"That was in the beginning. These last couple of months must have meant something to you."

He could have no concept of how much it had meant. She didn't think she'd ever felt more like a woman than she had since she'd met these two men. She'd learned to appreciate what it was to be desired, to inspire passion and hunger, to feel entirely feminine. The experience had reminded her that her body wasn't only a vessel with the potential to carry disease, but a thing of beauty to be celebrated.

"They have meant a lot to me." More than he could ever possibly fathom. "But I can't..."

The rest of what she'd been about to say was drowned out by the shrill peel of an alarm. A voice sounded over a PA system, relaying details of a warehouse fire in a neighboring suburb. Erica scurried to get out of the way as footfalls sounded on the cement floor and men started grabbing gear, heading for the truck.

Corey grasped her arm. "Erica, come to Griff's tonight. We need to talk."

She considered refusing, but now wasn't the time to explain why she had to. Corey and Griff had a job to do.

She had a job to do, as well, one she should have done weeks ago. Mutely, she nodded. A second later Griff's voice yelled out Corey's last name, and Corey raced to gather his heavy yellow jacket and helmet.

The men piled into the Firepac. The engine roared as it came to life. The siren wailed. Erica remained pressed up against the wall of the garage, as far out of the way as she could get. Before the truck pulled out of the station, Corey rolled down his window and stuck his head out.

She couldn't hear his voice above the cacophony, but she read his lips easily.

I love you, baby.

Erica closed her eyes on a gasp of pain as the vehicle sped away.

Corey was in love with an illusion. And it was well past time she shattered it.

Corey had a really bad feeling in his gut.

Part of it was due to the aftereffects of adrenaline, the mingling of excitement and fear that always swirled in his stomach when there was an emergency call. But the warehouse fire turned out to be minor and relatively easy to deal with.

Not what he would say about his personal life.

Although the job was fairly straightforward, the team had worked overtime to ensure the building was unoccupied and that there was no possibility of further flare-ups. By the time Corey arrived at Griff's house, the twilight was being swallowed by night's blackness.

As had become the custom, Corey let himself in. The absence of her scent confirmed what the empty car space in the driveway implied.

Erica wasn't here.

"Hey, Cor. Long day, huh?"

Griff's arms wound around him from behind. Corey smelled soap and shaving cream, the familiar brands Griff used that he would recognize anywhere. His smooth cheek was damp where it pressed against Corey's, his chest bare where it warmed the back of Corey's T-shirt.

Slipping a hand beneath the cotton, Griff found Corey's flat nipple and stroked it to a point. "Did you have fun giving Erica the grand tour this afternoon? Get her off out there between the trucks?"

The memory and the reality of Griff's tensile strength surrounding him made Corey's cock stir. As though he knew, Griff sent his other hand down to cup him through his jeans. "I knew it. You made me horny at work, you dirty bastard. I've wanted to fuck you for hours."

Corey groaned at the words, even as a part of him resented them. *Can't have you feeling any damn thing at work, can we?* The bulge in his pants filled Griff's hand, even as the annoyance took root.

It was always like this after they shared a shift. Corey nursing the thousand tiny injuries Griff had inflicted with his coldness, Griff soothing the pain with his hot desire, which he let out only when they were alone or with Erica. Within minutes Corey was usually moaning under the heat of Griff's hands or his tongue, his cock twitching with need until he was ready to beg for whatever scrap of attention it now suited Griff to give him.

He was vulnerable like he never had been before. This afternoon Erica's questions had forced him to face how much it did hurt that Griff had put such distance between them. Knowing they couldn't make out in the locker room was one thing. Accepting Griff's utter departure from the uncomplicated warmth of their previous friendship was another.

Griff kissed along Corey's neck, melting him and drawing every desperate need he tried to bury to the surface. He delved into Corey's jocks, stroking skin. "We're going to give it to you so good tonight, Erica and I. Or don't you want to wait? God knows I feel like I'm about to blow."

The solid nudge of Griff's erection fitted between Corey's ass cheeks as Griff tilted his hips. Corey almost succumbed to it, knowing Griff could make him lose his mind up against the kitchen counter, filling his ass and stroking his cock until he forgot all about how bad it sometimes felt to need him this much.

And then Erica would arrive and guess what they'd been doing. She'd get that soft smile on her face, the light of mischievous arousal in her eyes. He'd be at her mercy too, and her feminine caresses would open him up further, until the both of them had his heart gripped tight in their careless hands.

In a burst of frustrated movement, Corey broke free of Griff's embrace. "I can't do this anymore."

"Can't do what, exactly?"

"Any of it." Griff didn't say anything as Corey moved away and shoved back the hank of hair that always fell over his forehead. When he got himself more or less under control, Corey turned back to face Griff. "I don't think Erica's coming tonight."

Griff scowled. "Why not?"

"I'm pretty sure I fucked up when I told her I loved her."

Dead silence. Corey couldn't have read the look on Griff's face if his life depended on it. At length he asked, "What did she say?"

"She didn't exactly come racing after the truck to shout it back."

Griff made a sound somewhere between a scoff and a laugh. "You yelled it out the window on the way to a fire? Classy, mate."

"You can talk."

Griff tipped his head, conceding the point. "So that's it? She didn't fall at your feet right away so you're giving up on her?"

He made Corey sound like an immature dick. "*I'm* the only one who's been making an effort. I've given all I've got and I'm getting squat back."

"She'll come around. No woman in her right mind is going to turn down those baby blues of yours."

The sardonic inflection he gave the words stripped any flattery from them. They also completely dodged the fact Corey wasn't only referring to Erica's emotional distance, but Griff's too. "Maybe she isn't in her right mind. She's been fucked senseless because you wanted to make sure this whole thing stayed about sex."

Griff stalked into the kitchen, pulling a beer out of the fridge and popping the top. "I never did anything she didn't beg me for. But if you can't handle that she gets down and dirty for me in a way she doesn't for you, I guess I know what that means."

"What do you think it means?"

"I always said I'd walk away when it's time," Griff said. "It's time."

The announcement sucked all the air out of the room. Corey couldn't breathe, couldn't think. All he could do was stand there and feel the intense pain infiltrate his body and take over. Griff had told him he'd do this very thing one day, but Corey had dared to hope over the past couple of months that he'd change his mind.

"No."

As one they turned toward the doorway to see Erica standing there, her hand on the knob, wearing some tight black dress that barely covered her. If Corey felt like he'd been sucker punched before, now he knew he was down for the count. He remained speechless as she shut the door behind her and strode toward them—or prowled more like it, her heels clacking on the hardwood floor.

When had she learned to walk like that?

Erica reached his side and placed a hand softly against his chest. Beneath her fingers his heart was reborn, pounding with a new lease on life. "I thought you weren't going to come," Corey finally managed to choke out.

"I had to. Apparently it's my job to talk Griff out of making the biggest mistake of his life."

She turned toward Griff, who was staring at her body like it was buried treasure he'd been searching for his whole life. At the mention of his name, he blinked once and raised his eyes. The lust in them was obvious from clear across the room. "What's that?"

Erica stated unequivocally, "You're not going anywhere."

Chapter Fifteen

Well, he wasn't going anywhere right this second, Griff thought. The hugest erection he'd ever had in his life wouldn't let him breathe, let alone move.

He tightened further when Erica slid toward him on those impossibly high heels, the fabric of her dress hugging those ample curves like it never wanted to let go. Her smoky-dark eyes made him harder, her red lips caused him actual physical pain. Griff had to clutch the beer bottle tight in his fist to keep from grabbing her and pulling her closer.

"Of course I'm not going anywhere," he said. "This is my house."

The two of you can get the fuck out and leave me in peace.

Griff really wanted to say the words, anything to get Erica and Corey out of here so he could slam back about ten beers and forget what a fucking loser he was. But he couldn't, just as he'd been unable to walk away any of the countless times over the past two months he'd told himself to.

He'd done it again, fallen in love with a couple who were more into each other than him. Now he'd ended up outstaying his welcome.

Erica sidled up to him, forced his back against the fridge and pressed her luscious self all over his front. She'd made up her eyes with that black makeup, the look she'd sported the first time he'd had her here. He'd slipped a little in love with her that weekend, when she'd cried at what he and Corey had made her feel, when she'd given herself so completely, time and time again.

He hadn't wanted to admit it, but he'd been slipping a little more each time he saw her. "Tell Corey the truth, Dale."

Shit, he hated it when she called him that. Hated it because he loved that she was the only one who did. "The truth about what?"

"Why you can't let a single emotion show on your face when you're at work with him. He doesn't understand what it's like to hide how you feel, not like you and I do. You're hurting him."

Griff shut his eyes, wishing he could have avoided that. "He knows we have to stay professional. Sometimes it's a matter of life and death."

"But that's not why you treat him like he has the plague."

"I don't do that." From the other side of the kitchen counter, Griff sensed Corey's eyes on him, the accusation in them. *Shit.* He *did* do that. "I don't mean it to be that bad. I just..."

When he trailed off, Erica filled in. "You just can't let a single emotion show, because you're afraid then they'd all come tumbling out. That everyone at that place would see what I see—that you adore every hair on Corey's head, that you live for every flash of his smile, that the thought of sending him into a potentially life-threatening situation scares you half to death, that you can't bear the thought of—"

Griff slanted his mouth across hers, sticking his tongue right in there. As a method of shutting her up it was pretty fucking effective. She swallowed every last word she'd been prepared to say and kissed him back, her lips mobile and her tongue as wild as his. Griff searched blindly for a flat surface to put his beer on, only to find it taken from his hand.

Corey. The man Erica somehow guessed Griff loved more than life itself came to stand behind her, pressing into her back so she merged more fully with Griff's front. All those lush curves caressing every hard inch of him drove him wild. He shoved his hands under Erica's dress, cupping her ass and lifting her so her thighs clutched at his waist. Her wet heat scorched the front of his shorts. His knuckles brushed over Corey's cock as the other man fitted his crotch more intimately against Erica's ass.

Erica was right about everything. One small scratch on his cavalier surface and all was exposed. He loved Corey. He couldn't get enough of Erica's passion. He could no sooner walk out of their lives than he could run an Olympic marathon.

"No."

Erica wrenched her mouth from his, only to find Corey's waiting. He tilted her head back and devoured her, using more force than he usually did. Erica had to arch backward, giving Griff a fantastic view of the cleavage the dress made a point of displaying. Damn but she was gorgeous. She always had been, but lately she seemed to be working it for more impact.

Because of him, him and Corey.

Pleased at the thought, Griff cupped one magnificent mound in his hand and brushed his thumb over the tip. No barrier there. He groaned. The black corset he'd bought her with the half cups that went nowhere near containing Erica's generous flesh. *Please tell me it's that one.*

"*No*," Erica said again, freeing her mouth from Corey's with effort. "It's not supposed to be like this."

"Seems like it's supposed to be exactly like this." Griff let the truth infiltrate him.

"It has to be you and Corey. I want you to show Corey how you feel."

Griff met Corey's gaze, so bright blue with passion it took what little breath Griff had left in his lungs away. Corey already knew, it was there in his soft smile, in his *you are such a tool, why didn't you tell me?* expression. Corey knew because Erica said so, and the man had always been willing to believe every husky word the woman uttered.

"He knows, Red." Griff gave her butt a light pinch. "Because you meddled."

Her brown eyes flared with defiance. "Are you going to punish me for that?"

This particular hard-on was causing him serious agony, and her breathy suggestion only made it worse. But Griff recognized a woman using sex to deflect a man from the emotional turmoil broiling beneath the surface. He'd done that kind of thing himself often enough lately. "No." He gave her ass a gentle caress rather than the abrupt spank she'd tried to elicit. "We're going to make love to you."

"We don't make love," she spat. "We fuck."

Griff had made every effort to ensure that was all they ever did. Time to make reparations. "Not tonight."

He sent Corey a look the other man interpreted easily. Corey pulled Erica into his arms and carried her, over-the-threshold style, into Griff's bedroom.

Erica writhed against Corey as he set her on her feet, everything in her body straining to get away from him. Ordinarily Corey would have released her immediately. Being a big guy, he'd always been extra careful not to inadvertently use his strength against a woman.

But tonight he held her banded tight to him even when she elbowed his gut and scratched his arm and stomped on his boot with the heel of her shoe. He held her like he would an injured animal scared out of its mind, or the owner of a house that was burning to the ground. He drew her against him, her back to his front, ignoring the demands of his erection every time her butt wiggled against it.

"Shh." He stroked her hair and kissed her cheek. "It's going to be all right now, baby. I love you."

"No, no, *no*. You love Griff."

"I've got room in my heart for two."

"Stop it. Three people is too hard. Do what makes sense, Corey. Be a couple. Be happy."

"I'm happy right now because we're all together."

Griff came to stand before Erica, his golden skin and eyes shining like fireworks, every lean muscle displayed to perfection by the low-watt bulb of his bedside lamp. Damned if Corey didn't grow harder against Erica's backside, knowing as he did now that Griff was *his*. Griff loved him.

And Griff was looking at Erica with an amused smile, all his hard edges filed down to soft affection. "What was your plan, Red? Seduce me into admitting how much Corey meant to me and then..."

"You make love to *him*," she wailed. "Not me."

"Then you shouldn't have worn this dress, gorgeous."

"Promise him you won't leave, Dale. Please."

Griff showed her a lopsided smile. "Can't leave now even if I wanted to—which I never have. You made me show it, so now you've both got me."

"No."

It was barely a whisper now. The fight was leaking out of her.

Corey held her more securely when her legs weakened, taking her weight against his chest. "Don't be scared," he whispered. "We're not like the other guys. We're not going to abandon you."

"Oh, Corey. Stop being so damned sweet."

"He can't help it."

Corey's eyes flashed to Griff's. That affectionate expression was still in place, but this time it was all for him. Corey's heart fluttered like bird wings, beating faster as Griff moved in and kissed him. His lips were as thorough as they always were, his tongue as hot and knowing as it stroked his. But Corey sensed the shift in the gesture. Griff had never kissed him like he was giving his heart in the act.

And Corey lost his, completely. If this didn't work out, he knew it would break, unable to be repaired.

So make sure it works out.

Between his and Griff's body, Erica squirmed. As another attempt to escape, it was less than halfhearted. Her ass ground into his erection, giving away her arousal. She'd always loved to watch him and Griff together.

With a groan, Griff released him. "Take off her dress. I have to see what she's wearing underneath it."

Grasping the hem, Corey slid the dress up and off Erica's body. The corset was strapless, the boned bodice cinched in her waist while the lace-edged top came to rest just beneath her breasts, lifting them without covering their glorious, dusky pink peaks.

Corey had never seen anything so sexy. He had to release his hold on her a little so he could take a step back for a better view. His pants chafed his dick, he was so hard.

Griff's voice was hoarse. "And you figured we'd get a load of you in this thing and let you walk out the door?"

Blushing, Erica bowed her head. "I thought I could have one last time."

Griff's determined words echoed Corey's thoughts. "This will not be the last time, Erica."

Griff pulled her to him and took her mouth. Corey sensed the savagery he reined in. Griff's hands trembled on Erica's face—remained there, when Corey knew every instinct he possessed was screaming at him to grab and spread and thrust and fuck.

Moving to the bedside table, Corey took out the lube. They were going to need it because they both had to be in Erica.

Together.

There was a little—emphasis on little—pair of panties that matched the corset. Dropping to his knees, Corey slipped them off, noting how wet they were. He licked over her ass cheeks as he spread the cool lubricant over her hole.

She wiggled and moaned when he ventured inside her with his finger. Corey looked up to see Griff now playing with her breasts, his hands still gentle in a way they'd never been before. Corey inserted a second finger and stretched her a little, until she gasped and thrust her ass back into the invasion.

A zipper parted. Two pairs of hands, Griff's and Erica's, worked on stripping Griff's pants down. Griff kicked them off, his smooth erection thrusting proudly from the thatch of light brown curls, his balls heavy and tight. *Well, since you're down here.* Corey reached around Erica's hip and took hold of Griff's dick, stroking it up and down until Griff swore and rocked into his touch.

Glancing up he saw them both staring at him, watching the movement of his hand like it mesmerized them. Corey swiped the precome from Griff's slit and used it to coat Griff's shaft so he moved more easily along his tensile length. Corey smiled at Griff. "I got a bit better at this, yeah?"

Griff muttered something that didn't even sound like English. Erica threaded her fingers through Corey's hair, holding on for dear life while Corey kept up the in-and-out thrust of his fingers in her ass. He was the one on his knees but they were at his mercy, the two people he loved.

"Stop, or I'll lose it." Griff removed Corey's hand, his chest heaving. Corey was tempted to say *fuck you and your orders* and take Griff's cock into his mouth. He might try that one day, he thought with a smile.

But tonight was about Erica, so he stood and stripped off his shirt and shorts, drawing Erica back against his naked body. Her smooth ass cheeks cupped his hard-on, tempting him. He'd only taken her ass with his cock once. It had hurt her, so Corey hadn't been able to bring himself to go there again. Now, Corey took the condom Griff handed him and rolled it on, resting just the tip of his erection at the tiny entrance. "I want to be in your ass, Erica. Is it going to be okay?"

In response she ground against him. "Do it."

"I never want to hurt you. Not ever."

"Please. I like it."

She turned her head, embarrassed by her admission. Griff cupped her cheek and forced her to look into his eyes. "You enjoy a little pain with your pleasure. I fully intend to explore that fascinating prospect, you gorgeous little minx—another time. Right now it has to be all pleasure."

Sitting on the bed, Griff reached between Erica's legs and started playing with the treats awaiting him there. Corey heard the wet squelch of her pussy clutching at Griff's fingers and groaned, edging a scant inch inside of her lubricated asshole.

Even that partial breach was a burning pleasure for his dick. Her puckered ring banded his achy tip, squeezing him like a velvet vise. Pleasure and pain. He could see what Griff meant now. Maybe he could bring himself to spank Erica's beautiful backside one day, if she wanted him to. He'd do anything, *anything* she wanted.

"Oh yeah, you're so wet. Put your hands on my shoulders."

Erica did as Griff said, leaning forward and using his steady shoulders for purchase. The new angle opened her up further, and Corey sank another inch into her body. He clutched her hips and held his breath in an effort not to push too far, too fast.

He'd never felt anything so exquisite and yet so torturous as teetering on that brink.

"Erica's going to come soon." Griff nuzzled Erica's breasts as he continued stroking inside her with his finger. "Her pussy's clutching at me, her clit's quivering beneath my thumb."

Corey couldn't resist pushing a bit farther in, until Erica's gasp made him freeze. "Don't stop," she rasped. "I'm going to..."

"Tell Corey when you're coming so he can bury himself deep when that orgasm hits you."

"Yes." Erica gyrated between them responding to the twin assaults of Corey's cock and Griff's hand. "Yes, Corey, deeper. I'm coming, I'm coming."

Corey plunged home and Erica screamed, her ass slapping against his hips as she rode through the storm of her climax. Corey stared at the place where his cock drove in and out of her ass, holding on to his own orgasm like his life depended on it. *Not yet.* When they were both inside her, he'd let go. He wanted to feel those spasms rock him at the exact same moment Griff did.

Impatience made Griff's movements jerky as he ripped open a condom packet and sheathed himself. His gaze never left Erica's as he lay back on the bed, easing her on top of him. Corey moved too, desperate to stay seated within her body as Griff helped her straddle his hips. "Now both of us," Griff said huskily. "Like it's supposed to be."

Erica whimpered as with a tilt of his hips he entered her. Corey withdrew far enough for Griff to plunge in all the way, watching the agony and ecstasy play out over Griff's face. "Bloody hell, Red. The way you take me in so deep and easy is heaven. I could never bring myself to give it up."

As Griff stroked the hair away from Erica's face Corey saw it all in his friend's—his lover's—eyes. Corey held Erica around the waist with one arm and brushed his mouth over her ear. "He's in love with you, Erica. Griff's as crazy about you as I am."

Griff shot him a look that was probably supposed to warn Corey off. But he was too open now, as transparent as cling wrap after all he'd been forced to reveal tonight. By Erica, the intuitive, wonderful woman between them. Corey smiled. "You know it's true. You love her, you love me. You can't live without us."

"Shut up and make this woman come, or do I have to show you up?"

Corey rolled his eyes, happier than he'd ever been in his life. He'd bug Griff about his feelings later. He swirled his tongue around Erica's ear. "I love you, Erica. I love how brave you've been, how you came here ready to fight for my relationship with Griff. I love your eyes, and your mouth and this body. God, these breasts." Corey moved his hand upward so he could cup one in his hand. She hardened under the brush of his fingers. "I love these breasts."

She let out a choked sound. For a moment it almost sounded like a sob. "I know."

Moving his hand down, Corey delved into the curls at the juncture of her thighs. "I love this clit. Making you come is the easiest, most beautiful thing in the world."

"Oh, God, Corey. You make it impossible for a woman not to fall for you."

Music to his ears. "Have you fallen for me, baby?"

Corey circled a finger over the bud of nerves that ached for him, just as he ached for her. Reluctance came off her in waves, but she nodded.

Heart expanding, Corey turned her face so he could kiss her, delving into her mouth with his tongue the way he delved into her ass with his cock. He built up a steady rhythm, alternating entries with Griff who lay beneath Erica, tilting his hips and burying himself in her tight heat.

"Cor, can't last much longer."

Tension marked Griff's face as he watched the two people above him—Erica riding him with sensuous bows and twists of her body, Corey fucking her, seducing her with words. Griff always teased Corey that he was the youngest and horniest of the three of them, always impatient to blow his load. Not this time. This time he'd wait and watch the woman and man he loved turn themselves over to him completely.

Corey eased Erica forward, until she lay on top of Griff, breasts to chest. Immediately Griff took her mouth with his, as though he'd thirsted long years for the taste of her. Corey rocked into her, knowing each plunge made Erica's clit rub against Griff's body, knowing that and the way Griff made love to her mouth with his would make her feel incredible.

She whimpered and squirmed, thrusting her pussy forward and her ass back, begging for every inch of contact. Griff moaned into her mouth, his hips tilting one last time as together he and Erica gave over to ecstasy.

Only then did Corey let himself go, the hot seed jerking from his body.

Perfect. Everything was perfect.

The knowledge warmed Corey as he collapsed onto the mattress beside the two people he intended to spend the rest of his life with.

This was not going according to plan.

Erica had arrived at Griff's house, her intentions firm in her mind. Use her body to bring Griff and Corey together, force Griff to acknowledge his emotions. Perhaps, selfishly, allow herself this one final encounter with them. Then leave and never return.

It had all worked out exceptionally well—except for the leaving part.

Dark shrouded the room. Griff had turned the light off some time ago, signaling his intention to finally sleep. After being exhaustively made love to three times by two men, Erica hadn't possessed one iota of the energy required to escape while he and Corey dozed. Not the energy—or the will.

Now, the light of predawn filtered through the blinds. She could just make out the shape of Griff's taut body where it lay stretched out beside her, his arms flung above his head. Corey was pressed to her back, spooning her so close their heads shared a pillow. Fortunately the size of Griff's bed meant Erica never felt crowded sharing it with two such large men.

No. All she felt was safe.

Erica blinked back the sting of tears. Almost as though he hadn't been asleep at all, but attuned to her every emotional shift, Griff's hand came down from where it had been buried in his pillow to stroke over her hair.

His gentleness made the tears burn a path to the pillowcase. "You were supposed to keep me safe from him," she whispered.

Griff tilted his head, opened his eyes and looked at her. "From Corey?"

Erica nodded. "I knew he thought we could have something traditional, but with you there... It can never be permanent between three people."

"Who says?"

"What happened to walking away?"

Griff rasped, "You happened."

Biting her lip to keep the sob from bursting out of her throat, Erica buried her face in the pillow. "Damn you, Dale. I thought you were using me for sex."

"Haven't you worked out what a phony I can be, Red? I faked not being in love with Corey for five years."

Now he wasn't pretending anymore—not for Corey's benefit or hers. Griff had always been closed off emotionally, throughout this whole thing. It had given Erica tacit permission to do the same, even as she knew Corey offered so much and wanted, deserved, more in return than what she gave.

But Griff had opened himself up and been honest with both of them. Erica couldn't go on lying to them anymore.

"Tell me, Red." Griff gave her hair a slight tug, compelling her to face him once again. "Tell me what's keeping you from wanting this."

His voice husked on the words, and Erica's heart broke to think she could make the brash Dale Griffin feel vulnerable. "I want this more than you can possibly imagine."

For the first time Griff smiled. "You've got it, gorgeous."

Shaking her head, Erica sat up and scooted to the end of the bed. "You don't understand. You might not want *me*."

"I think we've both proven otherwise." Griff sat up too, drilling her with his gaze. "What's really going on?"

They weren't whispering any longer, and the noise and movement woke Corey. He propped on his elbow and looked at her with an adorable, sleepy expression. "What's up?"

Erica had to turn away from the sight of them, they were both so tempting. It would be easy to fall back into bed and keep pretending.

Right up until she booked herself into the hospital.

"Is it that dickhead Doug?" Griff asked. "He didn't want you so you assume that's about you instead of him?"

"It *was* about me," Erica said sadly.

"And your Dad leaving you? That was your fault too?"

"I was too much trouble."

"*Fuck.*" Corey sat bolt upright, his expression more thunderous than anything Griff had thrown at her. "You are no trouble, Erica. You're nothing but magic. How many times do I have to tell you I love you before you'll believe it?"

Sadly, Erica did believe it. At least she believed Corey loved who he *thought* she was. That was why she had to tell him everything, give him, both of them, a chance to back out. She owed them that and so much more.

No matter how dreadful the thought of possible rejection was to her.

She addressed her question to both of them. "Didn't you ever wonder that first night why a straight-laced type like me was willing to go home with two men I'd barely met?"

"I wondered," Griff said. "But I spent most of the time thanking my lucky stars."

"I wasn't myself. Something happened..." Erica swallowed. "I found a lump in my breast, and I was so terrified I was willing to do anything to forget what might lay ahead of me. I'd often fantasized about the two of you and I figured I had nothing to lose."

"A lump." Corey reached blindly for her hand, clutching it tight in his against the mattress. "Was it...is it..."

Erica shook her head. "I had a biopsy and it turned out to be benign. Can you believe that?"

"Christ, baby." Corey let out a sigh that shuddered audibly and brought her hand to his lips, kissing along her knuckles. "You scared the hell out of me."

"That day you came over," Erica said to Griff. "I was due to get the results."

Griff simply stared at her, barely appearing to breathe. There was a wealth of understanding in his eyes. He remembered as well as she did how frantic she'd been that day.

"Is that why you told me not to call you again? Because you thought you were going to get sick?" At Erica's nod Corey swore. "You would have needed me more than ever. Why didn't you tell me?"

Erica could have pointed out the obvious—that they barely knew each other then and he didn't owe her solace. Instead she said, "You don't know what it's like, watching someone battle cancer. I wouldn't have let you help."

"But you know what it's like," Griff deduced. "From your aunt."

"And my mother." Erica smiled sadly. "It runs in the family."

Griff's gaze never wavered. His expression didn't alter. But Erica sensed him taking it in, absorbing what a family history meant for *her*. His face was patently unreadable, but he *got* it.

Corey didn't.

"But you're all right," he said. "You must have been so scared, but it's over now. Promise me you won't keep a secret like that from me ever again."

Dragging her gaze away from Griff's, Erica met Corey's. "It's not over. It'll never be over for me."

She sensed his frustration in the tense set of his shoulders. "That's a bit fatalistic. We're here now, Griff and I. If you ever get scared again, you've got us to lean on."

"I've been using you from the start, don't you get that, Corey? All those times you called me, I hung on to the sound of your voice because it helped me forget what I was going through. I've still been using you these past months, to make me feel alive and womanly and sexy. All the things I might not feel the same way again after I..."

"After *what?*"

"I have to have an operation. It's called a prophylactic bilateral mastectomy. I have to, because I can't live my life searching for lumps anymore, waiting for cancer to win."

"A prophylactic bi... What is that?"

"They're going to take out my breast tissue—all of it. The only way I can be sure I don't get breast cancer is to have my breasts surgically removed."

It was as though time suspended, freezing everything in the room. Corey's features hardened in shock. Erica couldn't take her eyes away from him. The only thing that seemed to move was her heart. It hammered so fast she thought it might burst right out of her chest.

After what seemed an eternity, he reacted. His glance slid down, touching on her bare breasts for a fleeting instant before darting away. He'd never turned away from the sight of her naked body before. He was already picturing her without the part of her he apparently found most attractive. Picturing it and finding the image...

...repulsive.

Erica would never have thought it possible for a heart to truly break from little more than a look, to physically sever into parts that would never knit back together. Corey couldn't accept it. Just like Doug, like her father. He didn't want her unless she was easy to deal with and physically intact.

Her hands had never shaken this badly, not even when she'd first found the lump, or when she'd been the one to gently lower Aunt Claire's eyelids after she'd expelled her last breath. Erica swiped her black dress from the floor and dragged it on. Without the figure-shaping qualities of the corset, it no doubt looked indecent on her frame.

How could she possibly care?

"I know, it's weird." Somehow the shaking remained confined to her fingers, leaving her voice blessedly flat. "They'll do a reconstruction, but I won't be the same. I won't feel anything, for a start. And what the heck? I'll probably go a couple of sizes smaller. I might actually be able to take up jogging in comfort."

Erica had never felt the yen to jog in her life.

Corey's voice was as toneless as hers. "I don't think you should do this, Erica."

A flash of anger finally gave Erica the temerity to face him again. "It's not your choice. It's mine."

Chapter Sixteen

Cancer. *Cancer.*

The very word scared the shit out of Corey. Cancer killed people, and his Erica was not going to die, simple as that. Cancer was not going to ruin her life either, make her destroy her beautiful body this way. He couldn't fathom the fact she'd been going through this kind of hell and she'd never told him. All their confidences, everything they'd shared. What did any of it mean if she hadn't felt she could tell him *this*? Christ, he'd discovered he was bisexual and Erica was the first to know. Now Corey found out she'd honestly thought she might die or get really sick, and she hadn't said a single bloody word to him.

And she was going to do this *thing* to herself. Why? Because she was scared? Why hadn't she turned to him or Griff and talked to them about it?

"I don't get any say in it at all?" he rasped. "It didn't occur to you to discuss something this important with me?"

Her expression was shuttered. "It's not your problem."

He *loved* her. He'd given her everything he had in him. But she decided this was her problem to deal with alone. That *hurt*. "There must be another way. People get c..." His throat closed over the word. He didn't even want to link it in his mind to Erica, let alone voice it. "People get sick all the time but they have treatments. Chemotherapy and diet and..."

"Yes, Corey. I'm *aware* of the treatments. My mother endured every one available. They made her miserable. They stole her life years before she died. And she had to have a double mastectomy anyway. This way is better—it's preventative. I don't want chemo."

"You said the lump was benign," Corey pointed out. "Isn't this a non-issue? Why don't you wait until—"

"Do you have any idea what it's like to live with an axe hanging over your head? It's not living, Corey. I won't wait for cancer to attack me any longer."

"But you're so *beautiful*." Corey couldn't understand how someone so physically desirable would want to disfigure herself, all to avoid something that might not happen anyway. "There has to be another way."

"Corey, that's enough."

Corey sent Griff a sidelong glance. "You heard her, Griff. She's just going to..." ...*lop them off*. Christ, he couldn't bare the thought of his Erica going under a surgeon's knife, of anything about her changing so drastically. "Tell me you're not upset."

Griff's eyes narrowed. "Of course I'm fucking upset."

"So we need to stop her. She's afraid of facing something scary alone, but if we promise to be there for her, she won't be."

"You know what, Corey?" They both turned to Erica, stilling at the note of inevitability in her voice. "I've been alone a while, I think I can handle it. I dealt with a mother who was often too sick to play with me and being an only child because the chemotherapy she had after I was born made her infertile. I dealt with watching my aunt, whom I loved like a second mother, die in agony right before my eyes. I dealt with Doug leaving the *second* he found out there was an almost ninety percent chance the same thing would happen to me. And I can even deal with the fact that I probably won't have children because..."

Her voice cracked, and she had to clear her throat before continuing. "Because I'm genetically predisposed to ovarian cancer too, and the next thing I'll have to do is have them taken out. So you see, Corey, I've pretty much always been alone, and I figure I always will be. So forgive me for saying this, but I will live my life the way I see fit. What I do is none of your fucking business."

She stormed out before Corey could utter another word. Corey stumbled out of bed, grappling for his pants. He only had one leg in them when the front door slammed, announcing Erica's departure. He hurried to finish dressing but didn't chase after her. The sound of her car starting already pierced the morning quiet. Corey had no clue what to say to her anyway.

A ninety percent chance. What the fuck? Her odds had to be better than that.

She couldn't have children. That flayed Corey, made his knees weaken until he dropped onto the bed. He had to admit he'd imagined certain things about his future, the future he wanted to share with Erica and Griff. Kids had been a part of that picture. He adored his nieces and nephew and had always figured he'd have about five offspring of his own one day. He hadn't been able to stop himself envisaging Erica being the one to carry them, he and Griff both being fathers. Lots of kids these days had two dads, or two mums. It wasn't so crazy an idea.

But Erica had shut the door on that. She was going to have all the necessary equipment removed. Corey was devastated—for her and for him. Erica, with her difficult-to-ruffle demeanor and empathetic heart, would make a fantastic parent.

From behind him, the sound of Griff's voice emerged like the growl of a tiger from the depths of some dark cave. "What the fuck did you think you were doing?"

"Me?" Defensiveness reared instinctively at the venom underpinning the query. "Ask Erica that. She kept a huge secret from us for *months*. Aren't you pissed she didn't say anything?"

"I'm not surprised she didn't tell me." Griff climbed out of bed and pulled on his jeans with a couple of sharp jerks. "I haven't exactly been approachable. And you... I suppose she was right not to tell *you*."

Griff looked at him, so much disdain in the expression Corey tingled with mortified heat. "I was only trying to make her listen."

"No, you were freaking out."

"What do you expect? The woman I love starts throwing out words like mastectomy and c..."

"You can't even say it, you piss-weak prick. Erica's been dealing with *cancer* her whole fucking life and you can't even face it. There she was, trying to tell you about her darkest fears and her biggest life decisions, and you acted put out because you weren't going to get to play with her tits anymore."

Corey rose to his feet like a shot. "It was not like that."

"It sounded exactly like that to me, and obviously to Erica. She's been in agony these last few months—hell, *years*—and somehow you managed to make it about *you*."

"Bullshit." He hadn't done that. Had he? "Anyway, I didn't hear you saying a damn word."

Griff's teeth clenched. "Because I was trying not to say the *wrong fucking thing*."

Corey's own words filtered back to him. *People get sick all the time* like cancer was no biggie. *Didn't you think to discuss it with me?* like it was his decision, not hers.

Holy shit. He had made it about him.

"Face it, mate, you flinched."

"What?"

"Couldn't you see the way she was watching us when she told us all that? She was waiting to see how we'd react, waiting for us to be like Mr. Wonderful who dumped her when her aunt got sick. And you did it, you fucking idiot. You didn't understand. You proved that you wouldn't be there for her when she needed you."

"I was trying to *help* her!" Corey tried to hang on to a sense of indignation, but it was crumbling fast under the weight of suffocating panic. He was starting to realize how badly he'd stuffed up, and his stomach swirled like he might vomit.

"How, exactly, was that helping her?"

"You know what she's like. She tends to think the worst about a situation first, like she did with us. She didn't want a relationship with us, but we changed her mind. Maybe she'll change her mind about this."

Maybe, but as Griff had pointed out, that wasn't Corey's decision. Yet he'd acted like it was.

Corey had a sinking feeling that the only thing Erica would change her mind about now was him.

Griff pushed out a rough sigh, dropping his head back and staring at the ceiling as though the way out of this mess might be written up there. Divine guidance on his paintwork. Not likely.

He'd never felt so gutted, so helpless, so utterly furious with Corey. And yet if he really stretched his powers of logic, he understood why Corey had reacted the way he had. He was scared shitless because Erica and the prospect of terminal illness did not want to lock together in his mind, and he was grasping at any straw to try to convince himself the situation wasn't as bad as she'd made it sound.

Understanding it didn't lessen Griff's desire to punch the living snot out of the man he loved.

"If Erica was a smoker," Griff posed patiently. "Would you want her to give up?"

"Of course."

"Why?"

"Because everyone knows smoking gives you..."

"Cancer, Corey. You gotta wrap your mind around that."

Corey's voice was thready. "I don't think I can."

"Tough." Griff's ire returned. "You have to grow the fuck up, Wachawski."

"So now I'm immature."

"Right at this moment you are. In fact, you're kind of being a dick, when what Erica needs is a man."

Corey's eyes narrowed. "So now you think you can do a better job on your own."

Oh Lord help him, he really was going to hit the dense son of a bitch. "One more comment like that and I swear to God I'll shut you up for good."

"Fine. Whatever. I'll get out of your hair." Christ, he sounded twelve years old, proving Griff's point about the maturity of his behavior. Corey found his shirt and dragged it on. "I have to go to work."

Griff thought of stopping him, hell, of holding on to him so tight Corey let out all this anger and made way for what was really churning his gut—fear. The same fear that churned inside Griff because he'd finally fallen in love with a woman who was worth the risk to his heart, only to find out she was in danger. And not from something he could protect her from. Not something that could be prevented by a smoke alarm or a better-quality deadbolt. Something Griff couldn't see and couldn't fight for her.

He thought of stopping Corey, but he let him walk out the door, telling himself he needed time to get his own head together before he could help Corey work out what he felt. Sure as shit he needed time to figure out how to fix this, because the responsibility seemed to have fallen to him. Erica was too vulnerable and Corey was too confused for either of them to work it out on their own.

So it turned out, they needed him.

What a way to discover he was an integral cog in the machine that was their little love triangle.

The last day of high school for the year always meant sparsely populated classrooms and virtually deserted quadrangles. It had always seemed like a light, breezy day to Erica, even when the mercury often hit the high notes.

Today the empty school felt eerie. On the horizon black clouds trapped the summer heat to the ground and ramped up the humidity unbearably. It was a desolate, horrible day that thoroughly matched Erica's mood. Her eyes felt layered with sand although she hadn't cried when she'd left Griff's house that morning. A blessed numbing had taken over, allowing her to move through this day on autopilot.

Corey was gone, out of her life. If he didn't understand the most important thing about her, they couldn't have a meaningful connection. And Griff's place was with Corey.

She'd lost them both.

Nobody expected to learn anything on the last day, when exams had been sat and results handed out. The students who turned up usually did because they had nowhere else to go, no invitations to parties hosted by the cool kids to attend, no parents at home because they had to work. Kids Erica identified with.

So she played movies and let them watch or read their novels. She was sitting at the back of the class watching *10 Things I Hate About You* with the five children who'd turned up to second-last period when the classroom door swung open.

Erica's heart stopped when she saw Dale Griffin standing there.

His shorts and T-shirt looked unironed, his face unshaven. His expression was inscrutable as he walked into the room without a word and took the chair beside Erica, stretching his long legs out before him and crossing them at the ankles like he was settling in and about to order popcorn.

Erica's heart restarted with a vengeance. She wondered how he'd found out which room she was in but figured one of the admin staff would have been happy to reveal all if he flashed that confident smile of his. Even though he appeared wracked by exhaustion, he still looked damn good.

He was here to tell her he understood Corey's objection, perhaps agreed with it. He and Corey would move on together without her. Perhaps he felt the responsibility to say goodbye.

It hurt like hell on earth. Yesterday it was exactly what she'd decided had to happen. And then last night Griff had shown her what it was like to have his loyalty, his love, for the three of them to really *work*. To have it ripped away now would devastate as utterly as Corey's attitude had.

"It's all right, Griff," she murmured, her tone flat. She'd felt flat all day, as though she'd been run over by a steamroller. "I know what you're thinking and you don't have to be here."

"Thank God," he groaned in relief, bruising Erica's heart further. "Because I was just thinking how much I hate this movie. Let's go somewhere we can talk."

Erica set him a sharp look. "Pardon?"

"The movie, it sucks. This is what you call an English class?"

Erica decided not to get into the unofficial last-day-of-school no-work policy at Ashton Heights High. "It's based on *The Taming of the Shrew*. It's educational."

"Pfft. I mean, what's he doing there now? Singing to her in front of the whole school. You know a single high school kid who'd do that?"

Two rows in front of them, Tyler Hanley snorted. Griff made a gesture with his hand, as though the boy's barely disguised mirth proved his point.

"It's romantic," Erica hissed. "There's precious little romance in real life."

"I don't think it's romantic." Callie Pratt, who rarely said a word during class, was the one to speak. "I get sad now when I watch it, knowing Heath Ledger died. He was so young."

Erica sobered. "You're right, that is sad. Do you want me to turn it off, Callie?"

"'Sokay." The teenager shrugged.

A moment later Tyler started making pretend sobbing noises, teasing Callie for her admission. Griff grabbed a sheet of paper from a nearby desk and screwed it into a ball. Then he tossed it at Tyler's head.

"Hey!" Tyler exclaimed, shocked that some complete stranger, not even a teacher, had done such a thing.

Griff asked him, "Have you got your license yet?"

Tyler swallowed, his voice breaking a little at the intimidating look on Griff's face. "Next year."

"You know how many kids not much older than you I've seen wrapped around telephone poles because they thought dying young was something they didn't have to take seriously?"

"N-no."

"Hundreds, mate. That wasn't funny teasing Callie like that, was it?"

Mutely Tyler shook his head. At Griff's expectant look, the kid turned to Callie and muttered, "Sorry."

"You're forgiven, Tyler." Callie sent Griff a blushing smile before turning once again to face the TV screen.

Erica sat in silence for several minutes, Griff beside her not saying a word either. At length she observed, "You'd make a pretty intimidating teacher."

"I've done a few road-safety talks at high schools."

"You're really not supposed to throw wadded-up paper at the students' heads though."

"Rules suck. You know what else I think sucks?" Griff waited for her to turn his way. *"An Affair to Remember."*

That long-ago conversation was burned into Erica's memory. "You're really not a movie fan, are you?"

The censure in his eyes knocked her flat. "Terri should have told Nickie she had a problem so he could have helped her."

"Terri didn't want to be *helped*. She wanted to be *loved*."

"She was loved. Don't you remember how it ends? The second Nickie finds out the truth he kisses her and promises never to leave her. It made no difference to him."

Erica swiveled in her seat to stare at him, furious. "It's too bad that life isn't like that!"

"Corey stuffed up," Griff conceded, his gaze narrowed. "But that's what you were waiting for, wasn't it?"

"You think I *wanted* him to react like that?"

"Yeah. Because then you get to be right. All men are bastards who can't be relied on." He pressed his index finger to her temple. "Isn't that what you really think, up here?"

No. She wasn't that judgmental. Was she?

The silence stretched on, underpinned by the chatter of the film and the distant rumble of thunder. She thought of her father, how it had made her heart sing each time he'd called that first year, promising to be back. But he hadn't returned. He'd met another woman in Darwin and decided Erica was better off staying in school in Brisbane, but deep down she'd known the truth. He hadn't done it so she didn't have to move, but so he could escape the responsibility of a thirteen-year-old daughter.

She remembered the few lackluster relationships she'd had leading up to Doug, all men of the same type. Men who were so invested in their work they weren't willing to give love a proper chance. And Doug. He was nothing to her now. Not even a blip on her emotional radar. Doug's rejection hadn't made her feel like *this*, like he'd broken her.

Because she'd refused to invest her emotions in their relationship, as surely as he had.

"Miss Shannon?"

Erica turned to see Callie staring at her instead of the movie. All five students were. Tentatively Callie asked, "Do you think it's true? Can you ever really trust a man?"

Callie's parents had divorced recently. She was another child of a broken home who'd begun to think of commitment as an illusion. That men left, every damn time.

Yet Griff was here, a warm solid presence beside her. When had he taken hold of her hand? Erica had no idea, but he clutched it in his as though letting her go wasn't on his to-do list anytime soon.

"I don't know, Callie." Erica's voice quavered. "I've had some bad luck in that department."

Griff's voice was a low rumble, like the thunder outside. "Luck changes."

Callie looked at Griff. "It does?"

"Yeah." Griff smiled at the girl, making her teenaged blood rush to her face. "But you have to learn to put your money on the winners, instead of the losers."

Erica had been putting her money on sure losers all these years, and she'd thought Corey and Griff would be no different. She'd assumed anything she had with them was bound to be temporary—gorgeous firefighters didn't fall in love with ordinary, damaged English teachers. How could she have anticipated what had happened? She looked at Griff and saw the love shining from his eyes, love that had been there for a while, but veiled, just as she'd tried so hard to conceal her own feelings. The truth was there for her to see. He loved her.

The truth balmed her heart, soothed her soul. She wanted so much to cling to the belief that one look could change everything. But she knew Griff loved Corey too. If Corey truly couldn't accept her the way she was, flaws and all, Erica would never ask Griff to choose between her and the man he'd already loved for five years. She would have to release him.

Griff's appearance here today didn't really change anything.

Fingers trembling, Erica withdrew her hand from his. The tears that hadn't threatened all day welled in her eyes now as she excused herself and all but ran out of the classroom.

Corey really had thought Erica must be exaggerating when she'd laid out her situation. Everyone had a certain likelihood of getting cancer, but surely no one had to deal with odds so steep that removing perfectly healthy body parts was their only chance of avoiding it.

He'd gone online while he was changing for work at his apartment, searching frenetically for options he could present to Erica. He'd very quickly realized the depths of his idiocy. As if Erica wouldn't have already done the same thing. She wasn't stupid. She would have investigated every single option before landing on the one she had. Corey found out about the BCRA1 gene mutation and read the information with a growing sense of despair and dread, knowing those same emotions must have blackened Erica's thoughts for years.

Do you have any idea what it's like to live with an axe hanging over your head?

It shamed him now that he'd thought he did know what that meant. That occasionally risking his life on the job was the same thing. But he *chose* to be a firefighter, and with the kind of safety equipment they used the danger was minimal. Erica hadn't chosen this, and her risk was greater than anything Corey had faced for the fire service.

If she didn't have the operation—Corey made himself learn the term bilateral prophylactic mastectomy and even look at pictures—her chances of contracting cancer in her lifetime where around eighty-seven percent.

And he'd told her to wait, take her chances. What kind of life was that for her? *It's not living, Corey.*

Corey had never felt like a bigger idiot. He'd treated Erica as though she were crazy and had made Griff so angry he probably wouldn't speak to him again. He'd ripped apart everything he'd been trying to build with them, everything that he'd finally started to believe was coming together so perfectly. Because Erica had scared him with the C word.

He really was a piss-weak prick.

Now, having done his bit and helped Steve check the rig, Corey finally slipped into the break room. He'd already thought about calling Erica a hundred times, but was afraid she'd give him the short shrift he deserved. He hadn't yet worked out how he was going to make it up to her—or Griff. He needed something bigger than a simple "I was wrong".

But he had to make a start. He couldn't squander this chance at real happiness with Erica. He couldn't bear the thought of losing Griff either, and Corey was painfully aware that it was possible he could lose them both...to each other.

Finally he understood what it must have been like for Griff, having to watch Anna and Jack walk out of his life at the same time, and why he'd fought so hard to protect himself these past months.

Gathering the courage he should have shown this morning, Corey speed-dialed Erica's mobile number. The phone went straight to voicemail. Of course, she'd be in school now. When the beep sounded he began, "Baby, it's me. I just wanted to say..."

What? That you're a fucking moron who doesn't deserve her? That you'll do anything if she'd just give you another chance? What was it going to take?

All he could do was speak from the heart.

Corey was halfway through leaving his message when the shrill peel of the station alarm pierced the air. The disembodied voice of a Firecom dispatcher filtered out from the PA system. Corey was on his feet and getting into his turn-out gear by the time the details of a three-vehicle traffic incident were relayed. He stowed his phone in his bag, praying it was enough to pry open the door to Erica's heart. *Erica, please hang on. Forgive me. Let me be a part of your life. I want it as much as Griff does.*

The truck's siren wailed as the team pulled out of the station and into the afternoon traffic. When they arrived at the accident scene, any hope that their biggest problem would be angry city drivers died a quick death. The accident was bad, involving three vehicles, one of which was driven by a pregnant woman who looked about ready to pop.

Corey and Steve headed for the sedan. Corey introduced himself as though they were having a perfectly normal conversation. "My name's Corey and I'm with the Queensland Fire and Rescue Service. Can you hear me and understand what I'm saying?"

The woman nodded almost imperceptibly. "I hit...that truck."

"I can see that. Not to worry, we'll have you out of there in a jiff." A jiff was a nice vague term that suggested brevity, one

Griff tended to use in situations such as this and that Corey had picked up on over the years. Corey wished Griff was here now; he was so good with accident victims. Sometimes he actually managed to get them laughing.

Damn it to hell, he loved that man. Would love him still, even if he managed to steal Erica away.

Additional police crews arrived to deal with the traffic situation, the paramedics soon after. Corey and Steve set up the hydraulic extraction equipment, the device better known as the Jaws of Life. A light rain started falling partway through the maneuver, adding to the challenge of forcing the mangled door open with the spreader. By the time Corey managed to get the ram in position, the shower had turned into steady rain, hampering visibility.

In time, the ram did its work, moving the compressed dashboard apart enough that the pregnant driver's legs could be freed. Corey breathed a sigh of relief when he and the paramedic got her onto a stretcher and wheeled her away.

What happened next seemed surreal. Corey caught sight of a vehicle moving forward, when traffic had remained at a standstill during the entire operation. The car was looking for a way through the accident scene, moving up onto the median strip, travelling too damn fast. The roar of a V8 engine rent the air. The car was heading for the left-hand lane.

Where his accident victim was about to be loaded into the ambulance.

There wasn't enough room to get through. If that car kept speeding forward, it was going to crash into the ambulance, perhaps crush the stretcher, the paramedic and his pregnant victim.

Corey reacted faster than he could think, sprinting as quickly as his legs could take him. He screamed a warning. Through the haze of his vision he saw the female paramedic turn, her expression mystified. She hadn't seen the car yet. She wasn't going to make it out of the way in time.

Sami Lee

Flying at the stretcher, Corey managed to yank it backward. It rolled out of the path of the oncoming car but his own momentum couldn't be reversed as easily.

Corey could do nothing but brace for impact as he connected with the fast-moving hood of the V8.

Chapter Seventeen

Griff's mobile rang but he let it go to voicemail as he stalked after Erica. His swift strides took him out into the hall, to a row of grey metal lockers where she stood leaning with her head in her hands.

"He deserves another chance," he told her gruffly. "You blindsided him, Erica. You shocked the hell out of both of us, and the second Corey made a mistake you cut him out. Now you're trying to cut me out too, and I won't let you."

When she lifted her face, there were tears streaming down her cheeks. "Didn't you hear anything I said this morning?"

"I heard every damn word. I also saw how scared you were telling us that, how scared you've been all this time. Sweetheart, Corey's *crushed* that you thought you had to go through it on your own."

By the look on her face, by her parted lips, Griff could tell she had all her arguments lined up, about how she could handle anything by herself and that she was right not to tell Corey considering how he'd reacted. They were going to start going around in circles if he didn't do something to stop it.

So he stopped it the most efficient way he knew how. He drew her up against him and slanted his mouth over hers, smothering every objection, every stupid sacrifice she was trying to make. She moaned and melted against him as though all thought of protest went out of her mind the second his lips touched hers, consumed by the fire that was their attraction.

Their love.

Griff let it consume him too, warming all those places inside that had stayed cold for so long. He pressed her up against the lockers and kissed her until the metal at Erica's back shook, until he was out of breath and she was too.

He drew in a ragged gulp of air as he pulled back and stared into her face. "Is this what you're trying to save us from? How right it feels when we kiss? How perfectly our bodies fit together?"

The befuddled expression made way for sadness again, but Griff stopped that train of thought before she could let it take root. "Everyone's body changes with time, Erica. Yours will just change faster, and for the better, because that operation will keep you safe. And Corey and I want you safe more than we want anything in the world."

"He was repulsed," she whispered, pain strangling the words. "He won't be able to look at me."

"Corey loves you." He cupped her face so she had to hold his gaze. "I love you, Red. And love, for me, has never been about body parts. Do you think I wouldn't love Corey if he wasn't good looking and criminally well hung?"

A surprised laugh spurted out of her, mingling with the sob she'd been holding back. "Oh, Griff."

"You know I'd love him no matter what because it's his openness I love, his modesty and kindness, the fact he can't help letting his emotions get the better of him. Just like I love your bravery and your dignity and grace, and the fact you refuse to let your emotions rule you. You hold them in like you're doing everyone a favor with this stoic martyr shit. Aren't you sick of being on your own?" Griff leaned his forehead against hers and admitted with a shuddering breath. "I know I am. I want you and Corey in my life, and it's long past time I fought for that—for both of you. You hear that, Erica? I'm not giving up."

Her exhaled breath mingled with his, and Griff heard surrender in the sound. She weakened against him, the fight ebbing out of her. "Then I suppose it's lucky I love the fact you can be a stubborn, know-it-all a-hole."

"A-hole?" Griff chuckled, relieved beyond measure. It was going to be all right. He'd make sure of it. "After all the things you've said to me, you still can't curse for the life of you."

"Asshole then. You're an asshole, Dale Griffin."

"Well done, sweetheart." He held her tight to his length, breathing in her familiar scent like it was oxygen. "I'm your asshole. Don't forget it."

His phone rang again, the mobile bleating out the opening bars of "Smoke on the Water". The last thing he wanted to do was let Erica go, but the thought that it might be Corey had him reaching for the phone.

It wasn't Corey. "Griff, it's Steve."

Something in the other man's tone put Griff's instincts on high alert. A rolling sense of dread purled through him, and he knew, just *knew*, something was wrong. *Please God, please not Corey.* "What's happened?"

"There was an accident. We were at an MVA and a couple of kids hyped up on speed didn't like waiting in the jam with the cops hanging around. It was the strangest thing. They just freaked out and drove into the accident scene." Steve Waller's tone gave away how astonished he was by what he'd apparently seen. "They hit him."

Griff didn't have to ask who Steve was talking about, even though he probably would have been on the call list if any member of the team had been in an accident. His entire body froze even as his mind screamed.

"How bad is it?" He almost choked on the question. His blood performed a slow, painful thud as it travelled through his veins. If Waller told him Corey was dead, Griff felt sure it would stop altogether and he'd die too, in one blinding explosion of unspeakable agony.

"Pretty bad." Pretty bad meant he was still alive, but Griff wasn't ready to breathe quite yet. "He was thrown into the air a good way, landed fairly hard. He was still unconscious when they took him to hospital."

"Which one?" Griff listened to the details, already calculating how long it would take him to reach the inner-city hospital. "Has someone called his family?"

"We're on it. Griff..." Steve's voice broke. "They almost ran down one of the accident victims, a pregnant woman. Corey jumped in front of the car instead. He saved her life."

That's my Corey. He wouldn't have hesitated, Griff knew. Pride filled him even as his heart ached, suspended painfully in his chest.

"Dale."

He turned to see Erica staring at him with wide, terrified eyes. He muttered something to Steve and disconnected the call, realizing only then how tight he was holding her. So tight she wasn't breathing either. "It's Corey," he rasped.

Abruptly Erica shoved against him, escaping his hold and sprinting down the hall. She yelled for her friend Pam, who emerged from another classroom wearing a concerned expression. Pam must have agreed to watch Erica's class because a second later she was back. Without a word, Griff and Erica hurried from the school building.

Corey spent most of the night in surgery. Erica wouldn't have thought it possible to fall asleep in the most uncomfortable chairs ever invented, but sometime before dawn a nurse roused her from a doze she hadn't been aware of falling into. "Your friend's been taken to ICU. You can come through and see him now."

Erica's head was resting on Griff's shoulder. She turned to face him and saw he was awake, his hazel irises rimmed in pink. He didn't look as though he'd slept at all.

Throughout the long horrible night, they'd barely said a word to each other, neither of them wanting to voice the frightening possibility that Corey might not make it through. The very thought of it filled Erica with an aching sense of dread. As though Griff sensed it, he squeezed her hand. He hadn't let go of it since that phone call yesterday afternoon, and his constant touch was the only thing keeping her from screaming.

"The surgery went well." Erica wasn't mollified by the surgeon's opening statement. She was well acquainted with the tendency of medical professionals to lead with the good—and follow up with sucker punches. "He has a few broken bones, some cracked ribs and various lacerations and bruising. We've stopped the internal bleeding but the trauma to his head was significant. He's in a coma, but there's every chance he'll wake up in the next day or two. A coma is common with this kind of head injury."

Common or not, the thought of Corey lying unconscious in a hospital bed with all those injuries was sickening. A shudder tore through Erica, and Griff wound his arm around her shoulders, supporting her.

Supporting her, as she had never wanted him or Corey to have to do. Now she needed Griff more than she ever thought it possible to need another person. The thought of Corey so badly broken had felled her every inner strength more completely than anything she'd faced before.

Once the doctor moved away, the ICU nurse approached them. "You can go in to see him, but only for a few minutes."

He looked so much smaller lying in the hospital bed. Corey was a large man, but it was the power of his personality that made him seem like such a giant. Now, the crackling vivacity that Corey exuded like a life force was conspicuous by its absence. It was that, even more than the beeping of the heart-rate monitor and the damage to his body that broke Erica down.

She didn't care about the stupid fight they'd had. Griff was right—she'd sprung her news on them and then unfairly expected them to take it in their stride. The worries—self-centered worries—that had consumed her for weeks melted away in the face of this crisis. All that mattered now was Corey.

Erica sobbed his name, approaching the side of the bed tentatively and slipping her hand into his. His fingers remained lax and unresponsive on the mattress. "Please come back to us."

Beside her, she felt Griff's presence and knew he was silently pleading for the same thing.

Morning came and Corey's sister Sasha arrived, as did several guys from the fire station. Griff told everyone what was going on, over and over, his voice flat and lifeless.

The day wore on, endless hours characterized by barely tasted coffee and tense silences. As late afternoon approached and Corey still had not woken, Griff suggested gently, "Why don't I take you home, Erica. You can have a shower and grab something to eat."

The thought of food made her stomach roil. "I can't leave him."

"You need to rest."

"Are you going home?"

The look on his face said it all. Griff couldn't bring himself to leave any more than Erica could. Yet he said, "I'll go get us a change of clothes and then come straight back. Look out for him for me."

Erica sat in the waiting room while Corey's sister took her turn beside her brother's bed. The grey of an overcast day seeping into twilight filtered through the hospital windows. Appearing grimy and cold, it illuminated Erica's bitter self-recriminations.

Erica could kick herself for the time she'd wasted dithering, fixating on her own mortality and disregarding the risks Corey and Griff took every day on the job. All this time, they had been in as much danger as she had, but she'd been too self-involved to see it. Obsessed with her own problems, using them as an excuse to keep the two most amazing men she'd ever met at arm's length. Why? Because she didn't trust them to be there for her when she needed them.

She was ashamed of herself. Just watching the way the Ashton Heights firefighters had rallied around each other today proved how wrong she was. Corey and Griff were both the loyal type. They'd stick by her if she let them, no matter what she had to go through.

And what she had to go through was nothing compared to what lay ahead for Corey—if he woke up. Bile scored a path up her throat as the thought penetrated. Erica rushed out of the hospital, into the gardens, sure she was going to throw up. But she had barely eaten since lunch yesterday and soon the spinning sensation passed. She struggled to get ahold of herself. *Pam.* She ought to call Pam and give her an update. She'd left her hanging yesterday.

When Erica switched on her phone, there was a message that made her blood rush away like a fast-receding tide. Corey's disembodied voice filtered into her ear, forcing the bustle of the hospital and the city beyond to seep into the background.

I don't know what to say other than I love you. I lost my mind the second you mentioned cancer, and I've been trying to get it back since. The way I spoke to you was unforgivable. What I should have done was held you close and told you the truth— that no matter what, I'll be there. I'll help you through anything you have to go through because you're my girl and I'd rather die than let you down. I want to tell you all this in person, baby, if you'll agree to let me. I need you and Griff more than...

The rest of what he'd been about to say was drowned out by the shrill wail of a siren. The call he'd received that had taken him to the accident site where he'd been so badly injured. The thought that this message might be the last recording of Corey's voice made her knees buckle and a sob tear from her throat. Through her blurry vision she saw Griff running toward her, dropping the bag he held as he reached out his arms and caught her before she fell.

"He left me a m-message." Erica held on to the phone so hard her knuckles turned white. "The last thing Corey thought of me was that I might not forgive him for... I've been so selfish!"

"Shh, no," Griff crooned. "You were scared."

But it was nothing on how terrified she was now, merely contemplating the possibility that she wouldn't hear Corey's voice again. That he'd never smile at her and call her baby, or tease her about her love of corny chick flicks, or lift her effortlessly into his arms and swing her around until she was dizzy and laughing. "I can't bear it, Dale. I can't."

"He's going to get through this." Griff's announcement was decisive, as if he had the power to make it so. "He's fit and strong, and he has a hell of a motivation to get better—you."

"And you. It must have nearly killed you to play down how badly you felt today, to act like Corey's friend, but not his lover."

"Corey's family won't find out about that from me. He's got to decide if and when to tell them."

Without a thought, he'd sacrificed his own need to emote for Corey's sake. Erica had never felt more strongly about him than she did right now. "I love you, Dale Griffin. Lord help me, I love you both. What are we going to do if we lose him?"

Griff was undeniably strong but his weight sagged. It wasn't at all clear who was holding who up. "Don't even think about it. I love you, Red." Griff's laugh was pierced through with bitterness. "I love Corey too, and I never bloody told him."

"He knew." Which was more than Erica could say of herself. "But the last thing I said to him was that my life was none of his business. I need another chance to tell him how much he means to me."

"We'll get one—both of us."

Erica wished she could believe the certainty in Griff's voice was genuine, and not merely an attempt to reassure her.

Chapter Eighteen

"He should be awake by now."

Erica's words made the hair on Griff's nape prickle. It was a concern that neither of them had wanted to give voice to, although it hung between them like an airborne virus, ready to infect whatever buoyancy they'd managed to muster. The doctor's face had been impassive today as he'd checked Corey's vital signs, but Griff could tell he'd been hoping for better results.

"Corey's strong." How many times had Griff said those words in the last few days?

Erica responded as she always did. "I know."

The unspoken was as audible as the heart-rate monitor, as though they were telepathically linked.

But is he strong enough?

"Tell you what, I could go for a coffee. Feel like wandering down to the machine and getting me one?" Griff didn't think he could stomach another cup of the tasteless brew, but he had to keep Erica busy. He could hear her mind ticking over and coming up with nothing but devastating conclusions. She was going to drive herself crazy.

"Okay." With obvious reluctance, she walked out of the room, giving Corey's motionless form a lingering look as she left. As though she feared he'd disappear while she was gone.

Unfortunately, Griff knew Corey wouldn't be hopping up out of bed and leaving anytime soon—or possibly ever.

Fuck. He'd promised himself he wouldn't even let himself think that. He had to stay positive or they were all sunk. But the prospect was there, undeniable. Comas were unpredictable.

Already Corey had been out for close to seventy-two hours. He might be like this for months or years.

Forever.

Brick by brick, Griff's fortitude started to crumble. The hot sting of tears came, their progress down his cheeks unstoppable. He barely managed to quash the urge to sob out loud. He cried in silence, knowing he'd have to gather his composure before Erica returned. If she saw him like this, she'd give up hope and that was all she had right now.

"Jesus, Corey," he rasped. "I don't want to be here without you. I fucking love you, mate. I always have."

Griff could vividly recall the day Corey had first walked into Ashton Heights fire station, as eager as a kid on his first day of school, flashing that irrepressible smile. Griff's relationship with Anna and Jack had already begun its painful decline, and Corey had been like a light in the gathering darkness. A balm to his soul who'd become an integral component of Griff's heart as the years went on.

Without Corey, Griff had no idea how his heart would keep beating.

Realizing Erica would be back any minute, Griff forcibly got ahold of himself. He wiped the moisture from his eyes with the heels of his hands. Then he saw Corey staring at him.

Griff's heart skipped. He wiped his eyes again, praying the tears hadn't blurred his vision to the point he'd hallucinated. But there they were—Corey's baby blues, open and aware. "Cor?"

His lips moved, but his voice was too threadbare to be heard. Griff hurried to the side of the bed, bending his head close to Corey's. "What is it?"

After a moment, Griff could make out one word. "...crying."

Griff laughed, the tears making a reappearance. "Hell yeah, I was crying. I thought I was going to lose you."

Corey's forehead scrunched, as though he couldn't quite comprehend that. Griff touched a hand to Corey's head, tentatively brushing up against the crepe bandage and wishing he could feel Corey's silken hair. "Don't drift off again yet, I have to get the nurse."

His head moved only slightly, but Griff easily interpreted the side-to-side motion. He remained by Corey's side, waiting patiently while he struggled to form the words. "Sorry," he choked out. Then, "Tell...Erica."

Griff smiled. "Do I look like the town crier? Tell her yourself."

The hospital bed was surrounded by medical professionals when Erica returned. Griff managed to catch the Styrofoam cups she held before they spilled their contents all over the floor. He held them out at his sides as Erica collapsed against his chest. "He's awake. He spoke to me."

She lifted her head. "What did he say?"

"He told me to tell you he was sorry."

"Oh, *Corey*."

"We have him back, Red. I know it."

Griff had never been more relieved in his life, nor more determined. Corey was going to need a lot of TLC on the road to recovery, and they were going to give it to him.

He and Erica.

Corey figured he knew what lab monkeys felt like. He was poked, prodded and examined, all while being trapped in a bed that had bars on both sides. Why they had to cage him in, he had no idea. He could barely move, let alone fall out of bloody bed.

His family came by to see him. His sister Sasha and his parents who'd cut short the first vacation they'd been on in ten years. Corey felt bad about that and resolved to help them pay for another trip, as soon as he got his life, and his credit card, back.

The drugs they gave him took the edge off the pain, but Corey could feel the assortment of injuries leaving their impression on his body. He'd be in hell once they cut off the morphine. Still, that would be about the time he was ready to get out of here. *That* he was looking forward to. There was only so much he could take of being the center of attention. But the doctors wouldn't give him a definitive time frame on his recovery, and Corey feared they didn't want to depress him with the prospect of Christmas spent staring out a hospital window.

His memory of the events leading up to his accident was hazy. He recalled nothing of the accident or the vehicle that had hit him or of pushing an accident victim's stretcher out of its path.

"You'll have to trust me then," Griff had said. "You're a hero."

Corey had scowled, both at the concept of heroism, which he never had been able to get his head around, and at the glow of admiration on Griff's face. Corey admired *him*. It had never been the other way around. Yet lately it seemed like Griff couldn't stop staring at him with a goofy look on his face, like he'd done something miraculous. Like he wanted to throw his arms around Corey and squeeze.

And Erica. Every time she saw him tears sprang to her eyes. She would straighten his sheets and try to fluff his pillow and ask the nurse a million questions about his feeding and sleeping habits. She kissed him over and over, but on the cheek or the hand, her brown eyes filled with...what? Concern, admiration, affection maybe. But love? Corey couldn't be sure. His memory of the day of the accident might be hazy, but he remembered one thing clearly. Erica screaming at him that her life was none of his business. Erica storming away from him, slamming the door. Griff yelling at him about what an idiot he was, how he'd let Erica down.

Were her visits about nothing more than obligation? He'd seen Erica and Griff hugging in the hallway a couple of times, clinging tight like a couple of shipwreck survivors. He'd witnessed the way Griff would kiss her on the forehead, his eyes closed like he wanted to concentrate all his attention on how she felt in his arms. He deduced from the details of their murmured conversations that Erica was staying at Griff's place. They were practically living together as a couple.

So where did that leave Corey?

Stuck in here, that's where. For weeks, maybe months, while Griff and Erica built a life together. Without him.

The notion was like a kick in the chest.

One day Erica came in doing her now-familiar Florence Nightingale impression. Corey watched her questioning the nurses, reading his chart, placing another vase of flowers on the windowsill and arranging the petals just so. Realization hit him like a fireball that sucked the oxygen out of his lungs.

Erica was used to taking care of sick people. She'd been doing it ever since she was a kid, with her mother, then more recently with her aunt. This was habit for her, a habit she should never have had to acquire. The last thing Corey wanted was to be one more person Erica had to take care of, someone she put her own needs aside for.

And she needed Griff, the man who hadn't said the wrong thing that day. The man who, when the chips were down, was always there for the people he loved. Griff loved Erica, there was no question of that. He'd stand by her no matter what. By comparison, Corey was the broken man in hospital who hadn't lent his support when she'd needed it most, and who couldn't even wrap his arms around her.

It was pretty obvious who Erica would be better off with.

She smiled at him as she approached the bed, her face radiant. *False cheer.* "How are you feeling today?"

"Like crap," Corey growled, thinking it was true right down to the core of his soul.

Erica's expression turned to one of concern. "Are they giving you enough painkillers? Do you want me to go see if they'll up the dose?"

"I'm on so many drugs I don't even know what day it is."

"It's Saturday. You've been in here for eight days."

She didn't look at him as she gave him the information, and Corey could feel the tension radiating from her. Over a week and he was only now starting to gain some lucidity, starting to talk in full sentences. A chunk of Erica's life that she'd put on hold so she could come here every day and sit by his bed. Keeping him company because she felt sorry for him. He saw the dark circles beneath her eyes. This was exhausting for her.

And it could go on for months. He had no idea when he was getting out of here or when he'd walk without support, let alone go back to work. He was practically an invalid.

"School must be finished," Corey muttered. "You should be out enjoying your holiday."

She laughed. "Right. When you're ready to put on your dancing shoes, you can come with me."

"I think we both know I won't be going anywhere with you."

His statement was curt and Corey noticed the way she flinched. "Not for a while, no," she conceded softly. "This is a bad day, isn't it?"

She must have experienced all this with her aunt—days when she was angry at her situation and took it out on the one person who was constantly there, reminding her of her own dependence. Guilt burrowed deeper in Corey's gut. He couldn't make Erica go through the same thing all over again. "You should go, Erica. I'm not in the mood for visitors."

Deterring her wasn't that easy. "If you're not in the mood to chat, I've brought a few magazines with me."

"Because flipping through the pages is going to be so easy."

His sarcasm made her glance at his battered shoulder, which he couldn't even move, and his other arm which was wrapped in a cast. A look of stark pain chased the brightness from her expression. "I can read them to you."

Jesus, he even had to be read to like a three-year-old. "No thanks."

"Okay." Tenderly, as though afraid of hurting him, Erica slipped her fingers through his where they rested on the mattress. "We don't have to talk. We'll just sit."

"Don't you get it, Erica? I don't want you in here at all." Corey curled his fingers inward, forming a fist so she couldn't hold his hand. One of the few movements he could make without hurting. Christ he was a mess. A beat-up, broken mess that Erica thought she had to clean up. "Leave me alone."

Corey turned away from the sight of her but still heard the sharp intake of breath. He sensed her anguish, as though his own multitude of agonies made him more sensitive to it. *Direct hit.* Corey didn't experience one iota of triumph.

At length, Erica announced tonelessly, "I'll come back when you're in a better frame of mind."

"Don't," Corey snapped, not looking at her.

Dead silence. Then a rustling sound as she picked up her bag and walked out.

The city view beyond the window grew blurry, and Corey shut his eyes. He heard voices in the hallway, recognized one of them as Griff's. A moment later his footfalls sounded on the linoleum. "What the fuck did you say to her?"

"You can piss off too." The strident tone Corey had been aiming for broke up like a space shuttle on re-entry. "I don't need either of you hanging around."

"I hate to point out the obvious, but you need both of us more than you ever have."

"I won't mess up your life. I won't be one more person Erica has to look after."

"Ah, Jesus." Griff grabbed one of the vinyl chairs from beside the bed, turned it around and straddled it. The softness in his golden eyes made Corey's heart flutter. "You idiot. She's here because she loves you."

"She's never said that."

"She's said it a thousand times over the past week. You've been in and out, Cor, barely able to comprehend anything. Trust me. The thought of losing you almost destroyed her." Griff's hand was tender and warm on Corey's cheek. "And me."

Corey saw the truth of it written on Griff's face and a memory came back to him. Griff sitting by his bed, his eyes red and shoulders shuddering. Corey's own eyes filled with tears. "Was I...was it really that bad?"

The nurses and doctors had told him more than once how lucky he was, but Corey figured they said that to everyone. The look of abject distress on Griff's face painted a more vivid picture. When Griff spoke, his voice was husky with emotion. "You could have died. Or stayed comatose or had brain damage. We didn't know how it was going to go until you woke up. And we were scared out of our minds."

Corey swallowed a lump of uneasiness as it formed in his throat. It was true, he'd come close to losing his life. The reality filled him with horror. What if he'd never seen Griff's face or heard Erica's voice again?

"I'm glad you had each other," he said at length. "Maybe the two of you can..."

"Don't even start," Griff cut him off. "We're not a couple. It's always been the three of us, you know that, Corey."

Corey shot him a steady look. "You're moving in together. I heard you two whispering about it."

"That you heard, but not the million times Erica begged God for your life or told you how much she loved you?" Griff shook his head, chuckling. "We're getting the house ready for you, you dickhead. When you get out of here you won't be going back to some third-floor apartment. Your parents are happy to have you at their place, but Erica and I want you with us. At least she wanted it that way until you told her to rack off a few minutes ago."

"But, Griff, she's had too much of this sort of thing in her life. And she has to have her operation too. She can't be taking care of me."

"Erica's talking about postponing her op."

"What?"

"She wants to focus all her attention on getting you well first."

"No," Corey croaked, distraught. "She can't do that."

"That's what I said but so far she could give a shit what I say about it. That's why I need you, Cor. With her stubbornness and her insecurities and her crazy notions about self-sacrifice, loving her is a bloody minefield. The work of two men, for sure."

Hope surged inside Corey before he could stop it. "But I'm a wreck."

"Temporarily."

"You don't have time to—"

"I've taken long service leave," Griff announced. "And I've put in for a transfer. When you get back to work at Ashton Heights—and you will, because no way did you work so hard to get in the service to quit—I won't be there."

A sense of desolation hollowed Corey out. The thought of not seeing Griff every day, of not being on his team, lessened the attraction of work altogether.

"I don't have a choice, Cor," Griff said, apparently noticing Corey's agitation. "Erica was right that night. I can't send you in to dangerous situations and not get distracted from the job. Especially not now. Almost losing you is something I won't forget." His voice broke on the last statement, and never had Corey been more certain of Griff's feelings for him. They were written all over his face. "Besides, I don't think we'd be allowed to work together anymore. I was a walking zombie for a while there, and I'm pretty sure all the guys have guessed why I was so upset about your accident."

"They know?"

"Waller's the only one who's said anything, but yeah, I think they know I'm head over heels for you."

The easy way Griff admitted it, after so many weeks of denial, made Corey's heart trip. *Head over heels.* It was an apt description. Corey felt like his insides were all mixed up, and not just because the accident had knocked him around. "What did Waller say?"

"He rolled his eyes and said, 'I'm not as dumb as I look, Griffin.'" They both laughed. Corey stopped that pretty quick because it hurt like hell. Griff grabbed his hand and held it, squeezing his fingers to let him know he ached almost as bad as Corey did, vicariously experiencing the pain. "Are you okay with people knowing about us?"

"I never had a problem with it. *You* did."

"Bullshit. I just got so used to hiding what you meant to me, I wasn't sure how to change that habit." Griff eyed him steadily. "I've been in love with you a long time, Cor."

Corey raised an eyebrow but he wasn't sure Griff saw it underneath the bandage on his head. "Really? How long?"

Griff's eyes narrowed. "Long enough."

"Are we talking about months here, or years?"

"You're gonna tease me about this now? You want to make a point of finding out which one of us sucks worse at this love stuff?"

The moment of happiness slipped away as quickly as it had come. "I sent her away."

"That was pretty dumb, but Erica's the generous type—luckily. Who else would put up with our shit?"

"I don't want to be a burden to her."

Griff rolled his eyes. Then he leaned over the bed and planted a soft kiss on Corey's lips. "Between the two of you, I have a feeling life's going to be a big old pain in the ass."

"Like you're so easy to deal with."

They both turned toward the doorway to see Erica standing there, frowning at Griff. Not a serious frown, but an exasperated furrow of her brow that barely concealed the adoration behind it. Corey's heart lifted. She was as crazy about Griff as he was, one of the many things that bound them and always would.

"You came back." He couldn't keep the lilt of desperate relief out of his voice. How could she keep forgiving him for screwing up?

"Of course I came back," Erica said, walking into the room with confident strides. "I've never seen anything so pathetic as you trying to bully a woman, Corey Wachawski."

Griff snorted. It was all he could do not to laugh out loud at the indignant look on Corey's face. It was a difficult thing, too, to keep from leaping out of his chair and scooping Erica up in his arms.

She'd decided on her own that Wachawski was full of shit, when Griff had figured he might have to chase her down and patch things up between the two of them again. He'd never been so proud of her.

Corey's gaze narrowed. "Pathetic?"

"That's right. There isn't a cruel bone in your body so stop trying to tell me you don't want me here when you know there's nowhere else I'd be."

"You have things you need to do, Erica," Corey pointed out. "Like have your operation, for one."

Erica glanced at Griff. "You told him?"

"Guilty." Griff smiled, unrepentant. "No secrets between the three of us, Red. Not anymore."

"Don't delay it, Erica," Corey said. "It's too important."

"*You're* important." A passionate fire lit her dark eyes as she moved to sit on the edge of Corey's bed. "I've wallowed in my own problems long enough. Don't you think I feel like an idiot for doing that, only to have this happen to you?"

"I won't have you spending all your time taking care of me and neglecting yourself."

"I'll make my own decisions about that, Corey. Right now, you're my priority."

Griff watched them staring each other down, two innately selfless souls competing for the title of martyr of the year. It was the most adorable thing he'd ever seen. Years of this lay ahead and the thought filled him with a happiness like he'd never known. Not with any of the women or the guys he'd fooled around with over the years. Not with Anna and Jack, with whom he hadn't really been one of *three.*

Sure sometimes, like now, Erica and Corey seemed like two peas in a pod, a bona fide, born-to-be-together couple. But somehow they managed to be that without excluding him. They hadn't meant to keep him out of it, neither one of them, and whatever fears he'd had about that were born of his own screwed-up psychosis, the past hurts that had stopped him letting down his shields.

Good thing he wasn't the only one in this trio who was screwed up. Lord knew no two people ever needed his particular brand of Dale Griffin-patented blunt rationale more than Corey and Erica.

They needed *him,* the both of them. And Griff wouldn't have it any other way.

"So what am I over here," he asked. "Chopped liver?"

They both turned toward him. "Pardon me?" Erica said.

"It might have escaped your notice, but I'm the only one in this room without any pressing medical problems. You think I can't handle the both of you being in hospital at the same time?"

Erica waved a hand. "I won't even be admitted unless there are complications. I'll be in and out in no time."

"Right. So have the damn procedure and get it over with."

"But Corey..."

"Corey's going to be on his back for a while. By the time he's up and about I want you home with me sporting a brand-new rack." He raked a gaze over her body, dressed today in a little floral skirt and a sleeveless white blouse that did great things for her voluptuous figure. "What size you going to go anyway?"

It amazed him, after all they'd been through, that he could still make Erica's cheeks turn that particular shade of crimson. "I thought I'd go a little smaller."

"What a shame."

"They'll be *fake*, Dale. Why on earth would size matter?"

"They make mighty pretty fake ones these days." At the look she sent him, he shrugged. "So I've heard."

"Heard." She looked doubtful. "Right."

"Come on, Red. If we can't talk openly about your boobs, we haven't come as far as I'd thought."

"Erica?"

Corey's prompt had Erica turning from Griff, her infuriated expression turning instantly to one of concern at the tone of his voice. "What's the matter? Are you thirsty? Tired? Do you need me to..."

"Baby, shh."

Griff saw the corners of Erica's eyes start to glisten. "I've missed you calling me that."

"I'm sorry I've acted like such a jerk. Today and that other day, before the accident."

"I know. I got your voicemail message. And Griff rightly pointed out I shouldn't have surprised you with news like that."

Corey sent him a glance filled with gratitude. Griff smiled, feeling pretty damn good about himself. Then Corey returned his attention to Erica. "I want you to have the mastectomy as soon as possible. I want you safe and healthy, or I'll worry every day and that's not good for my recovery."

Erica bit her lip and they could both see her thinking about it. Corey held her gaze and knew exactly what to say. "You will always be beautiful, no matter what."

Her voice was threadbare. "Oh, Corey."

"As soon as possible. Promise me."

Erica let out a shuddering breath. "All right. For you."

"I'll try not to be offended that you let him talk you into it, but not me," Griff drawled.

"Silly man." Erica gave him a reproachful look. "You know how much I love you, but Corey asks me things nicely instead of trying to push me around."

"You like me pushy. Where the hell would any of us be if I wasn't pushy?"

The three of them thought about it in heavy silence. Corey looked at him, and Griff knew he was recalling that first night when he'd only spoken to Erica based on Griff's empty threat of stealing her away. And the high color on Erica's cheeks told him she was remembering how he'd been the one to force her to admit her two-men-at-once fantasy—and every other fantasy that came after.

So maybe he was an asshole sometimes, but he'd played a part in bringing them to this place. And Corey and Erica didn't seem to mind who he was—in fact they loved him for it. It was a Christmas freaking miracle.

"You gotta do one more favor for me, Red."

Erica sighed. "I hesitate to say 'anything', but go ahead."

Taking her hand, he kissed her knuckles and let the love shine out of his eyes, feeling his heart swell in his chest when he saw the same depth of emotion reflected back. "Give Corey a kiss, will ya? Tell him you love him because he was too drugged out of his brain to hear you all those other times."

A surprised gasp escaped her lips. She turned toward Corey and all but leapt on him, careful not to touch him anywhere he might feel it in a way that wasn't pleasant. "Oh, Corey, of course I love you." She kissed him, making a loud smooching noise to make up for the fact she couldn't hug the life out of him. "I adore you."

She kissed him again and again, on the lips, on the cheek, on his poor bandaged head, while a laugh of pure joy bubbled out of Corey's chest. "I screwed up so many times, baby."

"So did I. I'll be better from now on."

"I'm the one who needs to improve."

"No way, you're wonderful."

"You're *perfect.*"

"I'm not. But I do love you. I'll never stop."

"I'm *crazy* about you."

They ceased trying to one-up each other's gushy declarations only when the sound of Griff's laughter caught their attention. Corey quirked his lips. "I'm crazy about you too."

Griff winked, his smile growing broader. "I know."

Corey rolled his eyes. "Jerk."

Maybe he was a jerk, but Griff realized Corey and Erica both loved him for it, as illogical as that may be. They loved him, accepted him, for who he was. Just as he knew who they were and loved them that way, warts, stubborn martyrdom and all. They were a team, Corey, Erica and him, one Griff was as pleased as punch to be on.

There was nothing in life more beautiful than that.

Epilogue

Eleven months later

"I did not."

"You so did."

"Bullshit."

"I swear to you, Griff," Corey huffed. "You can't cry bullshit every time I call you out for something you did."

"I wouldn't if I was guilty. Come on, Red, help me out." Griff turned his imploring gaze her way. "Tell Wachawski I did not eat the last Tim Tam."

Erica looked from one man to the other. Corey sat shirtless on the living room floor with Griff behind him on the couch, working out the nagging kink in Corey's shoulder. It still gave him grief, as did his right knee, but for the most part Corey had recovered remarkably well from his horrific accident. He'd even returned to the fire station, on a part-time basis at first. Last month, he'd been restored to full duties and it had put the bounce back in Corey's step.

And Griff had played a huge part in getting Corey into shape. He'd been watchful, encouraging, forceful and even downright pigheaded on the odd occasion Corey needed a kick up the rear to get him motivated again. That last task was the one he excelled at most.

At the other extreme, Erica had to admit she had a tendency to take it easy on Corey. If it were up to her, she'd probably still be tucking him in bed and feeding him pudding like she had when he'd first come home.

Home. Their home. She'd rented out her place and moved in with Griff right after she'd had her mastectomy, a week before

Corey was released from hospital into her and Griff's care. Griff had needed the help with Corey. Besides, Erica couldn't stand to be apart from either one of them for long.

She loved them so much that it filled her heart to bursting point. But she wasn't stupid. She was never going to admit that *she'd* eaten the last Tim Tam. "I've told you both before, I will not referee your little tiffs."

"Guys do not have *tiffs*," Griff pointed out, affronted. "We take it outside and thump each other."

Corey said, "Bring it on, tough guy."

Griff pretended to consider it but eventually shook his head. "Nup. You still couldn't take me. Not with this shoulder. Besides, I know what happened. You're the chocoholic around here."

"Maybe so, but you're a glutton."

"I'll take selfish prick, but not glutton," Griff retorted. "You should thank me for it. A while back when you and Erica were trying to out-martyr each other, it was my selfishness that got things back on track."

"You just keep telling yourself that, mate."

From his place on the living room floor, Corey sent Erica a secret smile. They both knew Griff was probably right, that without his prodding they might not have made it to this place, this wonderful position where they all meshed together in an unusual, sometimes frustrating, but always glorious tableau of impure domestic bliss.

Listening to the two of them spar, watching the way Griff's hands glided with easy familiarity over Corey's shoulders, Erica marveled at how ridiculously happy she was. Once upon a time she'd thought she might not find a single man willing to take her on post-mastectomy. She'd wound up with two.

It would be greedy in the extreme to wish for anything more, but Erica couldn't help it. She did want more, and she wasn't at all sure how Griff and Corey were going to react to her request.

The sitcom on television lost whatever mild interest it had held for her when Griff reached down and massaged Corey's pectoral muscles. He gave a nipple a playful tweak, and Corey laughed, their biscuit-related argument forgotten. Griff started nibbling a trail along Corey's neck, his manner both mischievous and seductive.

Seeing them together, the casual exchange of innate masculine strength, always provoked a sexual response in her. Griff knew it too, the scoundrel. He let his hands wander until they moved over the ridged muscles of Corey's abdomen, kept hard by the hours of core strength exercises he did. Corey sighed, letting his eyes drift closed, and his head fall back against Griff's chest. Griff tilted his head and kissed him, languorously, so Erica could see the erotic interplay of their twining tongues.

In no time at all, she was scandalously wet. She shifted on the armchair, the leather creaking beneath her and drawing Griff's attention. He paused in the act of kissing Corey to pin her with his laserlike gaze. "You want something, Red?"

The confusion of mind-numbing arousal made Erica forget caution. The truth was out before she could pull the words back. "I want a baby."

In perfect unison, Griff and Corey stilled. They both stared at her, wide-eyed and clearly gobsmacked. Erica was more than a little stunned herself. She'd meant to bring the subject up carefully, at an appropriate time—not like this.

Corey was the first to find his voice. "What did you say?"

There was little point in trying to backpedal now. They wouldn't let her anyway. "I've been discussing some of my other options with Dr. Singh, about the ovarian cancer. I don't want to make the mistake of putting off the inevitable only to find my luck runs out before I act. I'll need to have my ovaries removed at some point, in the next couple of years I should think. But before I do..." She trailed off with a shrug, hoping one of them would step in to help her out.

When they both remained silent and stock-still, Erica began to worry she'd made a serious error in judgment, destroyed her perfect life with the mere suggestion that it could be even better.

Swallowing her anxiety, Erica pushed on despite their silence. She'd promised herself months ago she'd never be backward in coming forward again. "I want to be pregnant, to have a baby and be a mother. Now might be my only chance."

Corey croaked, "Now?"

"As soon as possible."

"What about your genes, honey?" Griff asked gently. "I thought you were concerned about passing your problems on to your kids."

That was the part of this decision she'd struggled with the most. "I have to hope that in twenty or thirty years, my child will have better prospects than I have right now. That there may be a cure, or more palatable treatments available. If not..." Erica shrugged. "That's okay too. My life's pretty darn terrific. I wouldn't change anything about it. So, I guess all I really need to know is if either one of you is ready to be a father."

"Fuck yeah."

"I'll do it."

Corey and Griff glanced at each other.

Griff asked dubiously, "You?"

"Why not me?" Corey scowled.

"You're the youngest."

"So?"

"So, maybe this is *my* only chance."

"Charlie Chaplain was a hundred and two and he had a kid."

"He was seventy something, and I don't want to wait that long."

"What about me? You think because I'm only twenty-six I'm going to tire of this arrangement and go knock some other woman up?" Anger flared in Corey's voice. "I've got news for

263

you, this is it for me—you and Erica. I want to be an old man—Charlie Chaplin old, one hundred and freaking two—and still be arguing with you, and loving Erica. I have as much right to be this baby's father as you do."

Erica watched the exchange, amusement mingling with her love for them. She should have anticipated they'd fight each other for the right to be her sperm donor. They bickered to the death about Tim Tams. A baby was bound to generate some heated debate.

At length, Griff sighed and affectionately mussed Corey's hair. They called a truce with their eyes before Griff transferred his gaze to Erica. "How do you feel about twins? We'd get an egg each."

Erica laughed, so relieved that tears leaked from her eyes. "I think that would be very difficult to arrange."

Corey said, "Bummer."

Wiping the moisture from her cheeks, Erica hopped out of the chair and walked toward Griff's bedroom. They each had one but more often than not they were drawn to Griff's by the easterly breezes and the king-sized bed.

Stopping in the doorway, she cocked her hip and arched a brow at them. "Are you coming or do I need to buy a turkey baster?"

The mad scramble they completed in order to follow her was comical. Erica giggled, feeling giddy not only because she was amused, but because she was utterly, dizzily happy. She started undoing the buttons of her blouse, turning to face Corey and Griff as they entered the room.

"You know what I think?" she began. "I think that the way we share each other means we might never know who the guilty party is if I wind up pregnant."

Erica slipped the blouse from her shoulders, revealing her skimpy red lace bra. Her breasts might not be "real" but Corey and Griff certainly seemed to like looking at them, so Erica bought more fancy lingerie now than she ever had. With the reconstruction, she had opted to go a little smaller. It was more practical, and her new C cups fit into all manner of spunky little garments that she never would have gotten into before.

In a strange way, she was prouder of her fake boobs than she ever had been of her natural ones. They were a symbol of her life-changing decision, of her determination to live.

"Good God, baby." Corey's gaze remained riveted on her as she slipped out of her skirt, revealing the bra's matching red lace panties. "Are those new?"

"It's shameful how much money I spend on underwear these days."

"You can never spend too much on stuff like this." Griff stepped toward her and rubbed the material of her knickers between his thumb and forefinger. "But I have to warn you, these aren't going to last long. I'm so fucking hard for you I'm about to explode."

Capturing her mouth with his, Griff proved his statement with the brutal thrust of his tongue, the brash scrape of his teeth. At her other side, she felt Corey's warmth surround her as he slowly caressed her body, awaiting his turn with her mouth.

Yet when she drew away from Griff to offer herself, Corey placed a finger against her lips. "What are you saying, Erica? You don't care which one of us does this?"

"I'm saying you're both doing it. My baby will have two fathers. If it's not medically necessary, I don't need to know who provided the biological material."

He shook his head in amazement. "There's no one else like you, baby. We're so lucky to have you."

Corey did kiss her then, a long lingering kiss that had Erica slipping readily into that dreamy state of arousal that only Corey, with his soft mobile lips and loving manner, could generate. Griff was compelling in his own way, a different way. Griff was—

He thrust his hand inside her panties to cup her sodden folds.

Griff was *forceful*.

"I'm going to fuck this beautiful cunt so hard you'll be seeing stars for a week."

And blunt to the point of crass. Overconfident, overbearing and stubborn. And yes, often selfish.

Erica arched into his rough touch, loving every minute of the way he handled her. Loving everything about him.

"Get into bed, baby."

Erica extracted herself from their embrace to do Corey's bidding. She climbed onto the bed, facing them on her knees. Inch by tantalizing inch, she began to slip out of her panties. She smiled and licked her lips, astonished as always at the brazen female she'd become. "You know what I want first."

Corey smiled. Griff groaned as he watched her slow strip tease. "No, Red. I won't last tonight."

But Corey was already lowering to his knees on the floor, unzipping Griff's fly. He pushed the denim jeans down Griff's legs, causing his stiffness to bob as it was released from the confines of his clothes. Griff threw back his head and sighed his pleasure, unable to resist as Corey swallowed his long cock.

"Christ, Cor. Yes. I love the way you suck me." Griff rocked his hips to the rhythm of Corey's bobbing head, burying his red, throbbing penis to the back of Corey's throat. Erica's excitement spiked. Shucking her underwear, she spread her legs and started fingering her swollen clit. She kept her eyes wide open, watching Corey give Griff head and trying to control her lightning-fast response to the sight.

"No, God. Don't do that." Griff grabbed a hank of Corey's hair and pulled him away from his crotch. "You're trying to make me come before I get to Erica."

"A little healthy competition usually improves your performance."

Griff's smile was feral. "My performance doesn't need improving."

"Okay, okay. Show's over." She didn't want to orgasm without someone inside her, but even watching them try to outdo each other was impossibly arousing. "I need it now."

"Sorry, baby." Corey climbed onto the bed beside her. "Was I neglecting you? Come here and let me make up for it."

Corey dropped onto his back. His hands spanned her waist and, bum shoulder and all, he lifted her with ease, settling her over his hips. His erection pressed against her wet cleft, making Erica whimper. "Please, Corey."

He positioned her and entered swiftly, letting out a litany of curses as their bodies became one. He held her still, panting to control his reaction. "I've never been inside anyone without a condom. Jesus, Erica. It's unbelievable."

The sensation of Corey's flesh fitting so snugly inside her, with nothing between them, robbed Erica of speech. She could only act. Levering herself up and down, she reveled in the new, wonderful intimacy, in the tortured moans Corey emitted. She impaled herself again and again, taking every ion of ecstasy from the motion. Making love to Corey. Loving him.

From behind, Griff encircled her with his arms. Erica slowed her frantic movements so she could tilt her head and receive his kiss. His erection pressed into her ass cheek, promising another torrid ride ahead.

"So sexy," Griff muttered, grasping the straps of her bra and pulling them down. He fingered her nipples, filled his hands with her breasts before he stopped himself. There was a wealth of regret in his husky apology. "I'm sorry you can't feel anything, honey."

Erica shook her head. "You're wrong. I feel too much."

"But not here." He cupped her breast tenderly, as though it were real flesh capable of knowing his tenderness. "They do look great though. You chose well."

Erica smiled. Griff meant her reconstruction, but she thought of her choice to allow these two men into her life. She'd chosen better than well—she'd chosen to make fantasy reality. She'd chosen the dream, and had never once regretted it.

"How about if I touch you here?" Griff found her throbbing clit and stroked it. "Does that do anything for you?"

"Hmm. Oh, yes." She rocked into his hand, the motion changing the angle at which Corey penetrated her. His staff brushed against her cervix, activating the nerves in her G-spot. The combined sensations of Griff's knowing fingers and Corey's pistoning cock were her undoing. She exploded around Corey, thrust against Griff, bucking and thrashing as she climaxed.

Below her, Corey swore, grasped her hips and pulled her off him. Erica's internal walls protested the loss of him, clutching at the sudden emptiness. She looked into his eyes and saw a similar anguish there.

Tautly, he said, "Griff, do it."

And then Griff was inside her, filling the aching gap left by Corey. She was on her hands and knees, staring down into Corey's tense face, but it was Griff fucking her, shafting her from behind in marauding plunges that kept her hovering on the brink of a rolling orgasm.

Corey said, "I love watching Griff fuck you. I love watching you both come."

Behind her, Griff slowed his movements. His breathing was labored on her neck and Erica knew what it cost him to ask. "Cor, are you sure?"

In answer, Corey reached down between Erica's legs—not to touch her. From the strangled groan that rumbled against her shoulder Erica knew Corey had taken hold of Griff's balls.

"You're gonna make me blow my load first, you know that?"

Corey smiled. "I know. Give it to her, Griff. Give her your come."

Griff started pumping inside her again, the urgency mounting fast and high. He reached around and found her nerve center once more, playing with it as he thrust hard and rough inside her.

As Griff's cadence reached a crescendo, Corey stared into Erica's eyes. "I'm next, baby," he promised. "I'm next."

The mere thought of it made the sphere of regathering tension inside Erica rupture. She came in unison with Griff, who bit into her shoulder like an animal and pumped her full of his seed, a primal offering that added an edge to Erica's ecstasy.

This was sex at its most primitive, its most necessary.

She was satisfied, sated to within an inch of her sanity. But when Griff withdrew and Corey flipped her onto her back, Erica was ready for him, eager for him.

Without preamble, he spread her wide and buried himself deep. He groaned. "You're so hot, and still full of Griff's come. That's such a turn-on."

"Yes. Oh, yes, Corey." She didn't think she'd orgasm again, not when the last one had been so explosive. But it didn't matter to Erica. Watching the agony of lust on Corey's face, seeing the way their bodies joined as he jerked into her, was another kind of thrill. Erica reveled in her ability to satisfy both these incredible, virile men. Her womb tightened as Corey thrust his last and spilled his hot essence into her body.

All three of them lay flat out on the bed, sprawled together in blissful exhaustion. Erica could barely breathe, could hardly think. Only one thought occupied her numbed brain.

She might even now be pregnant, and she had no certainty who the father was.

Aunt Claire would have been aghast. But Erica had long since decided it was time to stop living her Aunt Claire's life and start embracing Erica Shannon's.

She didn't have a bad time of it, after all.

"Why'd ya do that?"

Erica understood the question Griff directed at Corey. They'd made such a contest about who was going to "get there first", and then Corey had simply handed the honor over.

Corey answered lazily. "I figured my guys would be faster swimmers anyway."

Griff threw back his head and laughed. Erica was too worn out to manage it, but she knew her smile wouldn't dim for a good long while.

Yes indeed. Erica Shannon had a lot to look forward to.

About the Author

Sami's been a secretary, sales assistant, bartender, waitress, student, tutor, human resource manager and administration officer, but at heart she's always been a writer. She enjoys creating emotional, sexy stories about the gorgeous, aggravating men who live in her head and the women who were made to steal them away from her.

Sami lives by the coast in Australia with her husband and two stupendous daughters. To learn more about Sami, please visit www.samilee.com, join her on Facebook or Twitter, or send an email to sami@samilee.com.

It's all about the story...

Romance

HORROR

www.samhainpublishing.com

CPSIA information can be obtained at www.ICGtesting.com
Printed in the USA
BVOW03s1215160414

350804BV00002B/88/P